GILDED
WINGS

FROM BESTSELLING AUTHOR
CAMEO RENAE

This book is dedicated to VICTORIA RAE SCHMITZ.
My beautiful and suddenly splendid editor. (Inside joke)
Seriously, she is amazing and this book would
not be the same without her.

YOU CAN
CHOOSE
YOUR PATH,
BUT YOUR
FATE
IS SEALED.

GILDED WINGS

ONE

HATE IS A VERY STRONG word. In fact, there are a myriad of reasons why one should avoid the vicious feeling. But at this very moment, I'd never felt more hatred toward another being. I couldn't stop the bubbling revulsion if I tried. Its dark tendrils spread through me like a cancer, grasping at every cell, seeping from every pore. It filled me with an unexplainable sadness and pain.

In just a single moment, I'd lost everything. My dreams and my future were shattered. He stole my free will and made me a slave. That's all I was now... a pawn who would eventually be used for destruction.

Lucifer had become the enemy of my soul. He took me to a place I never wanted to go; shrouded in darkness and internal suffering. Outwardly, I bore the marks of his fingers, which he'd wrapped tightly around my neck, nearly squeezing the life from me. The look of pure evil and murderous intent, burning bright in his wicked eyes, was imprinted in memory. It felt like a dream. I could only have wished it was, but the pain was too real.

Just outside my door I was surrounded by everyone I loved, and yet, I'd never felt more alone. They were so close, but I had become disconnected, muted, unwillingly sworn to silence. It was killing me inside, and I couldn't do anything about it. I had to submit. I had no choice. I wouldn't risk any of their lives. As much as I wanted to let them know why I was acting indifferent, I wouldn't speak a word.

Ethon tried to apologize before I left him, but even with the strong magic of the bond, I had a hard time forgiving. It wasn't something I could brush off and move on from. What happened in that tower was life altering, in the worst sense. I'd almost lost my life to his father. His *father*!

In essence I had lost it, but no one besides the few who were in that room, would ever know. Ethon knew what his father was plotting, regarding the bond, and yet he easily went along with it. I get he was probably afraid of his father, but still, he didn't even flinch. He wanted it, just as much as Lucifer did.

But the *big* question still remained…would I be able to live forever with him and be happy? Whether I liked it or not, Ethon was and would always be, connected to Lucifer.

If it was only Ethon, the answer would be different. The bond had joined us for a reason, and I knew Ethon really wanted to love and protect me. When I was with him, I truly felt it. If given a real chance, I think we could live happily ever after.

Unfortunately, everything changed tonight. I had a glimpse of our future and what it would become. The display between

Ethon and his father showed who was in control; and while Lucifer stripped everything from me, my bonded had remained quiet. He did nothing but say we would make it all work. How? How could it possibly work when I would not only be bound to him, but also to his evil father?

Lucian and Lucifer were almost identical. Each had dark, wicked hearts, and wouldn't hesitate to take control and power, no matter what the cost.

Regrettably, I happened to be the stupid 'prophesized child' who would supposedly bring change. Although it seemed absolutely ridiculous, I could already feel the change happening deep within. Every day my power grew in strength. Outwardly, I was the same girl, but just beneath the surface, I felt like a caterpillar slowly transforming, awaiting her chance to break free and spread my wings. I wondered if I would have wings. Ethon had them, and he was a Nephilim, so there was a chance.

And then, there was still a matter of the bond I shared with two different men. I couldn't help but think what my life would be like if Ethon or Kade weren't bonded to me. Would they have the same feelings? It was unlikely, considering without the bond, I probably wouldn't have ever met them.

Kade... the angel who was stripped of his immortality, for me—our bond broken. Nevertheless, a powerful connection remained between us. My heart ached as my thoughts focused on him. How the hell was I supposed to function normally around him? How could I look into his beautiful hazel eyes without sadness or pain? I knew he would want to hold or kiss me, but I couldn't allow myself to get too close. I had to keep him safe. I wasn't about to risk his life, when I knew he would easily give it for me.

I wouldn't allow it. Not over me.

The thought made my insides knot. A stabbing pain shot through my heart, and an even deeper hatred for the one who restrained me. I hated the fact I would never be able to tell Kade why we couldn't be together. I just had to be strong. I had to hold on, even though my heart was breaking, and the fibers of my life were steadily unraveling.

I pulled the blanket over my head, pushing my face deeper into my pillow, and screamed. There was one thing that might be able to put an end to all of the madness. It was a huge risk, but if it was even possible, it could change everything... or make it worse.

Uncertainty began to coil itself around me, daring to squeeze out whatever hope I had left. I just needed to find a way to make it out of this place without being seen.

I had to find a way to the portal for Midway. I needed to talk to the person in charge; the one responsible for making Kade mortal.

Everything good in my life had been stripped and I was drowning in darkness, but I was going to fight to get it back. There was a war waging inside of me. I could feel it pulsating through my veins. For better or worse, things were going to change. But this was my life, and nothing was going to stop me... even if it meant my death.

I closed my eyes knowing sleep wouldn't find me for some time, but eventually they became heavy, and darkness overtook me.

Sitting at the edge of a small lake, I dipped my feet in and out of the crystal clear water; appreciating the magical weather. The sun was shining, and the sky was the most unbelievable blue. It almost looked like a painting. The large tree behind me was providing the perfect amount of shade. The grass beneath me was bright green and feathery soft to the touch.

A few yards away, near the water's edge, two beautiful, children were playing. Their dark hair glimmering in the sun. The little boy was being chased around by an older girl. Their laughter filling the air, making me buzz with delight.

A large, strong hand found mine and squeezed. Leaning back, I breathed in the heady scent of my bonded. My soul mate. He was lying beside me, with one arm behind his head.

"Are the little devils behaving themselves?" he asked.

I turn to face him and use my free hand to draw circles up and down his chest. "Yes. They seem to enjoy this place, almost as much as we do."

"It's a shame we haven't flown here as a family more often." Turning his head, his mesmerizing eyes lock onto mine in earnest. "We'll have to remedy that in the future."

My eyes popped open. I sat up in the darkness, not knowing if what I had just experienced was a dream, or a premonition.

Whatever it was, it seemed genuine. I rested my hand to my heart, and took a slow, steadying breath.

It couldn't be real... could it? A tear escaped my eye and trailed down my cheek.

Dream or not, my plans were set.

Alone in the darkness, I whispered a prayer. "Can anyone hear me? I need some help, and a little guidance. What do I do next?"

A bright light illuminated from the bottom crack of my closet door. Gasping, I wondered if it was Lucifer. Holding my breath for what seemed like forever, I waited. The longer I sat there, the more compelled I felt to see what was behind the door.

Finally pushing the blanket off, I slowly stood from the bed. My heart hammered against my chest as I took my first few steps. Something, or someone, was there. As I placed my fingers to the knob, it was warm, unlike the room which was ice cold. The light still shone bright from under the door, actually warming my toes.

I slowly turned the knob, and my breath hitched as I pulled it open.

There was no one there, except for an indescribable sweet scent which wrapped itself around me, a dagger lying in the middle of the floor, glowing brightly. I bent down to pick it up and noticed it was resting on a piece of paper folded in half. I picked it up and unfolded it, reading the beautiful handwritten words.

Emma,

When worn, the Vestimentum Angelorum will aid you. Invisibility is a rare and wonderful gift, should you need it. The dagger will lead you wherever you need to travel. All you need to do is say the words aloud. When pointed in the right direction, it will remain lit.

I am always watching, and am hopeful our paths will cross one day.

With undying love,

Watching from above

I read the note a few times, and even pinched myself to be sure it was all real.

Things were about to change. There *was* someone looking out for me, and hopefully it was for my better interest. But what if it was Lucifer trying to set me up? Although, I didn't have a feeling it was him. Maybe it was my mysterious grandfather, or God himself? He was omnipotent, right?

These thoughts sent a rush of warmth through my veins, and the scent left in the room was of pure angel. There were no hints of smokiness. It was definitely someone from above.

"Thank you," I whispered, picking up and hugging the dagger and the note to my heart. The dagger was warm, sending a calmness cascading through me. I wasn't sure if I was doing the right thing. My greatest fear would be putting those I loved at an even greater risk.

But more than anything, I needed answers. I needed to know if I had a chance against Lucifer and Lucian.

All I had was hope. This mission needed to happen, not only for me, but for everyone I loved. I wouldn't risk everything on a whim, or something I wasn't sure would make a difference. I had one burning question, and the answer could possibly change everything.

Those around me probably had the answer I was looking for, but I would never ask them because they would have their own opinions. And I didn't want them to try and persuade me. This question needed to be kept secret. It was to be mine, and mine alone.

The super suit was clean and hung in the corner of my closet. I walked over and touched the fabric. Tingles vibrated through my fingers. *Magic.* It was the only way to explain it. I wondered if any normal human being would feel the same effects. I peeled off my pajamas and stepped into it, zipping it up. Immediately, its magic pulled me back together, mending my inner cracks and broken heart like a warm hug that never let go. I felt stronger, and suddenly positive I could actually pull this off.

What more did I need? I had this awesome suit of protection, the magical dagger, and the bloodstone amulet to alert me of danger. They were a triple threat, and I *almost* felt invincible. I was blessed to be in possession of such an amazing gift.

The only thing I was second-guessing at this point was going alone. No one would know where I was, or where I was heading. If anything should ever happen to me, it would be a while before they found out. And what if something happened and I needed help? No one would be there to come to my aid. My stomach began to twist with worry.

I still felt a small reassurance there was someone out there, watching over me. Even if they couldn't interfere, maybe they could let the others know if I needed help. I didn't want my mind to dwell on the negative. It would only pull me down from what I knew needed to be done.

I wished the dang portal was closer. Like in-my-room kind of close. That would be amazingly convenient. I could step in and be back before anyone knew I was gone. But of course, that wasn't the case. It seemed nothing was easy for me.

Taking a car was off limits because anyone of them, Fallen or Guardian, would catch me. This particular quest had to be done on foot. It was miles and miles away and would probably take days to get there. But first, I would have to head down to the kitchen and pack a few necessities for the journey.

Glancing over at the clock on my nightstand, its red numbers illuminated *1:17am*. No one should be up at this hour, but in a house full of immortals, anything could happen.

I slipped on my combat boots, and slung an empty backpack over my shoulder.

It was too risky to leave a note. I didn't want anyone to know of my plan anyway, especially Lucifer.

Taking in a deep breath, I opened my door and glanced both ways down the hall. It was dark and eerily quiet. Slipping out and shutting the door quietly behind me, I made my way down the stairs. I paused and looked at Kade's door; it was closed and the light was off.

How I wished I had a chance to talk to him. My insides ached to the core, knowing I hadn't seen or talked to him since the incident with Lucifer. I just hoped he'd understand. One day I would get the chance to explain everything to him.

I pushed the thought from my mind. I needed to focus and get moving before anyone woke up and saw me. Quickly making my way down the stairs, I headed straight for the kitchen. The hallway was dimly lit with nightlights, but the main kitchen lights were off. That was a good sign.

As soon as I stepped inside, I heard voices. They were right outside the door. I quickly ducked behind the counter, knowing I couldn't leave without being seen.

The door swung open and slammed shut, and then the light clicked on.

Dammit.

"I wonder what kind of goodies Miss Lily left? I hope she has a stash of her awesome cookies," Dom said. The fridge door opened, and I heard him rummaging about. "So, what? You want anything to eat?"

"Nah. I'm good."

My heart skipped a beat.

"Dude, just go to her room and give her a goodnight kiss," Dom jested.

"I can't. Did you see the time? She's been through a lot and needs rest."

"Yeah, but I think she'd rather have a visit from her Prince Charming. You should just seal the damn bond and get it over with, man."

"You know I can't do that."

"Why not? That bastard doesn't deserve her. They'll just use her, and you know it. The only way to keep her from them is to seal the bond."

"Dom, I can't seal the bond anymore. The bond between us was broken when I became mortal."

"I think that's bullshit. Everyone can see it in both of you, even if the bond was *supposedly* broken. It's so freaking obvious. How will you know unless you try?" Dom reasoned.

"Because I'm not her only bonded. And, I'm not even sure she knows who she wants to be with at this point. I won't force her to be with me. When he's near her, I can see the connection between them. And as much as it hurts to hear, Ethon has a point. He can protect her better than I could, he's immortal. I've already begun to age, and will eventually die. When I'm gone, Emma will remain here, alone."

"She'll always have me," Dom laughed. I could picture Kade rolling his eyes. "Dude, if you love her, you need to freaking fight for her. Mortal or immortal, don't just sit back and let someone else slip in the side door. You were her first bond. You need to get your shit together and figure out what you want. She might not know what she wants right now, but everyone can see you belong together.

"I mean, seriously. Can you see her spending eternity in hell with Ethon? Emma as Princess of the Underworld, with daddy

Devil watching and manipulating her every move? She'll never be happy, and once they find out about her, they won't sit back and let her choose. You can be sure they'll make sure she bonds with the little demon. We can't stand by and let that happen."

Damn, Dom totally rocked. He knew exactly what was going on, and I just hoped they'd be able to figure it all out, in case I failed.

Kade remained silent.

"Kade, you did what you had to. You're her Guardian, and you gave up your immortality for her. I know she sees that, and she'll make the right decision. Just don't bail out and make the choice easy for her. You love her. Just be sure *she* knows it, alright?"

"Alright," Kade answered. "Thanks, man. I will make sure she has no doubt, but I'm not going to force her either. I just want her to be happy, and to make her own decision. I guess I'll have to prove that actions speak louder than words."

"You already have, bro. Look at you. I think you've spoken loud and clear," Dom said in a more serious voice. "So, are you hungry now? I just found some roast beef, and I am totally making a sandwich."

I almost laughed out loud, but covered my mouth. He was too much.

"Sure, man. Why not?" Kade agreed.

There was no way I was going to get food or water with them here. I wondered if I should just head back up to my room. But I couldn't. I had to go. After hearing Kade and Dom's conversation,

I knew I needed to get to Midway as soon as possible. I needed to find some answers.

Starting to feel a little dizzy, I glanced down and realized I was invisible. The suit was aiding in my escape. To be sure, I stayed low to the ground and crawled my way out of the kitchen. As I exited the doorway, I stopped and turned back to look at him one last time.

Kade was standing at the counter, his beautiful face dimly lit by the kitchen light. He tried to smile while talking to Dom, but I could see his mind was elsewhere. His hazel eyes emitted a deep sadness, and I had to turn away.

It was time to leave.

I made my way toward the front door and when I touched the knob, I became terrified. I was leaving the safety and protection of my Guardians, and Samuel and Alaine. I would be out there all alone, with only the suit and dagger to guide me and keep me safe. *Am I making the right decision?* My mind said no, but my heart said yes. I'd learned to choose my heart. So far, it had never led me astray.

I took in a deep breath and turned the knob. The door squeaked as it opened and I paused. No one came, so I quickly slid out, quietly closing it behind me.

Outside, the air was cold and the sky was crystal clear; millions of sparkling stars gently illuminated the world around me. I glanced up to the tower and noticed the light was on. I could feel Ethon. He must be up.

I looked down at my arm and saw I was still invisible. Then something moved in the tower. It was Ethon, staring out the window right at me. Maybe he could feel me too. I quickly stepped back, pressing my back against the door and waited a few moments. When the feeling subsided, I checked again, and he was gone.

I felt bad for Ethon. Because of the bond, which found us compatible, I did have strong feelings for him. If it were just him in the picture, it would have been an easy decision. Easier, of course, without his evil incarnate father hovering above us.

Even though Ethon wasn't like him, he still grew up in that world. It was all he'd ever known, and some of it had to have rubbed off on him.

Soon, I would have to choose, but first, I had to get to my destination and make it back alive. Hopefully, with questions answered.

I unsheathed the dagger. Holding it to my lips, I whispered, "Where is the portal to Midway?"

Although the dagger was invisible in my grasp, I started to see a dim glow. As I moved it around, pointing it in different directions, the glow would disappear and then reappear straight ahead of me. I hoped it would be guiding me in the right direction. By the looks of it, I'd be starting my journey into the dark, unwelcoming forest.

A loud shrieking caw caused me to jump. I glanced up, and Ash was flying directly above. His glossy ebony wings were outspread, soaring in the dark, cold sky. Ash was Lucifer's eyes, and the thought of him watching me sent a skin-crawling shiver through my core. I started to second guess myself, but I couldn't let the fear overcome me.

I waited another few moments until he finally disappeared over the tower.

Taking a step forward, I was embarking on another journey, determined to find answers and hopeful to regain control of my future.

Once the whole crew found out I was missing, I knew they'd immediately start a search party. Moving quickly was key, especially with Lucian's legion out there. If they found me, I was as good as dead.

TWO

HURRIEDLY, I FOLLOWED THE DIM glow of the dagger which led me into the forest, further and further from my safe haven. There was no turning back now.

I ran through the never-ending spruce, as fast as my feet could carry me. Branches scratched and snapped at me; my heart and pulse thrummed faster and faster as I ran deeper into darkness. The dim glow from the moon and stars was almost immediately snuffed out by the thick boughs above, making it nearly impossible to see.

With the Fallen and Darkling on the prowl, I had to be smart and I couldn't let fear stop me.

The dagger led me deeper and deeper into darkness. My skin crawled, feeling as if hundreds of wicked eyes were on me, watching and waiting for a chance to rip me apart.

A sudden gust of wind and a shadow, darker than the dark above me, made me stop dead in my tracks. I took in a deep breath and held it, catching a familiar scent and along with it, the amulet began to emit warmth on my chest.

Fallen were here.

I pressed my back against a tree and stayed frozen.

"Do you smell it?" one asked in a low, gruff voice.

"Yes, but the scent... it's neither Fallen nor angel."

"What do you think it is?"

"I don't know, but I'm going to find out." The gruff voice boomed in laughter, sending goose bumps across my skin.

Two figures dove from the sky and hit the ground like thunder, making the ground quake. They reminded me of the Fallen we encountered in the forest on our way toward the North Pole. They were handsome with dark features and dark hair, but that meant nothing. These beautiful creatures were filled with evil. They must have been warriors because they wore some kind of armor over their chests. Their arms were bare and bulging with muscles.

I moved further into darkness, watching them carefully, holding the dagger tightly in my grasp.

"The smell is much stronger here. Maybe there is more than one. I'm catching a faint scent of Fallen."

"Do you think it could be one of the Nephilim?"

"It could be, though I thought we killed all the others. We could be wrong. There might be one trying to make it toward the dome of protection. Maybe we can find it and kill it before it reaches safety."

"What if it's one of *them* from the inside?"

"I doubt it. Coming outside of protection would be a death wish. This is probably one we missed. We better find it and kill it quickly. Lucian will give us an extra reward if we bring back its head. Maybe we'll get a day off."

Deep wicked laughter boomed through the forest.

"It's so close. I can smell it."

Bastards. I wasn't an *it.* I wish I had my power so I could kick their asses. Yes, coming out here was a death wish, but I did have some aid. The one who was "watching from above" wouldn't have left me the note if they didn't believe in me. I knew I was doing the right thing. I just needed to stay alive.

The Fallen crouched, sniffing the air. I tried not to breathe, but my breath wasn't what would give away my location. I slowly bent down and picked up a rock. As soon as it touched my fingers, it disappeared, and I thrust it as far as I could.

The Fallen immediately snapped toward the sound and took off. I ran in the opposite direction, as fast as I could. Assuming I was far enough away, I stopped and hid behind another bunch of trees. My lungs felt like they were going to explode.

I hoped and prayed one of my gifts would be wings. I needed them, especially right now. Oh, to be invisible and fly... I would definitely be a force to be reckoned with.

I quickly unsheathed my dagger and held it out in front of me. It was dark, and I swung it around until it started to glow.

A sudden overwhelming feeling crashed through me like a bolt of lightning, nearly bringing me to my knees.

Ethon.

He must have been looking for me because I'd been gone for over an hour.

"Who's there?" one of Lucian's Fallen asked. Damn they were fast.

"What are you two doing here?" Ethon asked.

"Well, look at this," one of the Fallen said darkly. "We are hunting, and it looks as if we caught ourselves a Nephilim after all."

"Are you threatening me?" Ethon questioned, without an ounce of fear in his voice.

I caught sight of him, faintly catching his silhouette, along with the other two. They were huge and towering over him. His eyes glowed a dark crimson, the color I'd witnessed when he was upset. Everything inside me wanted to run to his aid, but knew if I did, this whole deal would be off.

Nothing could stop me. I had to keep moving, but first, I had to make sure he was going to be okay.

"So, you're the bastard son of Lucifer. The eyes are unmistakable. If you think we are afraid of you, you've got another thing coming."

"You must be a special breed of stupid, because you should be *very* afraid. Especially of this bastard son and Nephilim," Ethon taunted in return.

The two Fallen roared with laughter, but he stood his ground.

"Before this night's end, we will have two Nephilim heads to present to Lucian. And with the head of Lucifer's son, it looks as if we might have an extended vacation," one jested in a condescending tone.

"Yes, maybe we might even get a whole century off," the other laughed.

Without speaking another word, Ethon lowered his head, his beautiful black wings expanding across his back and out to the sides. Before the Fallen knew what was happening, he jumped up and spun like a whirlwind. His wings, as sharp as blades, quickly and easily severed their heads. Both toppled to the ground, their lifeless bodies following behind with loud thuds. Their laughter was immediately silenced, and I could feel my lips turn upward as pride warmed my heart.

He was a killing machine, and I prayed he and Kade would never have an encounter.

Ethon tucked his wings behind his back and began to sniff the air, his eyes became a much softer red as he stepped closer in my direction. I pushed myself behind the tree.

"Emma, I know you're out here. *Please.* It's not safe. Let me take you back." He was pleading.

I wanted to answer him, but I couldn't. The pull of the bond was tugging at my heart; the fight was burdensome and exhausting. But I had to remain strong. It was essential for me to find answers before I made my final decision, and until I did, I'd have to keep my heart and mind guarded.

I hated how the bond toyed with my emotions.

"Alright then, Emma. You win. I don't know what you're up to or where you're headed, but please be safe." I glanced around the tree and watched him turn his back to me and walk away.

After a few steps, he paused. "I just hope you know, if I really wanted to find you, I could have – quite easily. Your Guardian sent me to find you and bring you back, but I won't interfere. You must be here for a reason." He paused, keeping his back to me. "The area is clear from Fallen. If you need to go, now is the time. The others will be coming soon. I will make sure no one harms you. All I ask is that when you return, we have a chance to talk. You at least owe me that much." With a flap of his wings, he was gone.

Dammit. Why did he have to be so freaking bad-boy perfect? He was really complicating things. Ethon and Kade were polar opposites, and I was equally attracted to both. Yes, the bond was magical and had chosen the perfect mate, but in my isolated case it was torturous, making it nearly impossible to choose between the two.

Once I made my choice, I knew a hole would forever remain in my heart. Both of them had a piece of it, and both were equally matched, except in mortality.

I sighed and tried to push it all out of my mind. I had to regain my focus and keep moving. Knowing Ethon was out there seemed to ease my fears.

I continued to move, steadily following the glow of the dagger, hoping it was leading me toward the portal. The suit kept me warm, but it didn't do anything for my thirst or hunger pains. After hours of walking, the lack of sleep also caught up to me. I had to stop and rest for a while.

Ahead of me, five spruce trees were somewhat intertwined, creating a small area of protection between them. I gathered bunches of spruce needles and placed them inside the area to act as a cushion. It wasn't nearly as comfortable as my bed, but it would work.

I could barely keep my eyes open and needed to rest, if even for an hour. I was still invisible as I curled up into the tight space, the dagger grasped tightly in my hand. Feeling safe and secure, I closed my eyes and immediately fell to sleep.

The snapping of branches nearby made me awake with a jump. I lifted the dagger in front of me, still invisible, but noticed the forest was dimly lit. The sun was beginning to rise.

I overslept. Pushing myself out of the space, I scanned the area and when I was sure it was clear, I stretched my tired muscles. As I turned, I noticed a brown satchel hanging on one of the branches of the tree next to me. I pulled it off and opened the flap. Inside was a small bag of assorted nuts, jerky, two bottles of water and Kade's blue flask.

What the heck was going on? Someone knew I was here, and also knew I was hungry and thirsty. It wasn't Ethon. Yes, he was out there, but I didn't get the feeling I usually had when he was near. This was someone else; there was a different scent in the air. It was someone I hadn't met yet. But how did they get Kade's flask? Did *he* send this person to me? My head spun like a whirlwind with even more unanswered questions.

I climbed back into the space and opened the satchel, taking out a piece of jerky and a few nuts. After I ate them, I began to feel a little better. The water was ice cold, and in no time I emptied a whole bottle. Next, I lifted the blue flask and placed it to my nose. A faint scent of Kade remained, warming my insides. I unscrewed the cap and placed it to my lips, taking a small sip. The magical liquid immediately worked its way through my cells, taking my aches, pains, and tiredness away. This was just what I needed to get moving.

After placing everything back in the satchel, I climbed out from the space, and slung it over my back. I had more than what I needed for this journey.

It would be another full day of walking, but at least the light made it much easier to travel. With a renewed vigor, I followed the light of the dagger. If I kept up a quick pace, I'd be at my destination in no time. I figured that I had traveled more than half the distance last night. The rest of the way should be easy.

No sooner than the thought left my mind, I felt heat on my chest. I glanced down at the bloodstone amulet, which was glowing bright red. I ducked behind a fallen tree and listened.

Nothing.

Just as I was about to peek from my hiding spot, a loud shriek sounded, shortly followed by the clanging of swords. I ran, not caring which direction I was heading.

As I looked toward the sky above, I gasped. At least a dozen pairs of black wings soared, darkening the sky above me. They knew I was here. They could smell me. With so many of them out there, I knew it was just a matter of time before they caught me. Even Ethon couldn't take on all of them by himself.

A battle was waging above me, and I wasn't sure who was fighting.

After a few more seconds, I felt Ethon arrive. Then, hearing Samuel's voice made my heart sink. They were fighting for me.

Fighting because I was out here. *What had I done?* They'd better not get hurt because of me.

"Emma!"

I turned and thought I was dreaming. I blinked my eyes a few times, but the vision didn't disappear. Kade was standing in the distance, looking directly at me.

"Kade?" I called out, but still questioning.

He ran over and wrapped his arms around me. "Thank God you're okay," he breathed. "Dammit, Emma. I've never been more terrified in all my life."

"How did you find me?"

"Ethon told me where you were. He and the others are dealing with the Fallen, and they wanted me to come and get you." He steadied my face in his hands. "Why did you leave?"

"I had to, and I'm not going back."

"Why? Why are you putting yourself in danger? I don't understand."

"I can't tell you." My heart was breaking, and a tear trickled down my face. "You just have to trust me."

"I do trust you, but you need to tell me why."

I shook my head. "I can't. I want to, but I can't. Please don't ask. You just have to believe me."

"Okay," he said, pulling me back into his arms, and kissing my forehead. "Can you at least tell me where you're headed?"

I stepped back and looked into his concerned eyes. "Midway."

"Midway? Why?"

"Please. I'll go alone, just tell me how much further it is."

"No way. You aren't going alone. I'm your Guardian and will take you there. I need to make sure you're safe. It's about ten miles away."

"Thank you," I whispered.

"You're welcome." He extended his hand toward me. "We better get moving."

Kade had me by the hand, running through the trees. I would never have been running this fast, but he seemed to know exactly where he was going. Ten miles. If we kept this up, we could be there in a few hours.

After running for what seemed like an hour, Kade stopped.

"Why are we stopping?" I panted.

"You need water and rest for just a minute, and then we'll get going again." He took the satchel and pulled out the blue flask. "Here, take a sip."

"I'm fine... and by the way, how did you know the flask was in there. Who brought it to me?" I questioned, looking deep into his eyes.

He paused, his eyes locking onto mine. "You have things you can't divulge at the moment, and so do I."

"Fair enough," I said, and he smiled.

I took a sip from the flask and instantly felt my heart and pulse rate slow. I felt good as new, and ready to run the rest of the way. "Your turn." I handed him the flask and he hesitated, but I stood firm. He finally took it and sipped, then twisted the cap back on.

"Where are the others?" I asked.

"Probably busy keeping the Fallen away. There were only a handful of them. Nothing they can't handle."

"Are you sure they'll be okay?" I asked.

"There hasn't been any Fallen who can beat our group. Especially with Samuel..." he paused, "and Ethon. They'll be just fine."

"That's good. I wouldn't want any of them to die over me."

"They'll be fine and those going up against them will get what's coming to them. Most of the time the Fallen are so filled with pride, it becomes their downfall."

"Well, I'm glad you're here. Thank you for coming for me, and not taking me back."

"I'm still yours... your Guardian that is. At least until you make your final decision." He flashed a half smile.

"Hey," I said, grabbing hold of his hand. "Yes, you are most definitely my Guardian, and right now I need you."

He glanced at me and nodded, then pulled me closer to him. "We really need to talk when we get back."

I sighed and nodded, knowing I was bound from telling him the truth. "I know."

He smiled, his eyes slowly slipping downward.

"What?"

"That suit. You know what it does to me," he said flirtatiously.

My face flushed with heat. "It's impenetrable," I answered.

"Nothing is completely impenetrable. There's always a weak spot."

"And *you* think you know where it is?"

"Oh, I'm pretty sure." He grinned and I blushed.

He softly lifted my chin with his fingers until my eyes met his. "Emma, I want you to know that my heart had never felt fulfilled, never felt whole, until I met you. After being in existence for nearly two centuries, you were the only one to unlock something deep inside of me; something I never knew I possessed. My heart is no longer my own. It now belongs to you, and will remain yours, even if you decide to give it back." Leaning forward, he leveled his beautiful eyes to mine. They were swirling with so much emotion. His closeness was my weakness. "I love you, Emma, and I would do anything to keep you safe and make you happy."

"I know. You've already proven yourself, and I cannot thank you enough," I looked deeper into his eyes, "And, I—"

He stopped me, by placing his finger to my lips. "You don't have to tell me you love me back. I know the strength of the bond, and how it only allows you to love your bonded. I didn't say it to you, expecting a response. I just wanted you to know in case—" he paused, weighing his words.

"In case what?" I questioned.

"It's nothing. I'm just rambling."

"Kade Anders, you better not be looking for a way out of my life," I said, grabbing hold of his arms, forcing him to look at me.

"Never," he assured, stepping closer.

As soon as his hazel eyes locked onto mine, I was captured. It was so damn hard to resist him, even without the bond. I wanted to step away. I didn't want to get too close, knowing I might have to break his heart - and mine. But I couldn't move. I was frozen under his bewitching spell.

He gently lifted his hands and placed them on either side of my face. I closed my eyes as his soft, warm lips pressed against mine. Lips, tongues, and breath intertwined. I had fallen hard for him, even without the bond.

I wrapped my fingers in his thick hair, locking him in place. There was something about him that took me to a high which was so damn hard to come down from.

Kade gently pulled back, leaving me breathless.

"I could do this all day, but we have to get moving." He rested his forehead against mine, wrapping me in a tight embrace.

"Yeah, good idea," I agreed.

I wished it were this easy, to stay encased and protected in his arms. But somewhere out there was another who was fighting for me, making sure I was safe. Even though my life had its few good moments, it had also been cruel and unfair. But it was the life destined to me, and I'd just have to wait and see how it all played out.

We continued on, and just when I thought we were in the clear, the ground thundered. I turned as a Fallen landed. His evil eyes were glaring at us with dark intentions.

"Emma, *run*," Kade ordered, stepping in front of me and unsheathing his sword.

"I'm not going anywhere without you," I answered.

"It's not debatable. Go now," he urged.

The Fallen growled. "She can run, but it will only be a matter of time before I catch her."

"Not if I kill you first, bastard." Kade crouched, ready to attack.

Behind us to the left I noticed something familiar. A ginormous tree stood out of place in the midst of the spruce trees. It wasn't the portal we were seeking, but I knew it was the portal to Ethon's secret place.

"Emma, you're not moving," Kade stressed.

"I told you, I'm not leaving you." There was no way I was going to leave him alone.

Three more Fallen dropped out from the sky, surrounding us. The suit wasn't making me invisible, but it was already too late. Even if I disappeared, they knew I was here. They were all herculean, towering over us.

"Just hand over the girl and we'll leave you alone," the first Fallen spoke.

"That's not going to happen," Kade answered.

"Then you will have to die."

"If it is my destiny to die saving the one I love, then I will do it with honor."

The Fallen shook his head and narrowed his eyes.

"Love," he spat. "It makes one weak."

"Oh, but you're wrong. Its love which gives me strength," Kade answered.

"Kade, don't," I begged.

"Do you have your dagger?" he asked, his eyes locked forward.

"Yes," I answered.

"Then use it, and don't be afraid," he said turning back, his eyes softening as they met mine.

"Kade!" I screamed, pulling him out of the way of the Fallen who had charged toward him. His sword whizzed right past Kade's head. He immediately turned and swung again, but Kade was ready, their swords clashing. Over and over the Fallen struck, but Kade countered, blocking his attacks, taking him further and further away from me.

Another Fallen rushed at me from behind. I automatically turned and ducked; his blade whizzing past my side, nearly missing its mark. As the momentum of his swing pulled him forward, I thrust my dagger upward, sinking it deep into his chest.

He dropped his weapon and fell to his knees, grasping for my neck. I leaned out of his reach, and yanked the blade free from his chest, using it to slice his neck.

He gasped, bringing his hand up over the gushing laceration.

I was in shock, watching him die from a wound I'd just delivered. Blood seeped through his fingers and down his chest. The sounds of his gasping and gurgling through the blood filling his lungs, made my stomach churn.

A scream from behind threw me back into the moment. I had to clear my head. We were in a battle. I twisted back and saw another Fallen charging at me. Without warning, I was thrust backward by an unseen force; my body slid under the advancing blade. I felt the breeze as it passed right over my face, slicing a few stray hairs.

I rolled to my hands and knees, scrambling to get to my feet. A bashing assault from behind knocked me flat. I rolled over as the Fallen's blade came crashing down, right on my chest.

I couldn't breathe. I couldn't scream. The pain was too agonizing.

"Emma!" Kade yelled.

I turned toward him. He tried to run, but was kicked in the gut and thrown further away.

The Fallen who dealt the blow bounded toward him, but Kade's rage had him back on his feet. With a quick twist and perfect precision, he sliced right through the Fallen's neck, severing the head from its owner.

Holding my breath, I glanced down to see if I'd been impaled. The suit kept the blade from piercing my chest and heart.

"Vestimentum Angelorum?" the Fallen who struck me asked in disbelief.

"Yeah, asshole. It's my super suit," I said, jumping up through the pain and thrusting my blade into his forehead. His eyes rolled back and he dropped to the ground. I quickly pulled the blade from his face and pushed it into his heart. It was easier than slicing off a head.

I dropped to my knees. The pain in my chest radiating.

Kade pulled his blade from the last one and ran over to me.

"Emma, are you okay?" He knelt down.

"Fine. I think he broke my ribs." My words were short and labored.

"I need to get you out of here," he said with urgency.

Two more Fallen landed and looked at their dead brothers. Their eyes locked onto us with burning revenge.

"Kade?" I turned toward him before someone grabbed me from behind, swooping me into the air.

"I've got you," Ethon said, holding me tightly.

In mere seconds we were at his safe haven. He slowly landed near the lake, laying me in the soft grass under the tree.

"You're safe," he said, gently letting go. "Are you hurt?"

"You need to go back and help him. They'll kill him," I pleaded. Tears fell from my eyes – a combination of pain and knowing Kade was out there alone.

"That would make things a whole lot easier for us," he smirked.

My stomach twisted at his disturbing response.

"If he dies out there, I—I will *never* forgive you," I snapped, my emotions seemed to be dulling the bond.

"Easy. I was only joking," he said rolling his eyes. "The other Guardians and your father were right behind me."

"I don't care. I need to make sure he's safe."

He sighed dramatically. "So you're taking role of Guardian now? Which is which?"

"If you don't go, I will." Pushing myself up, I groaned and fell backward as a stabbing pain shot through my chest.

"You cannot leave this place without me. You'll need wings. The exit is way up there," he noted, pointing to the distortion in the sky thirty feet above us.

"Ethon, please," I begged.

He stepped forward and knelt. "Let me fix you first."

I nodded, trying to hold back the tears of pain.

His eyes softened as he looked at me, and then they closed. When he opened them again, they were flaming, small wisps of smoke curled and twisted from the edges, disappearing as they touched the air. I would never get used to seeing him like this, all terrifyingly beautiful.

"Are you ready?" he softly spoke, slowly lifting his hands. They were glowing red with heat.

"Yes," I lied, knowing more pain would soon follow.

He laid his hands on my ribs. A heat, torched my insides, but only for a few moments. I gasped in pain as my ribs popped back into place, and only until the last one returned to its position, could I finally breathe freely.

I took in a deep breath, and watched him smile.

"Thank you," I said in all sincerity.

A crooked grin adorned his lips before he closed his eyes again. When they reopened, the flame was gone, replaced with his normal crimson color. "I have never met anyone in all my years who has broken as many ribs as you."

"Neither have I," I sighed, sitting up. "Thank you." As our eyes met, it was nearly impossible to turn away. The bond magnetized us, an invisible charm, seducing and luring us together.

Ethon ran his fingers down the side of my cheek, brushing a stray strand of hair behind my ear. "Can't you see what's right in front of you? Even with the bond, I can see your heart is torn," he sighed, and shook his head.

I swallowed hard and exhaled, knowing it was true.

"I can't help it. He was my first bond."

"Was. He *was* your first bond, and is not any longer. Now, you are bonded to me." He stood and walked away. "You don't understand, Emma. I could have any woman I choose. There is not one mortal who can resist me, but not one of them could ever satisfy me.

"I don't want, or need, anyone else but you. Can't you see that? Can't you feel it?" He turned and walked closer to me. "I want to spend the rest of my eternity with *you*." His fingers gently brushed my tears away.

"And what about your father, Ethon? He will always rule over us, and will always have a say. If we bond, I will be his slave for all eternity."

He closed his eyes. "He's not that bad, Emma."

"How can you say that? He tried to kill me," I said exasperated. Was this what I would have to look forward to? Him defending his father when he saw exactly what he did to me?

Ethon stepped forward and wrapped me in his arms. "I'm sorry. He shouldn't have touched you. Once we've sealed the bond, he will *never* touch you again. I promise."

I wanted to believe him, but given the circumstances, it was nearly impossible.

"Hey," he whispered. "I told you I would make you happy, and I plan on carrying out my word." He kissed the top of my head and stepped back. "I'll be right back. And, don't worry. No one can enter without me."

With a flap of his wings, he shot up and out of the portal.

My heart and mind twisted. I began to question my existence. All I did was bring pain and confusion. Angels and Fallen were fighting and dying because of me, and I was supposed to bring forth some kind of big change?

I sat next to the water's edge, wondering and waiting for him to return. I hoped they were all okay, and then it hit me. What would happen to me if anything happened to Ethon? How would I get out of here? The thought sent a wave of terror crashing through me, but before I had a meltdown, he appeared through the portal.

His beautiful black wings were extended as he landed. His raven black hair rustled lightly across his face, while crimson eyes steadied on mine.

"Don't worry. They're all safe. Your Guardian was injured, but it's only superficial. He'll heal up in no time. Your father took him back to Alaine."

I sighed in relief.

"Thank you," I breathed. But how was I going to get to Midway now?

"Come, I'll take you back."

"I can't go back. I need to do something alone. For myself."

"What is it? You can tell me," he said, coming close.

I shook my head and stepped back. "I can't."

"Why are you fighting? We will be bonded soon."

I had to make him believe I was still in total agreement with his father's pact. "Yes, I know. But there is something I need to do for myself, before the bond is sealed."

"Is it something I can help you with?"

"I wish you could, but this is something I need to do alone."

"Alright. I won't hold you back, unless there is a third immortal to whom you've been bonded?"

"No way! If there was another, I'd ask God to take me out himself."

Ethon laughed. "Come here, you." He extended his hand. I gasped as we touched, it was a rush.

"I can't imagine the feeling we will have sealing the bond," he whispered lightly in my ear. "It is something I am longing for." I swallowed the huge lump in my throat, taken back by his response. "And don't worry. I'm sure it will be beyond pleasurable for both of us."

I was speechless, and realized I had probably looked like a deer in headlights.

Ethon laughed loudly, and then kissed me quickly on the lips before ascending toward the portal. In seconds we were back outside. The bodies of the Fallen remained on the ground, headless.

He set me down near the rest of the Guardians. Only Dom, Malachi, and Alex were there.

"Well, there she is. We thought we'd never see you again, invisible girl," Malachi rolled his eyes.

I smiled. "It's good to see you too, Malachi."

"Emma, Emma, Emma. Do we need to lock you in your room?" Dom teased, heading over toward me. "And, damn. You always look so freaking hot in that garment."

Ethon stepped forward.

"I wouldn't do that if I were you," Dom said, wagging a finger at him.

"You have no idea what I could do to you. I only use restraint because of Emma," Ethon growled, his eyes burning bright.

I touched his arm and he turned to me, the flame almost immediately quenched. "It's okay. You can leave me with them. I'll be fine, and I'll be back soon. I promise."

He leaned over and hugged me. "Please be safe," he whispered, tucking a few strands of hair behind my ears.

"I will," I whispered back.

It was awkward and a bit unnerving hugging Ethon in front of the Guardians, but I needed him to know I'd be fine. As soon as we disconnected, he shot into the sky like a rocket. I knew he was gone because my whole body relaxed and became normal again.

"Little demon," Dom huffed. "I know you're bonded, but that is so freaking wrong."

"You don't have to tell me. I'm the one trying to deal and make sense of it all," I sighed.

"Hey, Emma!" Alexander chimed, pausing to wave before dragging a headless body over to a pile they'd started.

"Hey, Alex." I smiled and waved, then turned to Malachi. "Is Kade alright?"

"He's fine. He took a blow to his left shoulder, but it's not fatal. He'll need a few stiches and some rest, but he'll be fine in a few days."

"That's good," I exhaled.

"We need to get you back," Malachi said.

"You guys go on ahead. I'll take her back. She's safe with me," Dom said.

"You sure?" Alex asked.

"Very sure. I have a few things I'd like to discuss with Emma before we head back."

"Fine," Malachi said. "Emma, remember who you're talking to. Don't take it too personal… or too serious."

"I won't," I giggled, but inside started to wonder what this was all about.

After the bodies were stacked, Malachi and Alex left me and Dom alone.

"So, what do you want to talk about?"

"Kade told me about your secret quest, and since I'm his best bud, I figured I'd help out and take you to Midway."

"Really?" I squealed a little too loudly.

"Really. You know, I also had this amazing speech about the pros of hooking up with Kade, and the cons of bonding with the demon. But I think you're smart enough to figure it all out on your own. I mean, ultimately it is your decision, and no one can make it for you. So, I'll spare you – and me – the lecture," he said.

"Thanks, Dom," I said, hugging him tight.

"No problem. What are friends for?" He hugged me back. "Okay, follow me," he said, stepping around me. I smiled and followed after him.

The woods were quiet during our journey, and there were no signs of Fallen. It wasn't long before Dom stopped, standing in front of two perfectly symmetrical spruce trees.

"Are we here?"

"This is it." He extended his arm between the two trees, his hand and forearm disappeared. "The entrance to Midway. I think I will escort you, since you don't know your way around. Plus, they won't be too happy about seeing you there, and I might have some s'plaining to do," he said in his best Ricky Ricardo impersonation.

Laughing, I shook my head. "How could anyone forget you, Dom?"

"Yeah, it's hard. I mean, once you've seen these…" He flexed his biceps. "They're forever embedded in your mind."

"That's so true," I giggled.

"Have I been embedded into your mind?" His eyes narrowed and he wiggled his brow.

"Yes, Dom. You are, and will forever be, embedded in my mind," I laughed again, rolling my eyes.

"Well, that's good to know," he winked. "Shall we?" He offered his arm, and we stepped through the portal.

THREE

I WAS COMPLETELY DISORIENTED. GLANCING down, I noticed we were standing on white fluffy...clouds? Our feet were completely covered with the white mist, but when I stomped my foot, it was totally solid. I bent over to try and fan away the clouds to see what was beneath, but no matter how fast I fanned, the clouds wouldn't disappear.

"Yes, you are standing on a cloud, and no, don't ask. It's magic. You'll get used to it soon enough." Dom nudged me. "This place is called Midway because it rests just between heaven and earth."

"That's amazing," I whispered, grabbing onto his arm.

"Why are you whispering?" Dom whispered back.

"I'm not sure," I shrugged, answering again with a whisper.

Then, as I turned my head back to the front, three large doors appeared, suspended by magic.

Dom faced me. "Alright, Emma. What is your whole deal with wanting to come here? Was there someone specific you wanted to see, or were you hoping to get sent out on an assignment far, far away?"

"Although an assignment sounds tempting, I do want to see someone," I answered. "I need to speak to the person who changed Kade into a mortal."

His eyes narrowed on mine then furrowed in concern. "That would be Ephraim, but I hope you know Kade cannot be changed back into an immortal."

"Yes, I know," I sighed.

"Alright then. He would be just behind the first door on the right," he said, leading me toward a big white door. When we reached it, he knocked loudly three times and then pushed it open. As it nudged open, I heard voices. Once it swung all the way back, the voices stopped and I saw one of the figures disintegrate into thin air. I knew it was an angel because I saw the outline of its wings before they completely vanished.

"Who is it?" a deep voice echoed. "I don't have an appointment scheduled."

We stepped into a vast white room. It was empty, aside from a single desk sitting all lonesome in the middle. An elderly gentleman with ivory hair and a well-trimmed beard stood to meet us.

"Hey, Eph! Just the dude we needed to see," Dom shouted, waving.

The man's face stayed emotionless; his eyes were narrowed and his lips tightened.

"Dominic?"

"You know it. I'm baaack... and I bet you missed me," Dom chimed.

"As a matter of fact, I didn't. A century would have been too soon," Ephraim answered flatly, making me giggle. His eyes shot over to me; his face looked perturbed. I wondered if it was because we interrupted him. "Why have you brought the child? You know she is not allowed here," he said sternly.

"Oh, come on, Eph. She's cool," Dom chided.

"It's Ephraim," he stated.

"Look. Ephraim, pal, friend," Dom said slowly. "Emma just needs a few words with you, then I'll take her right back to where she belongs. You owe me a favor, and all I'm asking is that you give her a moment of your time."

Ephraim ran his fingers over his slick white hair and sighed. "Fine. But this has to be quick. I have a lot of work to do."

"Awesome. We'll call it even-steven then. I'll go and check on the guys waiting for their assignments. *So*," Dom said, stepping in between us. "Emma, this is Ephraim. Eph, this is Emma. And now that we've all been introduced, I'm out." Dom pivoted and walked through the door, leaving us alone.

My heart began to thump loudly in my chest. I'd never felt more nervous, and Ephraim's unpleasant welcome didn't help.

"Hi, I said," extending my hand.

He didn't reciprocate. Instead, he turned and walked away from me.

"What can I help you with?" he asked, heading behind his desk.

I sucked in a deep breath. "Do you know Kade Anders?" I asked.

"Kade? Yes. What of him?"

"Are you the one who made him mortal?"

He turned, and as his eyes locked onto mine I saw them soften just a bit.

"I realize you were bonded, but it was his decision, not mine. I am against immortals choosing the change. I tried to reason with him, but he was adamant. He believed it was the only way he could protect you."

My heart sank, and I could only imagine what Kade must have been thinking and considering at the moment he made his decision. It must have been terrifying. He had two choices, immortality or me... and he chose me. That action spoke louder than any word ever could. It wasn't a simple decision. It had altered his whole life, his whole existence. And he did it for *me*.

Ephraim cleared his throat, snapping me from my thoughts.

"Weren't you the one who told him our best bet was to go to Lucifer?"

"I was. But it was merely a suggestion. I never expected him to give up his immortality."

"I wanted to ask you a question about changing one from immortal to mortal," I asked.

He sighed. "If you came here thinking I can change him back into an immortal, I can't. Once it's been carried out... it is final."

"No one has ever been able to change back?" I questioned.

"No," he said, and then hesitated. "Actually, there has been one isolated case." He paused, his eyes staring blankly through me.

"What happened?" I pressed.

He was beginning to look put out. "Is this why you're here? To receive a lesson?"

"No," I hesitated.

His brow rose and his inquisitive eyes opened wider. "Then why have you come?"

"I've come to ask if you could do the same for me. Could I become mortal?"

His eyes narrowed with a look of confusion. "Child, you haven't transformed yet. I cannot undo what hasn't been done."

"But is it possible? Could you make me mortal once I've transformed?"

"Yes, yes." He breathed out heavily. "Every immortal has a choice, but once that choice is made, it cannot be reversed."

"I understand. But if I do decide, would I need to come back and see you?"

"Yes. Any Archangel can grant this wish."

I nodded. "Okay, thank you." I had my answer. It was the only way I could beat Lucifer. If I became mortal, he wouldn't be able to use me as a pawn. It was all I had, and would be my last course of action should all else fail.

"Is that all you came for?" he questioned.

"Yes," I nodded.

Ephraim's eyes softened as he looked at me.

"I know your struggle, child, but please remember your life is destined. You are part of a greater plan – a change that needs to take place. If you give up your power and immortality, there might be hundreds of others who will suffer because of it. Look within yourself and remember, you will not only have to live with the decision you make, but with its outcome as well."

Damn.

That was deep, and he was right. I suddenly felt the weight of the world on my shoulders.

The door swung open and Dom stepped in. "So, what'd I miss? Where's the party?"

"You didn't miss anything," I answered, with a half-smile.

"You can't fool me, Emma. I know something is up, and I think I deserve to know, especially for bringing you here."

I shook my head, and a tear escaped my eye.

"She cannot speak," Ephraim stated, looking directly at Dom. "Her tongue is tied, and she's been forced to silence. If she speaks to anyone, they risk death."

I gasped, shocked. My eyes darted to Ephraim. "How—?"

A warm smile graced his lips. "We see everything, child. It is my job to keep a watchful eye over those who have friends in high places," he winked.

"Friends? Who are my friends? Why don't they reveal themselves?" I questioned.

"Like I said before, we see, but cannot interfere. However, it's someone in a high position who has your best interest in mind."

"Okay, wait," Dom interjected. "I don't give a damn about her secret admirer. Well, I somewhat do, but that's beside the point. I want to know what the hell she's been silenced to. If she can't tell me, then you can," Dom said, standing in front of Ephraim. "Do they know? Did they find out about her?"

Ephraim gave a single nod.

"Shit," Dom cursed. "So what's their deal, Eph?"

"It's Ephraim," he said through gritted teeth. "She is to be bonded to the Nephilim before her transformation, and if she speaks of it to anyone, they will die. It was a pact made by Lucifer himself."

"Well, this complicates *everything*," Dom sighed, looking at me. A deep sadness swam in his bright green eyes. "You better make sure he doesn't force you into sealing the bond any sooner, Emma."

"Oh, I won't." But being alone with Ethon combined with the magic of the bond, it was hard to resist, especially when I was the only one resisting.

"He looked back at Ephraim. "I thought only immortals were given the gift of the bond, and they were only dealt after transformation."

"So did I. But things are different with her. She's not a full immortal. Neither is she Nephilim."

"See Emma, you've gone and thrown off the whole damn bonding system."

"Yeah," I sighed. "Lucky me."

"Well, we'll need to keep the demon occupied. No late night strolls in the labyrinth, or any alone time," Dom warned, beginning to sound like a big brother.

I grinned as the thought of Jeremy crossed my mind. If he knew what was going on, he would have probably said the same thing. "We need to get back in case Lucifer finds out what we're up to."

"I am not usually allowed to do this, but will make an exception this once. Come," Ephraim said, ushering me forward until we stood in front of his desk.

Dom stepped between us and patted Ephraim on the shoulder. "Thanks, Eph. And, don't worry, you probably won't be seeing me for a while."

"That's considerate of you," he answered before waving his hand in a circle, speaking a few words in their angelic language. Soon the space before him began swirling and I knew he was opening a portal.

"Where will this take us?" I asked.

"Back to your closet. You can change and get cleaned up without anyone knowing."

"I'll know," Dom said.

"I wasn't talking to you," Ephraim answered.

"Thank you, Ephraim," I said, hugging him.

He hugged me back. "Just stay alive until your transformation."

"Staying alive is not my greatest worry."

"Remember, your life is not your own. Your future is connected to people you have not even come into contact with yet. Individuals, whose lives will change, or be saved, because of your actions."

I nodded. That was a lot to swallow.

Dom grabbed hold of my hand, and we both stepped from Midway, straight into my dark bedroom closet. As I turned back, the portal disappeared.

"I better get out of here. We don't want the others to think there's something going on between us, if you know what I mean."

"Yes, Dom," I chuckled. I leaned forward and gave him a hug. His strong arms wrapped around me. "Thank you."

"No problem. And, don't worry. I'll do whatever I can to make sure you're safe, and will make sure Kade knows what's going on. Now, get out of that suit. It's making me a bit uncomfortable."

"Get out of here." I blushed, pushing him out.

"See ya, Emma," he said, leaving.

"Bye, Dom."

Unzipping the suit, I quickly stepped out from it and hung it back up. It had protected me yet again. This magical garment of the angels. Before I pulled a robe around me, I glanced down at my body. They whole right side and middle of my chest was marred in black and blue. Would this ever end? Would there ever come a time when I wouldn't have to worry about breaking or bruising anything? I mean, how many broken ribs can one girl take?

I pulled a pink, long-sleeved shirt off the hanger, and opened the drawer to get some jeans, then headed toward the bathroom. I needed a bath. There were splatters of dried blood on my hands, and I wanted it gone. After, I'd go check on Kade.

Before I stepped into the bathroom I felt dizzy, and grabbed onto the door knob to steady me. A rapping noise sounded at my window. My insides twisted in knots as I pulled the robe tightly around me and made my way toward it. I pulled back the curtain and let out a small shriek. Ethon was there, hovering right in front of the window. Without thinking, I unlatched it and swung it open.

"What are you doing here? You scared the crap out of me," I scolded.

He laughed. "I was on the rooftop, waiting for you to get back. I felt you arrive, and had to make sure you were alright," he noted, his crimson eyes flitting down my length.

"I thought you couldn't come near the house... you know, the barrier?"

"You were gone so Samuel has been inside the house with Alaine. He hasn't left yet. I think I have a few more minutes."

"If that," I laughed.

"Are you okay?"

"Yes, I'm fine, thank you. But I was just about to take a shower," I said, hugging my robe tight.

"Hmmm," he grinned.

"Hmmm, what?" I narrowed my eyes at him.

He jumped onto the sill and sat down, then wrapped his arms around me, pulling me right between his legs. I closed my eyes, trying to fight the bond, holding tightly to my robe. "One day soon, you will be mine. *All* mine. What I told you in the tower is true. I will do whatever I can to make you happy. We will be happy, and I will make sure you are fulfilled in every way. You are my bonded and my future mate, and one day we will rule the Underworld."

I looked into his crimson eyes and shook my head. "I don't want to rule the Underworld. I don't want to rule anything. I just want to live a normal life. A life where I get to choose my happiness."

"With the bond, you will be happy, no matter what," Ethon promised. "But, let's not worry about all of that right now." He brushed his hand down the side of my face.

I didn't want a no-matter-what kind of life. All it meant was the bond would be forcing my happiness, making it false. A lie. If I bonded with Ethon, everything real would be shrouded by the bond. But would I ever find real happiness in the midst of the madness? As long as Lucifer was alive, the answer was a resounding no. The fact he was immortal, and I would soon be one, made things worse. I couldn't see myself spending an eternity with Lucifer as my future father-in-law.

I forced a smile. I didn't want Ethon to know I had another option. It was mine to do with what I wanted. And, as long as Lucifer was around, I'd have to play along. I wrapped my arms around Ethon's neck.

"Right now I need a shower, and you need to get out of my room before someone sees you."

There was a knock on the door. "Emma? Are you alright in there? I heard a scream," Courtney called from behind the door.

"I guess that's my cue to leave," Ethon said, kissing me quickly before leaning backward out of the window.

"Ethon," I gasped, watching him push out and freefall. Halfway down, he kicked off the side of the house, and his black wings spread wide behind his back sending him soaring into the sky. He turned back to me and winked, then flapped once and was gone like a flash.

"Emma?" Courtney called again.

"Hold on," I called, locking the window and closing the shades. I was glad she unwittingly came to my rescue.

When I unlocked the door, Courtney stepped in. "Is everything okay?" she asked.

"Yep. Everything is fine," I smiled.

"Did you scream, or was I hearing things?"

"Yeah, umm... I thought I saw a spider," I lied.

"Oh, they suck. I hate spiders. I smashed one in the bathroom the other day. It was small and black and had hair on its body. Totally creeped me out," she shivered." Those things are nasty!"

"Yeah, they really are," I said, giggling.

"So how are you holding up? I bet you're missing your friends. I know I am," she grinned.

I guess Courtney didn't know I'd been missing. Good. I didn't feel like explaining myself to everyone, and she would've had a million questions.

I smiled. "I do miss them. So, have you heard from Jeremy?"

"Yeah. He texted me a few hours ago, when they landed in L.A. He said there was some crazy turbulence and Leah almost puked." She giggled.

I laughed. "Yeah, Leah has a very weak stomach. We went to the fair once, and she puked on the merry-go-round. She never rode anything else since. I'm surprised she had the guts to fly here."

"Wow, that sucks. I love rides, but haven't been to the fair since I was eight."

"Do they have a fair in Alaska?" I asked.

"Yep. It's in August and a long way from here, in a town called Palmer."

"Well, August is three months away. Maybe we can beg Alaine to take us there. I think we all need a break." I smiled, just around the same time reality hit. There was no way Alaine would allow me to leave the protection of this place. Not with all things wicked and evil lurking right outside our door. I had a sinking feeling I'd have to be holed up here until my transformation. Yeah, this was totally going to suck.

"Well, enjoy your shower. I'm glad the spider didn't bite you," she said, stepping back. "Hey, since it's dark and overcast, would you like to watch a movie in my room after lunch?"

"Sure," I answered. I was glad I still had Courtney and Caleb to keep me company. Having them here would help keep my time and mind occupied.

"Awesome." She waved and closed the door behind her.

FOUR

I QUICKLY SLIPPED INTO THE bathroom hoping to avoid any further interruptions. I needed to wash the whole eventful morning off of me.

I stepped into the shower and let the steamy hot water pound down on my aching muscles, and as it did, it melted away the stress and made me feel a bit more relaxed. I scrubbed the blood and grime from my hands and nails, and stood under the showerhead for a good twenty minutes, wishing it would wash away the black and blue on my chest. Unfortunately, bruises didn't wash away, but they would be gone in a few days.

After my shower, I changed into blue jeans and the long-sleeved shirt, and decided I would first go and check on Kade. Then I'd head down to the kitchen to see what Miss Lily was whipping up for lunch. My stomach growled at the thought.

As I made my way down the stairs, Alaine was exiting Kade's room. When she turned and her eyes met mine, I saw a mixed look of relief and sadness.

"Emma," she said, rushing toward me with open arms. I automatically fell into her embrace. She hugged me tight for a moment then stepped back, looking me over. "Are you okay? Are you injured?"

"No, I'm fine," I said.

"Kade said you were struck by one of the Fallen. Are you sure you aren't hurt?" she pressed.

I smiled. "Yes. The suit protected me from impending death."

"Thank God," she sighed, hugging me again. "Do you want me to check them just in case?"

"No, I promise I'm fine. But thank you."

"Alright," she said softly, her eyes still showing concern. "Now, would you care to tell me why you decided to sneak out of the house without letting anyone know? It's dangerous out there, *especially* during these times."

"I know. But I had a huge question I needed answered."

She sighed and rested her hands on my shoulders. "You know you can always come to me or Samuel if you have any questions. We are here for you, and will answer them to the best of our ability or knowledge."

"I know, but this wasn't something either of you could answer. I had to go to Midway." I stared into her deep brown eyes. "Right now, the information I have is for me, but when the time comes, I will share it with you and Samuel. I promise."

"Oh, Emma. That's fine, but please promise me you won't run off again. You need to stay within the protective barrier," she begged.

"I won't," I agreed.

"When you're ready to share, I'll be waiting. Did you find the answers you were seeking?"

"I did," I reassured.

"Good. I'm just glad you've come back to us safely. I'll have to go tell Samuel you're okay. He's been worried sick."

The thought of their concern brought a smile to my face. They had never stopped loving or worrying about me, and the warm thought settled in my heart.

"Thank you," I breathed.

"Just promise you won't do anything that will put you in harm's way. You and Samuel are my life. If anything happened to you—" Tears pooled in her beautiful brown eyes.

"I promise to let you or someone else know the next time I leave," I said softly, hugging her.

"Good," she said wiping away her tears. "Kade is fine. I just stitched him up. Malachi is in the room with him if that's where you were heading."

"I was. I just wanted to make sure he was alright. Have you seen Dom?"

"No, I haven't seen him, but he could be out in the cottage. I'm headed there now to see Samuel. Did you need him?"

"Nope. Just wondering," I said.

"Alright. I'll see you later, sweetheart," Alaine said, kissing the top of my head, before heading downstairs.

I guess Dom hadn't talked to Kade yet, which sort of put a damper on visiting him, especially with Malachi there. I had a feeling he was going to start the interrogation as soon as I stepped in the room. I didn't blame him though. Maybe Kade told him I was headed to Midway. But still, Kade didn't know the reason why.

I stood there for a few moments, debating whether I should go in or not. It was killing me because I was still sworn to silence.

What the hell. I would have to face them either now or later. I just wished Dom had already talked to them.

I walked down the hall and stood in front of Kade's door, then raised my hand and knocked.

"Enter at your own risk," Malachi said in a deep, scary voice.

I paused when the door swung open. Kade was standing there, shirtless. My face immediately flushed with heat as I glanced down at his perfect body.

"Emma, you're back," he said, stepping forward. It was then I noticed the stitches on his right shoulder.

I gasped. "Are you alright?"

"Totally fine. Especially knowing you're back safely. Did Dom take you to Midway?"

"Yes," I whispered. "Thank you."

"It's still my duty to make sure you're safe. I just wish I could have taken you."

"It's alright. Everything happens for a reason."

I was kind of glad Kade wasn't the one who took me. Knowing him, he would have stayed right by my side, questioning my question. I didn't really want anyone else to know. And, after talking to Ephraim, I wasn't completely sure what I was going to do. Becoming mortal would be the easiest path. It would mean freedom from any bond, and would completely set me free from Lucifer and Lucian.

On the other hand, becoming mortal would set me apart from my new family of immortals. Samuel and Alaine would be devastated to watch me grow old and die, way before their time. The only person who would benefit from me being mortal, would be Kade.

In the back of my mind I now wondered about the countless people who would benefit from my transformation. The one burning question was…what would I become?

Even though it was my destiny, I did have a choice. I could either run from it, or embrace it. As much as I wanted to be free from it all, I now had a responsibility. There were lives who were entrusted to me. Lives I had never met, and might not ever meet. And those who were already a part of my life.

Kade stepped forward and reached for my hand. "You have a worried look on your face. Want to talk?"

Those were the words I was hoping to avoid.

"Actually, I'm starving. I was just heading down to see what Miss Lily has for lunch. Would you care to join me?" I asked, trying to change the subject.

A wide smile graced his beautiful mouth. "Of course. I'm hungry too." He twisted his head into the room. "Hey Malachi, care to join us for lunch?"

"I thought you'd never ask," he uttered gruffly.

Kade ducked back in for a second and came back out, pulling a tight fitted black t-shirt over his head, then offered me his arm. I happily threaded mine through his and off we went. Malachi followed behind us.

"So did you guys run into any problems on your way to Midway?" he asked.

"Nope. It was all clear from the time we left you and Alex."

"Did Dom behave?"

"Does Dom ever behave?"

"Good point."

"Ephraim wasn't too thrilled to see him," I said, giggling as I remembered his face as soon as Dom entered the room.

"Yeah, Dom definitely knows how to make friends," Malachi noted sarcastically. "The worst part is, he enjoys it."

"I noticed," I agreed. Dom was carefree and snarky, but those were also some of his best qualities.

"Emma, are you going to answer the burning question everyone wants to know? You know, about why you went?" Malachi asked bluntly.

I didn't turn back, but instead shrugged. I knew he didn't care about idle chat. He wanted straight forward answers. I exhaled. "I just needed to ask a few questions, and wanted to hear the answers for myself. It's something personal." I hoped that answer was good enough, though it was still vague.

"What question?" He pressed.

Dammit. He wasn't going to relent.

"There was a reason I left alone and didn't tell anyone where I was going. If I wanted you to know, I would have already said something," I answered.

"I didn't mean to interfere. We're all responsible for your protection, and it seems you always try and put yourself in harm's way. It's like you have a death wish or something."

"I have to agree with him on that one," Kade added. "We need to know when you decide to leave the barrier. We can't protect you if we don't know where you are." He grabbed my hand and squeezed. "I wouldn't be able to live knowing something happened to you and I wasn't there to help."

"I know. I'm sorry. But, I wasn't really alone. I did have some help."

"Who?" Malachi jumped back in.

"I don't know. When I prayed for help, I received an answer. The dagger, the suit, and the bloodstone amulet came to me for protection and guidance."

"While that's all well and good, those things can't block a sword to your neck," Malachi said, huffing loudly behind us.

"They *did* help me kill two Fallen," I mentioned with a little bit of pride.

"That's true, Malachi. I saw it with my own two eyes. She kicked some ass. I've never seen anyone move the way she does. It was like she had eyes in the back of her head, and predicted strikes before they even happened." He squeezed my hand again.

"I missed one," I sighed, "But the suit did keep me from being impaled."

Kade's eyes immediately found mine and he stopped me at the bottom of the stairs. "That's right. You were in a lot of pain. Do you need Malachi to fix you?"

"No, I'm fine," I said.

"Emma, it's no problem. I can take a look."

"You should let him. It sounded like you broke something," Kade insisted.

"I did break a few ribs, but they've already been mended," I said, dancing around the reason why.

"How? Even immortals need assistance putting broken bones back before they can heal properly." Malachi wasn't going to let this go.

I swallowed hard, not wanting to give an answer, but Malachi was pressing. I closed my eyes and debated, then decided to answer. At least it was one thing I could tell the truth about, even though I knew Kade wouldn't want to hear it.

"Ethon fixed me," I said softly, pulling Kade along, trying to avoid any more chatter.

"Wait... *what?*" Malachi snapped. "He's a healer too?"

"Yep," I answered quickly.

"That can't be. All the Nephilim I heard of only have one gift. Look at Alaine. Hers is invisibility and nothing else. Are you sure he's a Nephilim?"

"Well, he is related to the ruler of the Underworld. That should count for something more, right?" I added.

"I don't know. Sounds kind of fishy to me. Frankly, I seriously don't give a damn, unless he crosses me... then things could get ugly."

"Yeah, that would be a real tragedy," I acknowledged with an over exaggerated nod of my head.

"Damn right," Malachi added. "I'll knock that demon straight back to the depths of hell, in a hand basket."

"Hand basket?"

"You've heard of the saying, 'to hell in a handbasket' haven't you?"

"Yes," I said, rolling my eyes.

I knew the conversation must have been killing Kade. Ethon could not only fly, fight, and protect me, but he could also heal me. Right now, he had the advantage and Kade knew it.

He looked over to me as we entered the kitchen, his eyes glimmering. "As long as you aren't in any pain, I'm good with it." His smile instantly brightened the room and my mood.

"Well, if it isn't the lovebirds," Miss Lily welcomed. "And hello, Malachi."

"Hey, Miss Lily. So what you got cookin' today?" he asked.

"I'm not really cooking. I'm just throwing together some deli sandwiches, chips, and potato salad."

"Sounds good to me, and I must say, you're looking very pretty today," Kade added.

"Why, Mr. Anders. You really have a way of making this old lady feel nice inside." Her face lit up with a large toothy grin. "Now, you all head into the dining room, and I'll bring out the platters in just a bit."

"You don't have to tell me twice," Malachi said, scooting past us.

As soon as we entered, we were greeted with a boisterous voice. "Hey you beautiful people... except for the big, brawny, tanned guy in the front who looks somewhat akin to a pit bull."

"Keep that mouth moving, Dom," Malachi threatened.

"It's early. I'm just getting started," Dom stated, showing all his teeth in an exaggerated grin. He then turned to me and winked which made me blush.

Malachi walked past him, slapping him on the shoulder extra hard.

"Crap. Now I'll have your huge paw print on my shoulder for the next few hours," Dom huffed.

"Yep. I've marked you, bitch."

"Dude, that makes me very uncomfortable. But I always knew deep down inside, you wanted to mark me as yours."

"Don't freaking flatter yourself."

"Oh, but you're the lucky one, broseph."

Malachi turned to us, his eyes narrowed, the vein in the middle of his forehead protruding. "I seriously can't wait until this assignment is done so I can be reassigned with someone normal."

"Normal is boring. Which explains a lot about your personality."

Malachi clenched his teeth and switched topics. "I heard Ephraim was ecstatic to see you."

"Yeah, that guy loves me. He just can't stand too much awesomeness in one room."

"No, Dom. He just can't stand you. Period."

"Not true. He just doesn't know how to handle all of this," he said. His chair screeched back as he stood and started flexing. "I don't blame him though. Not many do."

"Sit down before you get a cramp," Malachi barked.

"You're the one cramping my style, dude. Chillax."

"What the hell is chillax?"

"You know... chill out and relax. Dude, it's a mortal word that's been around for ages, so you should obviously know it by now."

"Hey guys," Alex greeted, entering the room with Thomas behind him. "Did we miss anything?"

"Nope," Kade said. "Just the normal blabbering banter between Dom and Malachi."

"Ah, shucks," he chuckled.

"Hey Emma," Thomas chimed. "It seems like forever since I've seen you. How have you been?"

"Good," I answered with a squeak, unsure of my word choice.

"Yeah, right. This chick is damn lucky to be alive. She seriously has like nine lives," Dom blurted.

Miss Lily came into the room just in time with the first platter of sub sandwiches. I was glad she set the first tray in between the cluster of hungry Guardians. That would keep their minds and mouths occupied for a while.

I just hoped Dom would be able to talk to them soon and explain all the craziness, and without anyone from the outside finding out. I hoped Lucifer didn't really have the threat of eyes and ears everywhere, like he threatened me with. I was afraid one of his goons would hear about my trip to Midway. All I could do was pray it would all blow over soon.

FIVE

FTER LUNCH, KADE WALKED ME back upstairs. "What are your plans? Not that there's tons to do."

"I actually promised to watch a movie with Courtney. Wanna come?" I asked, batting my eyes.

"No, thanks. I'll pass," he said, scrunching his nose and running his fingers through his hair. I didn't blame him. "I'll probably head over to the cabin and play some chess with the guys. It seems Samuel is the reigning King and needs to be dethroned." He smiled, making my heart pitter-patter.

"Alright, Mr. Dethroner. I'll see you later."

I smiled at him, he smiled back, and the world seemed to pause around us. No one made a move; no one took a first step. We just stood there, frozen, staring at each other. I couldn't tear my eyes away from his. The color was like none I'd ever seen before. He was wearing black, which seemed to make them pop even more. Specks of yellow swirled within the blue and green. It was mesmerizing.

"Awkward," Caleb exasperated, as he passed by us. We were so into each other we didn't even notice him leave his room.

I laughed and blushed, then looked down to break the connection.

"Since we can't leave the house, how about I show something you haven't seen before? Alaine would want you to know anyway. It's a secret tunnel that leads through the house. Maybe we can get lost for a bit," he said softly, his fingers brushing lightly across my hand.

"I'd like that," I said, not able to turn him down.

"Alright, after dinner," he said with a crooked grin.

"Wait." A thought of fear shot through me. "The Darkling can't get into this secret tunnel, can they?"

"No. It's completely Darkling and Fallen safe. You'll see." He winked, making my knees weak.

"Good to know." I exhaled in relief. I knew I shouldn't be putting myself in a position of getting any closer to him, but I couldn't resist. There was no way for me to say no. Not to him.

Plus, we were prisoners here, housed under the same roof. How the hell were we supposed to stay away from each other when his room was less than a football field away from me?

Yeah. Impossible.

"Alright, dinner and a tour," he said, turning and walking away.

"I'll be there!" I said, on my way up to my room. As soon as I took the turn, Courtney's head was peering at me from her room down the hall.

"Are you coming?" she asked.

"Aren't you hungry? I didn't see you at lunch."

"That's because I went down earlier and raided the kitchen. Miss Lily gave me food and snacks."

"Sounds great. Let me go and change into something a little more comfortable and I'll be right over."

"Alright. You don't have to knock. Just come in," she said, disappearing into her room.

I ducked into my room and headed for my dresser. It was a little chilly inside, so I decided to put on some sweat pants and a sweatshirt. When I opened my drawer, I noticed there were a few new hoodies. They must have been from Alaine. I pulled the first one out. It was grey with *Hidden Wings* written in a fancy font with feathers falling around it. It was so cool, and totally true for the new world I was living in. All the angels and Fallen did have hidden wings. I wondered if it was a premonition. Would I have hidden wings one day? I guess I'd have to wait five months to find out.

I took in a deep breath and exhaled. The thought was ridiculous.

Slipping into my sweatpants and new hoodie, I headed toward Courtney's room and pushed the door open. The floor was covered with pillows, popcorn, licorice, gummy bears, lemon heads, peppermints, and even an apple.

She smiled as my eyes caught sight of the apple. "That's in case you get another healthy craving. I wouldn't want you to leave and get lost on your way to the kitchen again. See, I thought of everything," she said slyly.

I laughed. "Yes, you have. But...I don't know. That apple I came back with the last time was pretty darn sweet," I grinned.

She rolled her eyes. "Should I go ask the sweet apple if he wants to come join us?"

"I already did and he politely declined. He needs to dethrone the King chess player in the cottage."

"Wha—?" she asked with a scrunched up nose.

"Nevermind," I giggled. "He didn't want to join us this time."

"Oh well. His loss," she sighed. "Cool hoodie. Where'd you get it?" She asked.

"I think Alaine must have bought it for me. When I opened my drawer, it was there."

"I'm going to ask her to get me one. Then we can be the Hidden Wingirls."

"Sure," I laughed.

"I saw Ethon the other day, when I visited Caleb. I glanced out his window, and Ethon was standing out near the entrance of the labyrinth; just staring blankly into it. He didn't move. I sat there and watched him for a good five minutes. He looked lost, almost sad. I felt really bad for him. But then—" her voice raised and she started to get excited. Her hands spread out to her sides. "All of a sudden he spread out his arms and two humongous black wings appeared out of his back! I was freaking out. And then he took off into the sky so fast, I don't even know where he went. I thought I was going crazy.

"I tried to tell Caleb, but he just rolled his eyes and said, 'what's new?'. That pissed me off, but then I realized, there is a lot more going on than people are telling me. I know about the angels, Fallen, and those horrible Darkling monsters, but now I'm finding out they have wings that magically appear. Hidden wings! Oh my God. Do they all have wings? Can they all fly?"

"No," I said quickly, before she had a meltdown. "All of the Guardians don't have wings. They supposedly have to earn them, and it takes five hundred years. The only ones who do have wings around us are Ethon, Samuel, and the goons… Bane and Azzah. Everyone else is basically normal."

"Samuel has wings? Are they black or white? They must be black because he is one of the Fallen, right?"

"Right," I nodded. "All of their wings are black."

Her face beamed with confirmation. "So, if you get wings when you transform, what color will they be? Since Alaine doesn't have wings, and Samuel has black wings, will yours be black too?"

"I don't know, but that's a good question. One that will take another five months to find out."

"Well, if you get wings, I call dibs on the first ride."

"Oh gosh. If I get wings, you'll definitely have more than one ride. That much I can promise," I said, shooting her a thumbs-up.

"Yay! Well, here's to hidden wings," she said, raising her sparkling apple cider bottle. I grabbed mine.

"Hidden wings!" I cheered, clinking our bottles together.

She grinned. "What do you want to watch? I have two new movies; *The Hobbit* or *The Sound of Music.*"

"Hmmm." I had to think about it a minute. "I'm feeling like a little Julie Andrews."

Her face scrunched up. "I didn't expect you to say that. I seriously thought you'd choose the hobbits over the nun."

I laughed. "I only chose *The Sound of Music* because it was my mom's favorite. We'd watch it on her birthday every year, and she'd sing all the songs out loud."

"She sounds like a wonderful person," Courtney said softly.

"She was." I breathed out, fighting back tears which stung my eyes at her memory.

Courtney walked up to the player and stuck the DVD in. She then plopped on her pillows, grabbed some popcorn and Pepsi and settled in. I did the same, except I chose a handful of peppermints, a chocolate bar, and a Dr. Pepper.

As the movie started to play, I felt a heat on my chest. Puzzled, I looked down to see the bloodstone amulet glowing bright red. I touched it and it zapped me.

"Ouch," I gasped. That never happened to me before.

"What?" Courtney asked, looking at me with a bewildered look.

A sudden hair-raising scream vibrated around us. As I turned to look out the window, something large was hurling toward us. I dropped to the ground as it collided with the window. Glass exploded, shattering everywhere. Courtney screamed and covered her face. I shielded her with my body from the shards of glass being thrust around the room. A large rock, about a foot round, slammed into the wall directly in front of us and rolled back touching my foot.

Fear gripped me as a familiar, horrifying stench filled the room.

It can't be.

I looked up as long decrepit fingers reached inside her window.

The Darkling were here.

"Courtney, *run!*" I screamed, but she didn't budge. She took one look at the Darkling climbing through her window and lost it. I jumped up and grabbed her arms, yanking her with me, dragging her out the door. "Help!" I screamed at the top of my lungs, to anyone who could hear me. "Help!"

"Emma, release the barrier!" Ethon's voice boomed from outside.

"I don't know how!" I yelled back.

"Emma, what's wrong?" Kade called, running from his room. Thank God he hadn't gone to the cabin yet.

"Darkling in Courtney's room," I was out of breath, and those were the only words I could push out before dragging Courtney to my room. I pulled her in and slammed the door shut, locking it behind us. I left her screaming against the door, and ran to my closet. Grabbing the dagger, it instantly started to tingle in my hand. I ran over to my window and looked out. It was clear, but I did see some movement within the Labyrinth.

Is this Lucian's attack?

I ran back toward Courtney and moved her off to the side, away from the door.

"You're safe here," I whispered, not sure if we really were. I took a deep breath, unlocked the door, and cracked it open. Kade ran past my room, making me jump. He had his sword in hand, and I soon heard a Darkling scream in pain.

I knew there were more Darkling than just one, and Kade would need my help. At least until the rest of the Guardians came.

Courtney was huddled in the corner with her head between her legs, rocking back and forth, wailing.

"Courtney, honey, I need to go," I said.

She grabbed hold of my arm. "You can't leave me. Please don't leave me here."

"I'll be right back. I promise," I said, grasping the dagger. "If you can, I need you to go downstairs and get the others. We need help, and I need you to be strong for me. Can you do that?"

She nodded with tears pouring down her cheeks. "Yes." She wiped her face and stood.

"You're so brave, Courtney. Now, run straight to Alaine. She'll gather all the others, and make sure you and Caleb are safe."

"What about you?" she asked, squeezing my arm.

"Don't worry about me. I'll be fine. Just get to Alaine as quickly as you can. Okay?"

"Okay," she said, taking in a deep breath.

I opened the door again and peeked out. It was clear, but I could hear Kade fighting the Darkling in Courtney's room.

"Go!" I urged, exiting the room first. Courtney ran out from behind me and bolted down the stairs. I turned and ran down the hall to help Kade. The smell of Darkling was overpowering, the burning stench made my stomach twist.

When I entered the room, there were three headless Darkling sprawled out on the floor, but there were a lot more wrestling Kade to get in.

"Emma!" Ethon shouted with urgency in his voice.

"Kade, do you know how to release the barrier?"

"No. Only Alaine, James, and Samuel can release it."

Dammit.

The sky was dark and overcast. That's why the Darkling were coming out during the daytime. The last time they attacked was in the same kind of weather. How could we ever feel safe, knowing they could crawl into our windows at any given time?

"Ethon. Go get Samuel!" I shouted.

He didn't answer, so I assumed he left to get him.

I rushed to the window, helping Kade by slaying the Darkling as they attempted to come in. I kicked a few in the chest, sending them flying back out. Below the third-story window was already a pile of wounded and dead Darkling. I thought we had the advantage, until I heard more glass shattering in one of the adjacent rooms.

My amulet became so hot, it burned my chest.

As I turned around, I was met with a Darkling standing at the door. Its long stringy hair hung in front of its blackened eyes. It snarled and snapped at me, crouching down like it was about to strike. I noticed it didn't have any weapon in its hand, but its sharpened fingernails looked just as dangerous. Besides that, the Darkling were super-fast and strong.

"Kade. They're in the room." I said, cautiously.

I could hear him struggling with all of the Darkling still trying to get in through the window. As I readied myself to fight the one crouched in front of me, four more appeared behind it, in the doorway.

It was at this very moment I wished I had slipped into my super suit.

I felt my heart beat quicken, and held the dagger tightly in my grasp, knowing it was the only form of protection I had.

"Kade?" I knew I couldn't fight all five of them.

"Emma. You're going to need to fight," he spoke loudly, thrusting his dagger into the neck of a Darkling snapping at his arm. "Don't you dare let them take you."

The Darkling who was crouched, bared its rotted teeth. Their odor violated my nostrils, making me want to gag. Swallowing hard I whispered quietly to my dagger. "I need your help. Now more than ever."

I felt the dagger warm and then it started to glow.

The Darkling pounced at me, and I swung. The dagger pierced its neck, slicing through it easily. Black tar-like blood spewed everywhere, and gushed from the open wound in its neck.

The Darkling dropped and grabbed its injury, its eyes wide with shock. I felt the dagger trying to raise my arm, and as I lifted it above my head it swiftly thrust my hand downward, plunging the blade into the Darkling's left eye.

It let out a horrendous, hair-raising scream. I closed my eyes and held tight to the dagger, yanking it out from the socket. Its eyes turned white, and it fell backward, limp.

One down, four to go.

The black blood on the blade of my dagger started to drip off, like rain on a newly polished car, leaving it spotless and ready for its next victim. I stood there in awe, and then noticed the Darklings' eyes narrowing on my magical dagger. They growled and glanced at each other, deciding on their next move. Only one let out a horrifying growl and charged forward. I dodged it, stepping to the side, while pushing my dagger into the side of its head. As I pulled it free, the next Darkling pounced forward, not giving me time to prepare for my follow up move. It slammed into me, its arms wrapped around my legs, thrusting me back toward the window.

I couldn't breathe and struggled to kick myself free from its grasp, but it held on tight, slowly crawling to my chest. Straddling me, its face hovered over mine. This stench made me wince. Lunging forward, it moved to bite my shoulder, but Kade pulled it off me by its hair. When I was safe, he threw the Darkling against the wall. It turned and glared at him, but in a second, Kade severed his head. He caught the head before it hit the ground, then turned and flung it, like a bowling ball, at a Darkling entering through the window. The force knocked it backward, dropping it down to the ground below.

"Thank you," I panted.

"Anytime," he answered. He then turned and sliced off the hand of another Darkling trying to enter. I heard its scream as it fell.

The fourth Darkling in the room paused and took a few steps backward. I sprung up and moved to the side of Kade as it charged forward. It dove at me, and I jumped out of the way and landed on a pile of pillows. The Darkling just missed me, and crashed through the wall and into the next room, leaving a huge hole. The last Darkling standing pounced on top of me, pinning me down. I struggled to free myself, but he was too strong. I raised the dagger and stabbed its thigh, it's scream pierced my ears, making them ache. The black evil eyes locked onto mine were filled with rage and hate. It raised its fist in the air. I closed my eyes and shielded my face from the oncoming blow. But it never came.

I opened my eyes, and Dominic was standing behind the Darkling with his arm in his hand. He glanced down me and winked. "Looks like you need some help," he said.

"Always right on time," I exhaled, smiling.

He picked the Darkling up and flung it across the room. It crashed into Courtney's dresser, breaking it in half. In a flash he was after it, jumping on its chest and pushing his blade into its heart. It went limp.

Malachi ran in next and came over to me, offering me his hand. He pulled me up to my feet. "You alright?" he asked.

"Yes. There's a live one in that room," I said pointing to the hole.

Without saying another word he rushed through the hole. Immediately following were sounds of banging, crashing, and screams from the Darkling.

Kade was still fighting the endless Darkling parade attempting to climb through the window, but he managed to hold them back.

Outside in the sky, I witnessed Samuel battling with another Fallen. He must not have released the barrier, because they weren't coming any closer than about one hundred yards.

"Emma," Kade called. "Put on your suit."

He was right. I needed the extra protection. Just as I turned to run, a Darkling flew at me from the doorway. I screamed and Malachi came charging out from the hole, tackling him. The two of them were hurled across the room and tumbled into Courtney's closet.

I heard more fighting going on outside Courtney's room, and in the distance, the shouts of Thomas and Alex's voices. Then, Alaine's frantic voice yelled Courtney's name. Her cries became desperate and sent a shiver up my spine.

I grasped my dagger and ran for the doorway, yelling and thrusting it at an oncoming Darkling. He dodged my attempt and grabbed my legs. I hit the ground hard, and the dagger was jolted from my grasp, flying under Courtney's bed. I wrestled with the Darkling who quickly overpowered me, and began slamming his fists into my chest.

Freaking bitch!

It landed a direct hit to my bruised ribs. Agonizing pain gripped my chest. I couldn't breathe, and was forced to take short gasps for air. I wanted to call for help, but I couldn't get the breath necessary to push any words out.

Malachi came charging back out from the closet and dove for the Darkling, tackling him off me. They both crashed and tumbled back through the hole in the other room.

Thomas and Alexander finally entered, and assisted Kade at the window.

"We've got this man," Thomas said.

I couldn't move. Pain. Sharp, excruciating pain radiated in my chest. It was nearly unbearable. It felt like my ribs were broken, but I wasn't sure. I was surprised I still had any ribs left at all, they'd been broken so many times.

Kade was suddenly over me, scooping me up into his arms. He took off running, out of the room, toward the end of the hall. He stopped abruptly and kicked open the last door on the left, then carried me into the bathroom, carefully laying me on the floor before locking the door behind us.

He then went to the sink cabinet, and yanked it away from the wall. Right behind it was a small latched door. He unlatched it and pushed it open, then picked me up and carried me in, setting me back down. He then pulled the sink back into place, and closed the trap door, locking it from the inside. We were draped in pitch-black.

I could hear him feeling around the walls. "Where the hell is it?" he muttered, under his breath. "There it is." A flashlight clicked on and we had light.

SIX

W E WERE IN A PASSAGEWAY in between the walls. It was tall and wide enough for any full sized person to stand and walk comfortably. I could hear banging and muffled growls and screams, but they seemed so far away.

"Don't worry. We're safe here. These walls are reinforced with steel," he assured me.

I couldn't answer him, and knew I had a look of fear and pain in my eyes. I could barely breathe, and was still trying to breathe without pain.

"Where are you hurt?" he asked.

I pointed to my chest, and he carefully lifted my sweatshirt. When he reached my ribcage, his eyes pressed closed.

"Dammit. Did they break your ribs again?"

I shook my head, not completely sure.

"Let me get you to the safe room." He picked me up again and carried me down through a small maze of openings. He ended at the front of a large metal door. He set me down, and as soon as he did, I collapsed forward.

"Emma," he gasped, catching me before I hit the ground. Gently setting me down, he then opened the door, and clicked on a light. Picking me up, he carried me over to one of the two beds, and carefully laid me down.

"I thought I'd be bringing you down here after dinner, but I guess now is better than ever," he said with a sad grin.

He headed over to a wall and opened up a cabinet. "I left my vial in my room, but I think Alaine keeps some here, he said lifting a few bottles and reading their contents. "Here we go," he said happily, unscrewing the top of a clear bottle. He made his way over to me and carefully lifted my head, then placed the vial to my lips. I took a sip, and instantly, started to feel tingly. The tingles continued down to my ribs, soon making them numb.

"Thank you," I said through my deep breaths.

"I'm glad it helps. I can't bear to see you in pain."

I smiled at him. "And what about you?"

"I'm fine." He smiled.

"I noticed you locked the bathroom door from the inside. What if the others try and get in?"

"There is more than one entrance to this place. It's like a maze to throw off the Darkling, in case they get in. I guess Alaine has a thing with secret mazes."

I grinned. He shifted, and I noticed blood dripping down his arm. As I followed the trail of crimson, I noticed a rip in his shirt, and a gash about three inches long on his bicep which continued across to his chest. It looked deep, and I could see his flesh.

"You're hurt," I said tugging at his arm. "Let me see that."

"No, it's fine. Just a scratch."

"A scratch? That is not a scratch," I said, pulling him closer. I sat up and took in a deep breath. My ribs felt much better, so I stood up from the bed. "Sit," I instructed.

He narrowed his eyes and plopped down on the bed in front of me. "It's nothing, really. I was just scraped by some damn shards of glass when I pushed a Darkling out the window." He tried to make light of it.

I leaned over for a closer look and swallowed as I saw the depth of the wound. "It's pretty bad and needs to be taken care of immediately," I sighed. I took the vial from his hand. "I'll need you to take your shirt off." He glanced at me with a crooked grin, so I held up the vial and smiled. "So I can apply the medicine."

"Sure," he exhaled, pulling his shirt over his head. My eyes wandered to his chest and continued down to his perfect abs, lingering there a little too long. "Ahem." He cleared his throat, making me blush.

I lifted his muscular arm with my hand, and slowly poured the liquid magic over the wound. I watched in awe as the tissue began to mend right before my eyes, but it was so deep it would still need a bandage, or possibly stitches. I then moved to his chest, which wasn't nearly as bad. "You'll have to lean back a bit."

He obliged, his eyes never leaving mine. I swallowed hard trying not to look directly at him. I knew if I did, at this close proximity, I'd be a goner. I focused on his chest, and poured the liquid over the cut. It wasn't deep, so it instantly sealed. I gasped, instinctually grazing my fingers over the healed wound.

Kade took hold of my hand, and our eyes connected. That was it. My heart did a twist, and before I knew it, he let himself fall backward, bringing me on top of him. He locked his arms tightly around me, our bodies fit perfectly together, our faces inches apart.

We were alone, the two of us, secluded in a safe room, far from the others. The only sound in the room was that of our hard breathing. This was something real, something true, something the bond didn't have any part in. I looked deep into his beautiful eyes, and saw something I'd never seen before.

Unconditional love.

A rush of sadness overwhelmed me as I thought of a life without him in it.

"Emma?" Kade whispered. My emotions took over, and tears instantly welled, burning my eyes and spilling out onto his cheek.

"I'm sorry," I sobbed. I shook my head and rolled to my back, off to the side of him.

"What's the matter?" His chest pressed up against my side, and his fingers gently brushed the dampened hair from my cheeks.

"Nothing," I lied.

"You know you can tell me anything," he said.

"No, I can't. I wish I could, but… I can't." I wept openly, feeling horrible. My insides ached with not being able to tell him why I couldn't speak.

"Why? I don't understand." His saddened eyes gazed longingly into mine, tearing my heart apart.

I turned away from him, but everything inside me wanted to turn toward him, feel his arms wrap around me, and tell me everything was going to be okay.

Instead I whispered, "I'm sorry."

"Is it because you don't want to be with me?" His voice sounded weak. "If it's true just tell me now. I will promise to stay away."

Hot tears streamed from my eyes as my heart was being pulverized over and over again. I knew this would happen if we were ever alone. It was too much to bear. This burden was wearing me down.

I turned to face him and placed my hand softly on his cheek. "Never. Wanting to be apart from you is the furthest thing from the truth. I *do* want to be with you. You have been there for me, guarding and protecting me when I didn't even know your name. You held my hand when I needed you most, and even gave your life for me. It's never been a matter of if I *want* to be with you. I do. But there are some major complications now, and I – I just can't deal with it anymore. Please don't make me talk about it," I sobbed.

From the day he walked into my room at the hospital and our eyes connected, so did our hearts. Yes, the bond played a huge part of it, but even without the bond, it was still there and very strong between us.

"Hey, it's alright," he said sitting up, pulling me into his arms.

My head rested against his chest. This was exactly where I wanted to be, enveloped in his warmth and love. I pressed myself closer to him, breathing in his sweet scent.

"You don't have to say anything, Emma. I just want you to know that I'll be here for you. Always," he reassured. "I know you're scared. But I am too... of losing you. You don't ever have to be afraid of giving your heart to me. I will make sure to fill it with love, at least for the rest of *my* life," he said, then frowned. "But I am preparing my heart for the most reasonable choice because I know Ethon can protect you, and take care of you for the rest of *your* life."

"You will always have a part of my heart," I said, hugging him tight. Everything inside of me was warring, fighting hard not to say a word. I wanted to tell him the truth.

"And you have all of mine." He kissed my forehead.

"Kade," I sobbed.

"Don't worry," he whispered. "Everything's going to be alright."

I hoped he was right. There was something about his eyes. They emitted so much love, sincerity, and tenderness. They spoke so loud, without him uttering a single word. I wrapped my arms around his neck and pressed my lips against his.

I felt him smile against my lips, then he kissed me harder. His kiss was like a magic potion, making me dizzy, sending tingles to every part of my body. His fingers gently grazed the small of my back, making me quiver. I placed my hands on his back, and paused for a moment as I felt his scars.

"It's okay," he whispered.

I nodded, and pressed my lips back to his. He rolled over, pinning me under his weight. His hands steadied my head as he continued to deepen the kiss.

His knee pressed between mine, pushing my legs apart. Then, he settled his body on top of mine. It felt so right, like we were a perfect fit.

His fingers found their way under the hem of my shirt, tracing patterns along my sides. I felt a moan escape my lips, and Kade pulled back.

"What's the matter?" I asked, wondering if I did something wrong.

"We can't get too carried away. I made a vow to Samuel and Alaine," he sighed.

"A vow? What vow?" I questioned.

"Not to defile you."

"Did they force you take that vow?" I asked.

He shrugged. "Maybe. Still, it's something I take seriously. But believe me, it's taking everything within my power to stop."

I sighed. "I know exactly what you mean." We both looked longingly into each other's eyes, then broke out into laughter.

"We're a mess," I said, hugging him again.

"A hot mess." He chuckled. "How the hell did we end up here?"

"I don't know," I replied, shaking my head. "But I'm glad you're here with me."

He leaned forward and kissed me again. "I am too."

"Do you think everyone's alright?" I asked. "I can't hear anything."

"That's because this room is completely secure and heavily protected. All we can do is pray they all make it safely. At least they're only dealing with the Darkling, so I think they'll be fine. It seems as if Lucian is still testing our strength."

"Why would he keep testing it?"

"He's finding our weak spots and trying to wear us down before he attacks. His goal is to make sure when he does attack, he wins."

"Do you think it'll be soon?" I questioned. I still had a ways to go before my transformation.

"I don't know. But we need to take extra careful measures. You can't be alone anymore. Especially knowing the Darkling can scale these walls."

"I know. Just the thought of it makes me terrified. I don't think I'll ever feel safe being alone again."

"As long as I have breath, I'll guard over you."

"Thank you," I said, wholeheartedly. I knew he meant what he said. His eyes never lied.

Voices echoed from down the hall. One of them was Alaine's, and the other sounded like Courtney. Alaine entered the room first, her brow was furrowed, her eyes red, and she was spattered with black blood. As soon as her eyes found mine, she sighed in relief.

"Thank God you're here," she said, rushing over to me, wrapping me in a hug.

"Yes, Kade brought me here after I was injured."

"You're injured?" she questioned.

"Not anymore. He gave me the healing potion and I'm good as new."

Thomas entered next, carrying Courtney in his arms, and Caleb right behind him.

"Set her on the bed," Alaine said, heading to the sink and washing her hands. "Kade, are you injured?"

"No. I'm fine," he said, glancing over to me with a grin.

We quickly shuffled off the bed to make room. Courtney was whimpering, and her hands, clasped tightly over her right eye, were covered in blood.

"What happened?" I asked, very concerned.

"My bag, please," she noted to Thomas before answering me. "She was hit with a stone thrown through the downstairs window."

"Oh my God," I gasped.

"Let me see darling," Alaine spoke softly, trying to coax Courtney to settle down and let her see the wound. After a few moments, Courtney slowly let Alaine take her hands away.

When she revealed her injury, I held my breath and turned into Kade's arms.

Her right eye was badly bruised and was swollen shut. Right above her eye, a large piece of skin was missing, and I noticed it hanging off her forehead.

"Is there anymore potion left?" Alaine asked calmly.

I turned and handed Alaine what was left in the vial. There was still half a bottle, which was more than enough. She slowly lifted Courtney's head and made her drink. She moaned as the liquid took effect. Alaine then poured some of it on the hanging flesh and the wound, placing them back together. I assumed the liquid would knit the skin back together.

Courtney was still whimpering, but not nearly as bad as when she first came in. The potion was taking effect.

Alaine dug through her small medical bag and pulled out a small plastic bag. She ripped it open and pulled out a blue pack, then crushed the contents inside of it, and instructed Courtney to hold it over her eyes.

"It's cold," she exhaled.

"Yes, it's an ice pack which will help take down the swelling. Keep it on until I say."

"Alright." Courtney sighed. As she held the patch over her eyes, Alaine pulled a needle and thread from her medical bag.

I knew she would need stitches, but this was something I couldn't watch. That's probably why Alaine told her to hold the pack over her eyes, so she wouldn't see and freak out.

"Hold still," Alaine said. I'm just going to fix your injury.

I went to Courtney's side, and held onto her hand.

She squeezed my fingers. "Emma?" she asked.

"I'm right here," I answered.

"Those stupid monsters didn't let us finish our movie."

I laughed. "Well, I think Julie Andrews can wait for another day."

"I think I need a new room," she said softly.

"Don't worry," Alaine answered. "We'll fix your room, and it will be better than ever."

"Good," she said through a yawn. "I feel so sleepy."

"Then rest," Alaine said.

"Aren't you supposed to keep people with a concussion awake?" I asked.

"Yes, but the potion will help with any internal damage. Sleep is what she needs," Alaine said softly.

I nodded, impressed at how much she knew. One day I hoped to know just as much as she did, so I could also help others.

In a matter of seconds, Courtney's mouth drooped open. She was fast asleep.

"That didn't take long." Thomas laughed.

"She's had a rough day. I'm glad she's sleeping. Sometimes the potion will do what is best for the patient. In her case it was sleep."

"I'll take some of whatever she had," Caleb said, huddled in a corner. He was so quiet I'd forgotten he'd come in, and he was obviously shaken.

"You were brave, little man," Thomas said, patting him on the shoulder. "You pulled your sister away from harm. You're a real life hero."

Caleb smiled.

After Alaine finished stitching Courtney's head, she called Caleb over to an adjacent twin bed.

"Are you hurt?" she asked.

"No," he answered softly. "Are those creatures going to be coming after us forever?"

Alaine closed her eyes and shook her head. She sucked in a deep breath and knelt beside him. "No, not forever." Her answer was simple, but I could still see fear embedded in Caleb's eyes.

"But how? There are so many of them. They're going to kill us one day." His eyes pooled with tears.

"I would never allow it," Alaine promised. "We will find a way to either eliminate them, or keep them away. But for now, you also need to rest," she said, nodding to Thomas.

Thomas came and stood behind Caleb and placed his hands on his shoulders. "Don't worry, little man. We've got your back," he assured. Caleb nodded, then Thomas leaned over and whispered in his ear.

I watched Caleb's eyes get heavy, before they rolled back and closed. Thomas laid him back on the pillow and Alaine threw a blanket over him.

"Gotta love the sleeper," I said quietly. Thomas grinned.

"It's not safe for them to stay here anymore," she noted sadly. "I'll have to make arrangements for them to stay with someone far away from this madness. At least until it's finally dealt with."

"I'm so sorry," I said. "If I hadn't come here, none of this would have happened."

Ever since the accident, trouble – in its most horrific forms – followed me, and put everyone around me in danger. Caleb was kidnapped, Courtney was injured, Kade was now mortal and had to endure pain and suffering, and even Ethon was now brought into the mix. All because of me.

"That's not true," Kade said, still holding me.

"No, it is. This whole house is in danger because Lucian and Lucifer want me. What if you just send me away? They shouldn't have to go away from their home, or be put into any more danger," I said, glancing at Courtney and Caleb. I couldn't bear to look at Courtney's battered face.

Alaine walked over to me and laid her hand on my shoulder. "Emma, they would have come anyway. You aren't the only one Lucian wants. I'm also on his list." She took hold of my hand. "We are in this together. And we will finish this, *together*. Alright?"

"Alright," I sighed. I knew she was right.

"Thomas, we need to get back and help."

"How is it out there?" Kade asked.

"They are holding their own. This is the most Darkling I've seen in a long time. Lucian must be planning his attack soon. He actually might have, if anyone had taken down the barrier. Thank goodness it's still intact."

"Yes," I breathed, remembering how Ethon yelled for me to release the barrier. But I quickly squashed the thought of it being malicious because I knew he only wanted to get inside so he could help me.

"We'll discuss it all later," she said, then turned to Kade. "Kade, thank you for bringing Emma to safety. Time and time again, you have proven yourself. Please stay here with them," she said, smiling at him with admiration.

"I will," he promised.

"Be back soon," Thomas winked before ducking out, and Alaine followed.

SEVEN

KADE AND I SAT ON a small couch in the corner and waited, while Caleb and Courtney snored away. I was glad they were both safe, but I had a feeling Courtney would totally freak out when she woke and saw her stitches.

Alaine said they would have to leave. I didn't blame her for wanting to send them away to safety, but the thought of not having them around made me sad. My last connections to the human world would be leaving me, and I'd have to deal with the constant madness without them.

It wasn't too long before Alaine returned with the rest of the Guardians.

"Well, it's good to know all the humans are safe," Dom said, entering the room.

Kade huffed.

"Glad to see you're all safe too," I said.

Everyone entered the room and looked battle weary. James glanced at us and nodded, then stood against the wall. Thomas and Alexander plopped themselves down on the ground, and Malachi stood next to James. Dom walked over to Caleb's bed, pushed his legs over and sat on the edge.

"Rude," Alex chuckled.

Dom glanced over to him.

"You have some Darkling crap on your mouth."

Alex touched his mouth and when he felt the tarry blood, he began gagging.

"Dude, what the hell did you do? Slice an artery and stand there for a shower?" Dom teased.

Alex ran over to a small sink, loaded his hands with soap and began scrubbing his face. We all laughed because Alex *was* covered in Darkling blood.

"Shit this stuff is sticky, and it freaking stinks. I need a shower, like ASAP."

Alaine stood in the center of the room, and everyone fell silent.

"You all fought brave today, and I am eternally thankful for each of you."

"It's why we're here," Thomas said.

"Yeah. You, Emma, and even the two snoring humanoids have become family to us," Dom added.

"Thank you," Alaine smiled, but her smile looked a bit sad. "As you have become part of ours. But I've quickly realized it's not safe here for us anymore. This house is too large and I cannot make sure of everyone's safety with so many ways to enter. I will be sending Courtney and Caleb to stay with a friend of mine in Washington. She offered help if I ever needed it. The rest of us will have to find another safe house. Someplace we can put a barrier over. Someplace where we can fight easily, if needed."

"I think I might know of a place," Dom said, his face became serious. Everyone turned their attention to him. "It was used as a safe house a long time ago. It's far from civilization and located in the Oregon woods." He turned to Alaine. "It was set up by your birth father, to protect and keep your birth mother safe during her pregnancy. It's the place your life started, Alaine. It's been unoccupied ever since, but there has been someone assigned to the place, who has been caretaking it."

"How do you know this, Dominic?" Alaine asked.

"It was also the place where my bonded was murdered. She fought, defending your mother, and gave her life to save hers." Dom's lips trembled and his eyes bore so much sadness. He dropped his head down. "It's a safe house. An option, in case you need it."

Alaine walked up to him, leaned over and took hold of his hands. "I'm sorry for the pain you've endured, Dominic. I know what it feels like to lose a soul mate. I never expected mine to come back to me. She must have been an outstanding woman, and I will be forever grateful, to both of you. I will consider this option, but it might be too painful to revisit, for both of us."

"Thank you," he said, softly. "I battle with her loss every day, especially seeing new hearts being bonded." He turned to look at me and Kade. "Don't let true love and happiness slip away. There are some things you have to fight for, no matter what."

Kade reached over and took my hand, interlocking our fingers. We both turned and looked into each other's eyes, and then he smiled.

"Okay, you two can just stop with the freaking cuteness already. I was just stating general facts, not necessarily aiming it at you," Dom sighed and rolled his eyes.

Everyone laughed. "And, since I have all of your attention, I might as well keep this going. We have a major complication. One that involves our little darling over there." Dom gestured toward me.

I knew at that moment what he wanted to say. "I—I don't know if I should be here for this," I said, my heart twisting.

"Emma," Dom stated, "they can't hear us in here, and besides... none of us fear him more than we fear doing our job incorrectly."

"What is this about?" Alaine questioned.

"Yeah, Dom. Just spit it out already," Malachi added, and everyone agreed.

"Lucifer has bound Emma with an unbreakable oath. He made her agree to bond with Ethon before her transformation, and told her that if she speaks of it to anyone... they will die."

"Is this true?" Kade asked, turning toward me.

With tear-filled eyes, I nodded.

"No, no, no. That is not going to happen," Alaine huffed.

Kade disagreed. "If he bound her, she has to fulfill her word. I've heard stories of those who didn't keep their pacts with Lucifer. They suffered horrible deaths, which could not be stopped because they were bound to him. Once you make a deal with the Devil... it's sealed."

"Emma," Alaine turned to me and spoke so softly. "Did you make such a pact with Lucifer?"

I nodded, unable to speak.

"Why? Why in God's name would you do that?" Malachi asked.

I turned and looked into Kade's eyes.

"He threatened to kill him. I wouldn't allow it because I love him. He already gave up everything for me, so... I did the same."

"Dammit, Emma." Kade wrapped me in his arms and held me tight. "You shouldn't have done that. Your happiness means more to me than anything else."

"Don't you see?" I leaned back and looked at him. "You *are* my happiness. And, if you were ever taken from me, I would never be able to find it again."

"Sorry to interrupt this unbelievably moving moment," Alex broke in. "But what about the other dude, Ethon? The bond did choose him too. So now what? What are we supposed to do?"

"I don't know," Alaine sighed. "We'll have to find a way, but this really complicates things. There is something else I need to tell you all, something about Emma's true birth date."

"What do you mean my *true* birth date?" I gasped.

She walked over to me. "To keep your true identity hidden, Victoria and Christian decided to give you another birthday. A false one to celebrate. The date they chose was the birthday of your grandmother, Jane Wilder."

My mind began whirling with question. "So I wasn't born on October fifteenth?"

Alaine paused, then looked up at me. "No. You were born July fifteenth, three months earlier."

"July fifteenth? That's in a *month*," I shrieked, starting to hyperventilate. Everything around me began to spin.

"Hey, hey, hey," Kade said, steadying me. "I think she's gonna faint."

"Holy shit, Alaine. This does complicate things," Malachi cursed.

"Lucifer must know this, and he'll be watching, expecting her to seal the bond sooner than later," James noted.

"I know. We need to find a way to eliminate the pact, no matter what it takes," Alaine said.

"I don't think there is a way, Alaine. Unless, she does decide to be with Ethon," James cut back in. "The bond isn't just a simple matter. The tie it has between each heart will complicate things, and is something she cannot deny."

"That's true," Dom added. "But it should be *her* decision, and not forced by some wicked psycho. He threatened her, making her agree to the bond, or he would kill Kade. Shouldn't there be something within the heaven and hell handbooks that goes against that? Yes, she and Ethon are connected by the bond, but until it is sealed, we still have a chance."

They all murmured amongst themselves.

"Until such time, we will have to play along. It's vital they don't have any inclination that we have this information, and Emma will still have to play her part with Ethon. My greatest fear is that Lucifer will try and find any way to carry out his pact early... by either having her seal the bond with Ethon, or worse. Emma, you will have to separate yourself from Kade as well. I know it will be hard, but it is necessary. They have to believe you will carry out your part of the pact, and should we not find a way... you *will* have to carry it out."

"There has to be a way," Dom exhaled loudly.

"If there is, I will find it," Alaine said, and I believed her. She would do anything to keep me safe. "We have a lot of cleaning up to do. I'll need each of you to do another thorough sweep of the house. Check everywhere, we can't afford to have any stray Darkling lurking about. From now on, the barrier will stay up, and we will take turns watching the perimeter. I will make arrangements for Caleb and Courtney, and until we find a suitable safe house, Emma will need to be guarded at all times."

The room agreed.

"And remember... whatever happens in the safe room, *stays* in the safe room," Dom exclaimed.

"Yes," Alaine agreed. "Be safe, all of you."

Everyone left and Alaine walked over to me. "Don't worry, sweetheart. We are all here for you, and will fight for whatever you choose."

"Thank you," I said.

"You two wait here until we make sure the house is clear. I'll send a few of the guys back to let you know, and to collect Caleb and Courtney."

I nodded, then she leaned over and kissed my forehead.

"Have faith," she said as she exited.

When the door closed, Kade turned to me and grabbed me by both arms.

"I might not have the chance to say this again. I love you. You have become the best part of my life. From the moment I open my eyes, until the moment I lay my head down to sleep, you are on my mind. And even in my dreams, you are there. I love you. With every cell in my body, I love you. But, you need to listen to me," he paused.

"Kade," I breathed.

"No," he shook his head. "I need you to live, even if it's without me."

"I can't," I cried.

"Listen to me, Emma," he said, grasping my face in his hands. His body and words were desperate and urgent. "I've witnessed Lucifer's power, and have seen firsthand what happens to those who break his pacts. He tortures them without mercy, and no one can stop it. I will not let that happen to you. You need to do whatever you have to do to stay alive. Even if that means sealing the bond with Ethon."

"Why?" I sobbed. "Why doesn't God intervene? Why does he sit back and watch this madness take place? Does he know how many hearts are breaking?"

"I don't know," he said sadly. "I wish I had all the answers for you."

He stopped and cradled my face, gently stroking my cheeks with his thumbs, wiping away my tears. The passion in his eyes burned like I'd never seen before, but they were also filled with devotion and tenderness.

He didn't speak. He didn't need to. I reveled in the way he could look at me with so much love. He was the most selfless person I'd ever met, and he loved *me*. What did I ever do to deserve anyone so special?

"I'm so sorry, Emma," he whispered, resting his forehead against mine.

"Why?" I asked, breathing in his sweet scent.

"Because you should have been mine. We were supposed to seal the bond and be soul mates for all eternity."

I shook my head, but inside I did wish things were different. I wished he were still immortal, and I wished we could spend the rest of eternity loving each other. But the dream had been shattered. For him, there was no eternity, and that left a hole in my heart that could never be mended.

"You did what you thought was right," I said, twisting my hands in his thick dark hair.

"I did what I knew was right, yet it did nothing in the end. I was injured before you even started the quest, and look... you still made it out safely without me. If I would have known, if I were given a second chance, I would have chosen differently."

"Don't beat yourself up for something that cannot be changed."

"It haunts me every single day. Every time I look at you, and know I could have loved you for an eternity, it kills me inside."

"Then make me forget. Make us both forget. Right now."

I pulled his face closer, and he pressed his mouth to mine, kissing me ever so gently. His velvety tongue ran over the length of my lips, and then his mouth crashed down on mine with a sudden urgency. Heat blazed between us as his hands wrapped around the back of my neck, holding me in place. His kiss was eager, and his passion matched mine.

Pulling me to his lap, I straddled him and his arms wrapped around my waist. He kissed me like it was the last time he'd ever kiss me again.

I gave in. I wanted him like I'd never wanted him before. He pulled away, his tongue and lips leaving tingling sensations as they trailed down my neck and across my chest. I moaned in pleasure, and he found my lips once again. Desire burned within me, and I craved his touch. Moving against him, I wanted nothing more than to feel his skin against mine – to feel his gentle touch all over my body.

My heart filled with desire and flowed from my lips. "I love you, Kade," I breathed.

He paused, panting. His eyes burning with desire, locked onto mine. "That's all I've ever wanted since the day we met. It's all I've ever needed."

He kissed me again, and then Caleb snorted, throwing us right back into reality.

I sighed and rested my head on his shoulder. "We're hopeless, aren't we?"

"Yes. But at least we're together for now."

"I don't think I can be away from you," I admitted.

"Don't worry. I'll find a way," he winked.

Kade always had a way of making me smile. A thought crossed my mind and I randomly blurted out a question. "Do you think it will hurt?"

His eyes went wide, before narrowing. "What are you talking about?"

"I'm sorry," I giggled. "My transformation. Do you think my *transformation* will hurt?"

"I don't know. I never transformed. I was born immortal, remember?" he said, then his gaze went distant for a moment. "But I'm sure Alaine can tell you, or even Ethon." He said Ethon's name like it had left a bitter taste on his tongue.

"I never wanted to seal any bond before my birthday. I had a vision of how I wanted my first time to be. I was going to be married, and have a real wedding with everyone I ever loved there. And after, a romantic honeymoon. The thought of it being forced before my birthday terrifies me."

"The thought that it will most likely be Ethon terrifies me."

I shook my head.

"I thought I had more time, but I just lost three months of my life."

"Yeah, thirty days isn't much time. Let's hope Alaine finds a loophole. She seems to have a knack for finding information."

"Yeah," I sighed. "I am hoping."

We wrapped our arms around each other, not knowing if this would be our last embrace. All we could do was hold on to hope. And for this brief moment in time, I just wanted him to hold me.

EIGHT

THE HOUSE WAS CLEARED OF the Darkling and cleaned top to bottom, but the stench lingered for at least a week. Courtney and Caleb stayed downstairs in Alaine's study, carefully guarded by James, while Alaine made all the necessary arrangements for them.

Workers had come in to fix all the damage done during the attack. Alaine tried to explain that the house had been broken into while we were away on a vacation, and they bought her story. Within three weeks everything was fixed. Although the house looked nearly new, the atmosphere wasn't the same. It had been violated, and its scars were masked with drywall and paint. The truth would remain secret, and only remembered by those who endured the horrors.

In the morning, my adopted siblings would be flying to Washington to stay with Alaine's friend, Krystal Kross. She supposedly had a beautiful home and had taken a month vacation for their arrival. She'd stayed in this house for a few months to assist Kade with his burns while we were on our quest to the Underworld.

At least it wasn't like they were heading off to meet a total stranger. They actually spent quite a bit of time together, and were both fond of Krystal. Caleb wasn't too keen on the idea of being away, but he knew he needed to go wherever Courtney went. Even though he didn't show it, he was a very thoughtful brother.

My true birthday was only a week away. Time was flying way too quickly, and because of the renovations, things were pretty quiet. The Fallen and Darkling weren't seen, the barrier stayed up, and I had a Guardian with me at all times.

I hadn't spoken to Ethon in weeks. He and his goons stayed in the tower, but I knew when he was close. I could always feel the buzz of the bond pulling at me, trying to connect us. I peeked out the window on a few occasions and watched him hover just along the outside of the barrier. His eyes were always downtrodden and glancing toward my window. It was times like those which made me sad, and made me feel like I should talk to him. One day I would, but at the moment, I was bound to the house.

On this particular day, Thomas was on guard, and had fallen asleep on my floor. There was a faint tapping on my window. When I pulled back the curtain a few inches, Ethon was there hovering right outside the barrier. I finally gave in, sucked in a deep breath, pulled back the curtain, and opened the window.

"Hey you," he said with a sad grin.

"Hey," I replied, in a soft whisper, with a single wave which felt awkward.

"If it weren't for the bond, I would have thought you were dead," he remarked.

"I know, and I'm so sorry. I was healing. My ribs were bashed by one of the Darkling, and I thought I'd broken them again. But I guess they were just bruised," I explained.

"Your ribs, again?" he asked with a look of concern. "Do you want me to make sure they aren't broken?"

"No, but thank you. They're actually feeling a lot better now," I grinned. "So, how did you tap on my window?" I was curious because I knew he couldn't pass the barrier.

He opened his palm, and showed me a few small stones.

"Ahhh," I giggled. "So, how have you been?"

"Being away from you is nearly unbearable," he sighed, and then grinned. He was shirtless, his sculpted shoulders, chest, and abs were flexing with each flap of his wings to keep him steady. "We need to talk."

I'd known this was coming.

"I can't at this very moment. The barrier is up and Alaine and Samuel won't let me leave." This was the truth.

"You'll be safe with me and everyone knows it. They just won't admit it. And, we really need to talk. I'll take you to my secret place," he said, raising his brow.

"That sounds very tempting, but after the attack I'm now under constant guard," I said, thumbing back to Thomas, who was still out cold.

Ethon's eyes narrowed and his crimson red eyes began to burn a little brighter, but he quickly quenched it when his eyes glanced back at me. "Well, they can't keep you away from me forever. Your transformation is near, and we have a matter to take care of before my father sends his wrath."

"You would never allow him to hurt me, right?" I questioned him, looking into his eyes for truth.

"No, Emma. I would never allow him to harm you. I would die before that happened," he answered.

I turned back to Thomas who hadn't moved an inch. His mouth was still hanging wide open, and his face was half-hanging off the pillow. I knew Ethon would never put me in harm's way, and I really needed to talk to him. Time was running out and I had so many questions to ask him. I also wanted to see his eyes as he answered them, and see his sincerity.

I still had my little secret, which could only be fulfilled *after* my transformation. So literally and technically, I was pretty much screwed – unless Alaine found a loophole. I basically had two options. Either seal the bond with Ethon before my transformation, or run and attempt to hide from everyone, hoping no one would find me until my transformation was over.

With both Lucifer and Lucian out there, and the experience I had with my recent quest, running away wasn't the best or smartest option. Especially, if I was going to be alone. I was a magnet for the Fallen, and it seemed like even when I was invisible, they could smell me from miles away.

I needed to know Ethon would stand up against his father for me if he ever had to. I wasn't brought into existence to become anyone's pawn, especially Lucifer's. Hell if I would live the rest of my life as his slave. That was simply not going to happen. My freedom was something I'd fight for to the death.

I looked into Ethon's fiery crimson eyes. "I will meet you on one condition," I finally whispered.

He grinned. "Anything."

"You have to promise we will not seal any bonds yet." I knew with the power of the bond, it would be hard to fight, but I had to make sure he didn't try and force me to seal the bond.

"You have my word," he answered straightforwardly. Honesty emanated from his eyes.

"Alright," I uttered quietly. "Meet me at the front door. Midnight."

Ethon smiled and I was hit with a wave of happiness through the bond.

"I'll be there. Thank you, Emma." With a single flap of his beautiful black wings, he shot off into the sky.

I hoped I was doing the right thing. Alaine would kill me if she ever found out I was leaving the house, but then again, she was also the one who told me I had to play the part and make Ethon believe we would still be bonded before my transformation. I just needed to keep my head straight with him. Ethon and I together and alone... that was a lethal combination. I just hoped we could rationally discuss the future and I could get as much information as I could get from him before I returned.

Thomas was protecting me for the whole today, which meant he would also be here during the night. He was taking a nap. Would he even be able to sleep tonight? I wish I had the power to put the sleeper on him, just long enough for me to sneak past him. Maybe if I put on my super suit under my pajamas after my shower it would help me disappear. I was slowly learning how to wield the magic of the suit and now, with just a thought, I could disappear. It was like the more I wore it, the greater the connection became. I was glad because over the next week, I'd need it more than ever.

Aside from all the craziness, tonight was Caleb and Courtney's farewell dinner. Even though it was only for a few weeks, Alaine thought it fitting to throw together a little party in the ballroom, just to lighten the mood. She knew how much everyone enjoyed parties there, especially Courtney.

Thomas interrupted my thoughts, stretching and yawning. "Hey, you"

"Hey," I answered. "You were out cold."

"Yeah, I didn't get much sleep last night in the cabin. Those guys snore like a pack of wild buffalo."

"What?" I giggled. "Have you ever heard a pack of wild buffalo snore?"

"No, but I can imagine they sound very similar to the sounds the guys made last night in the cabin."

My giggle turned into a laugh. "Well, Alex was here last night and he said it was the best night's sleep he'd had in a long time."

"I couldn't agree with him more. I'm glad I'll finally get a chance to sleep in peace, unless... do *you* snore?"

"Me?" I squeaked. "No way. Until Malachi and Dominic slept in here, this was a snore free zone."

"Well, just in case I do happen to snore tonight—" he threw me a small, unopened package.

"What's this?" I asked.

"Earplugs. I have a box full of them."

I laughed. "Well, thanks. I wish I had these a few nights ago. They would have come in very handy." I pulled open my nightstand drawer and dropped them inside. "Hey, Thomas?"

"Yeah?" he asked.

"What do you think you'll do after this assignment is over?"

He glanced at me and shrugged. "Go back to Midway and wait for my next assignment."

I nodded. "How long have you known, Kade?"

"Well, until this assignment, I never knew him personally. I knew *of* him, I mean, everyone in Grandia knows about Kade because he is the son of Raphael the Archangel."

His words brought a smile to my lips. "You've met his parents?" I asked.

"No. His dad is kind of a big deal though. He's a healer, and is sent out on a lot of missions. I've heard he's super cool though, like Kade."

"And, what do you think about Ethon?" I wanted to see what he thought and was trying to make small talk instead of the awkward dead silence.

He puffed and shook his head. "There isn't much to say. Your bond with him is the worst possible scenario. He happens to be the *son* of our greatest enemy."

"Yeah," I sighed. I guess I already knew asking any of the Guardians this question would end with the same answer. None of them would choose Ethon.

"Look, Emma. If you're looking for my opinion, I'm sorry. I shouldn't be offering you my advice because it's biased. I will always choose my brother."

"I know. Thanks for being honest," I said.

"Hey, no problem," he said, with a smile. "Still friends?" His brow raised.

"Of course we are," I said, tossing a pillow at him. He caught it, fluffed it, and lay back down.

I couldn't wait for dinner to arrive, and it seemed like the seconds ticked by extra slow. It was casual, so I decided to wear my jeans and a nice, caramel brown, long-sleeved top. I wore my hair down, and applied some simple make-up. Thomas left the room for an hour so I could get ready, but he said he would be just outside my door.

Right before dinner, there was a knock.

"Are you ready?" he asked through the door.

"Yep. I'll be right there" I answered, giving myself a quick spray of perfume, one I remembered Kade liked. When I opened the door, Thomas stood there looking very dashing. His blond hair was neatly combed back, and he had on jeans and button down blue shirt, which made the blue in his eyes stand out. He must have gotten one of the other guys to stand guard for a while so he could change.

"You look good," he said, offering me his arm.

"Why, thanks. So do you," I responded. "I didn't think I would be escorted to this event. This is cool." I looped my arm around his.

"Yeah, I have my moments," he said. "Plus, I'm still on baby-sitting duty."

I gasped and narrowed my eyes on him.

"Babysitting?" I snarled.

"I'm kidding!" he laughed, holding his hands up in surrender.

"You better be."

As we walked down the stairs, Henry rounded the corner with a tray of yummy desserts.

"Emma. How are you, dear?" His warm smile instantly put a smile on my face.

"Henry! When did you get back?" I asked. It had felt like forever since I'd seen him last. He'd been away tending to his sick sister in England, before coming down with the same illness himself.

"Just this morning," he chimed.

"It looks like you're feeling much better," Thomas added.

"Yes, much. It's good to be back with all of my favorite people."

"Well, it's great to have you back, Henry," I said.

He gave a little nod and proceeded down the hall toward the ballroom.

When we entered, I felt like I had been transported to another place. The room was bright and cheerful, beautifully decorated with balloons, flowers, and centerpieces in vivid colors. There was no way anyone could feel sad in this setting.

Courtney and Caleb were already seated, picking on some snacks, and as soon as Courtney saw me, she waved me over.

"Well, I guess you're safe here," Thomas said, letting me go.

"Thank you," I said.

"Yeah, no problem. I'll be watching you, and will come to collect you at the end of the night," he said with an over exaggerated wink.

"Fine." I giggled, rolling my eyes, heading for Courtney.

"Emma," she exclaimed, waving. "Come, sit next to me."

I was glad to see a smile on her face. The past few weeks had been really hard on everyone, especially them. I finally made my way over and sat in the seat next to her. She had a scar from the wound on her forehead, and her bruises were almost completely gone.

She leaned over close. "I can't believe we're leaving for a few weeks."

"It's only to keep you safe. You saw what happened. Alaine wouldn't be able to forgive herself if anything ever happened to you or Caleb. You're her life."

"So are you," she said.

"I know, but you've been with her longer than I have. She practically raised you."

"Yeah, " she sighed, then turned toward me. "But I'm really worried about you."

"Why?" I asked, seeing the troubled look.

"I had a horrible nightmare last night about you and it scared me," she whispered.

"What was it about?" I asked. She paused. "It's alright, it was only a dream," I whispered back. But deep inside I knew, especially in this crazy new world, dreams sometimes did come true.

She exhaled. "It was pitch black and I could hear you screaming, calling out for help. It sounded like you were hurt. I tried to find my way through the darkness to get to you, and no matter how hard I tried, I couldn't find you. I yelled and yelled for you, but you kept screaming in pain. It made me so sick inside. And then, all of a sudden I saw you, lying in a pool of blood, and your eyes were red. No matter how fast I ran toward you, I couldn't get to you. You looked helpless and in so much pain.

"I woke up crying, and had to turn my night light on. I slept with it on for the rest of the night. I don't want anything to happen to you, Emma," she said, leaning over and hugging me tightly.

I hugged her back. "Hey, don't worry about me. I have Samuel, Alaine, and six of the best Guardians watching over me. I'll be just fine," I said, trying to be optimistic.

"I know, but there are a lot more of those monsters out there. Caleb told me there were thousands."

"Which is true, but look at how many of them attacked us, and they were all killed. They can't defeat our guys. They're the best warriors out there, trained to fight and protect us. You don't have to worry. We'll be just fine."

"I hope so," she breathed, a single tear trickled down her cheek. "I just can't wait until this is all over."

"Me too, Courtney. Me too." I grabbed her hand and squeezed it.

Glancing at the tray in front of us, I was about to grab a small pastry puff when Courtney nudged me.

"Hey, look who just walked in," she said, discreetly nodding toward the entry.

As soon as I saw him, my heart beat a little quicker and my insides fluttered with butterflies.

Kade.

I hadn't seen him in almost a week, and even when I tried, I couldn't tear my eyes away. He was with the rest of the Guardians, but he stood out of the pack. I felt the edges of my lips rise as I watched him laugh and talk to the others as they walked in. Seeing him was like drinking an ice cold cup of water on the hottest day. It quenched the fires of stress. His presence always made my world feel complete.

"You're in love with him now, aren't you?" Courtney questioned in a soft whisper.

"What?" I turned towards her cheesy smile, and remembered the first day I arrived here. We were in this very room when she asked me if I was in love with Kade. My answer at the time was no, because I barely knew him. But a lot had happened since then. That short time between then and now seemed like an eternity.

He combed his fingers through his thick brown hair. Every time he did that, it took my breath away. I was crazy about him - the way he carried himself, his perfect smile, his glimmering eyes, his charisma.

He was standing right under the flawless statue, carved from his likeness. A perfect reminder of who he really was... *my* Guardian angel. Kade turned and our eyes connected. His hazel eyes were gleaming just as bright as his beautiful smile. For that brief moment in time, we were frozen. One heart captured by the other.

"Well?" she asked again, her eyes intently watching me.

A smile rose even higher on my lips. My eyes still locked onto his. "Yes." I answered assuredly. "I *am* in love with him."

"I knew it. I just wanted to hear you say it," she giggled.

"I know where my true heart lies," I breathed out loud, but the words were meant for me. The feelings I had with Kade were just as strong as the bond itself, if not stronger. The pull between us wasn't one that needed to be forced, it just *was*.

"Then, why don't you two just be together?" she asked.

"I wish it were that simple," I sighed.

"Well, maybe it is and you're just complicating it more than you should," she said, shrugging.

I turned to her and grinned. "I'm really gonna miss you, little sister."

Her smile rose from ear to ear. "It's only for a few weeks. And when I get back, we are going to do more sisterly things."

"Deal."

When I looked back I noticed the guys walking toward the tables, but Kade stayed back. He discreetly motioned for me to come, then proceeded to walk back out into the hallway.

"Hey, I'll be right back," I said, leaning over to Courtney. "I need to use the restroom."

"Alright. I'll save your seat," she chimed.

I stood and proceeded to walk out, when Thomas called, "Hey where are you going?"

"To the bathroom. Do you care to follow me?" I asked, a little snarky in hopes he would say no.

"Nope. I think you've got this. Don't wander, and come right back," he replied.

"Yes, sir," I saluted.

"Funny," he said, unamused.

I laughed and quickly made my way toward the hall, sighing in relief.

Kade wasn't there when I exited, but I saw him glance around the corner of the foyer and wink. I quickly made my way toward him, my heart pitter-pattering, my knees shaking.

Before I reached the end, I quickly glanced behind me to make sure no one was following. The hall was empty.

As soon as I rounded the corner, I was enveloped in his embrace. His warm lips pressed against mine for a quick moment, stealing my breath. "I've missed you," he whispered, hugging me closer.

"I've missed you, too," I said, hugging him back. His sweet scent wrapped around me.

The feeling of being in his arms was like nothing else in the world.

"How are you holding up?" he asked.

"As fine as any person could be in my shoes," I sighed. "Alaine still doesn't have any answers, and I'm really starting to get worried."

"We still have a week. Samuel left this morning to do some of his own searching."

"Where did he go?" I gasped. I hadn't seen him since the attack, and knowing he was out there alone made me worry.

"I don't know. He didn't say. He just told us he'd be back, and I don't think he wanted anyone to know where he was going. Samuel's good at being hidden. He's done it for so long, I wouldn't worry about him too much."

I nodded, my mind tormented at the thought of him ever getting hurt.

"Hey," he whispered, steadying my face to meet his. "He'll be fine, and we still have time."

I forced a smile, nodding again. I wrapped my arms around his neck and brought him down until our faces were an inch apart.

"Kiss me?"

"You never have to ask," he breathed.

I pressed my lips to his, and an inferno erupted between us. Passion and longing filled me, and poured out to him. His gentle hands held my face, while soft wet lips claimed mine, making the world around us fade away.

Floating high on a cloud, and never wanted it to end, but his lips left mine much too soon, lingered painfully close. I could feel his breath brush across my lips, making me tingle.

"We should get back," he said softly, pressing his lips against mine again. "They'll come out looking for you."

"Mhmmm," I nodded, humming against his mouth. It was the only thing I could do, since he'd left me dizzy and speechless.

He quickly kissed the tip of my nose and chuckled.

"Thank you," I whispered.

"For what?" he questioned.

"For finding a way. I really needed this. I needed you."

"We both did," he answered.

I kissed him one more time before releasing him. "I'll see you inside."

He winked. "I'll be there in a minute."

During dinner I tried to keep my head in the moment, but it kept spinning and spinning with unwanted stress. *Kade, Ethon, Samuel, Lucian, Lucifer.* I felt like I was headed on a downward spiral, out of control, ready to crash and burn.

Before I knew it, dinner was over. I was sitting there for over an hour, and the whole thing was a complete blur. I vaguely remembered laughing and smiling but didn't remember why.

Would this ever end? Would I be able to enjoy my life without stress or worry?

I hugged Courtney and Caleb goodnight, feeling bad I hadn't given them my full attention, but they didn't even seem to notice.

"Have a safe flight," I said to Courtney as she stood up from the table.

She hugged me back. "Thank you. Please be safe, Emma."

"I'll try," I smiled.

"You better do a little more than try," Caleb answered. "I'm looking forward to hearing good news before we get back."

"Alright. I'll do my best to stay alive until you get back," I said, holding my hand out to him for a shake. "Good?"

"That'll do," he said, forgoing the hand and leaning over to hug me.

Alaine stepped forward and wrapped me in her arms. "Try and get some rest, sweetheart," she said, softly kissing my cheek. "You look very tired."

I nodded. "I will."

She smiled then escorted Courtney and Caleb out.

I doubted I'd get to see them off because they were leaving at five in the morning. By that time, I should be back, tucked safely in bed, sleeping.

James, Alex, and Malachi also left early, trying to get back to the cabin so they could claim a bed to sleep on. I guess with only two beds in the cabin, the rest had to sleep on the floor.

I glanced around and noticed Kade standing in a corner of the room, casually chatting with Thomas and Dominic. Henry was walking a few caterers out, and one man was clearing the tables.

Looking at the scene, I all of a sudden felt so lost and alone. And the only thing that could remedy my loneliness was Kade's touch. His touch was like an elixir which I craved. I wanted nothing more than to be wrapped in his arms, a blanket of strength and love. Arms that offered me hope, tenderly caressing the wounds and scars no one else could see.

Here he was standing in the same room, less than one hundred steps away, and because of the stupid bond, we weren't allowed to be together – for both of our sakes.

That was some grade A bullshit.

My emotions quickly overwhelmed me, sending a flow of tears down my cheeks, filled with anger and uncertainty. I wasn't going to let fear rule my life. Not anymore.

I walked toward him and without speaking, wrapped my arms around his neck and buried my face in his chest and cried.

"Hey, what happened?" Dom questioned, with a bit of anger in his words. "Whose ass do we need to kick?"

I shook my head, unable to answer.

Kade wrapped his arms around me. "She'll be fine. Can you guys give us a minute?"

"Sure," Thomas answered. "Come on, Dom."

"I'm serious, man. If there is someone messing with her, you let me know. I'll take care of it. Quick and easy," Dom said.

"Alright. Thanks, man," Kade answered.

"Let's go," Thomas said. I heard Dom exhale, then their footsteps walking away.

"Hey, what's the matter?" Kade whispered softly in my ear.

"I need you. I feel like my world is falling apart, and you're the only one who can hold me together. I just need you to hold me. *Please*. Only for a little while."

He laid his head on mine. "I'll hold you as long as you need, and even longer if you'll let me."

That's all I wanted. His embrace was magical. It warmed me and made me feel as if it were mending all of my broken pieces.

We stood silent, anchored to each other for a lengthy amount of time, and he never once loosened his arms around me. He held me tight, slowly rocking side to side. His steady heartbeat against my ear nearly put me to sleep. I felt so relaxed for the first time in a long time, and wished I could have stayed in his arms forever. It was my safe place. In his arms, I felt peaceful. His love was free, unconstrained, and came with no worry.

When I finally felt strong enough to let go, I slowly released my arms from his neck. "Thank you, for always being here when I need you," I breathed.

"These arms are yours, and hugs will always be free." His crooked grin made my heart swell.

"Well, that's a good thing because I think I'll need a lot more of them in the near future."

"Just speak the word, and I'll be there," he said, then placed his fingers on my chin and steadied our eyes on each other. "And if you *ever* need me, don't hesitate to ask. Alright?"

"Alright," I answered.

"Sleep sweet, my Emma," he breathed, kissing my forehead before letting me go.

"Sleep sweet," I returned.

Thomas walked me back to my room, and put a movie on the laptop as he made his bed on the floor. I rolled up the super suit as I was getting ready to shower, tucking it into my pajamas before I carried it into the bathroom. Thankfully, Thomas was too preoccupied to notice.

I stood in the shower, letting the hot water pound down on top of my head, hoping it would numb the growing pain.

Am I doing the right thing going with Ethon?

If I didn't go, it was possible things could quickly turn south. Lucifer had to believe that no one knew about his plan. I still didn't know how connected Ethon really was with his father, and really didn't want to find out.

I needed Ethon and Lucifer to believe I was still going ahead with the plan, and was intent to seal the bond between us. If either of them found out anyone knew about the plan, it would mean the deal was off. Then I, along with everyone in this house, was as good as dead. It terrified me, and was why I needed to see him. I wasn't going to risk any lives in this house.

NINE

FTER MY SHOWER, I SLIPPED into the super suit and then threw on my pajamas. The top part of the suit was sticking out from the collar, but I doubted Thomas would notice. Just to be sure, I brushed my long, damp hair over it.

When I exited the bathroom, he was lying on the ground half-asleep, watching some movie I'd never seen.

"Do you mind if I turn in early?" I asked.

It was actually already ten, and not very early. But this way I had two hours for him to fall asleep.

"Not at all. I was just about to crash. Don't forget your earplugs."

I pulled open the drawer and reached in. "Got them," I said, waving them in the air.

"Perfect. And don't worry, I've got mine... just in case," he winked.

"Good night, Thomas," I said, then clicked off the light.

"Good night, Emma," he answered.

I rolled over and pulled the blanket over me, pretending to go to sleep. My stomach twisted, and my pulse raced as I watched the clock, trying to lay as still as possible. It took an hour and twenty-two minutes before Thomas fell asleep. I knew because his breathing became heavy and loud. He didn't snore, but I could tell he wasn't awake.

When the clock turned to 11:50pm, I slowly pushed the blanket off and sat up. The bed creaked, making Thomas snort, but he rolled over and quickly fell back to sleep.

Slowly, I stood from the bed trying to keep my breath even and my legs from shaking. I quietly tiptoed past him and he didn't move.

I had this.

I was a few steps from the door when something grabbed my leg. I threw my hand over my mouth and screamed.

"Where do you think you're going?"

"Thomas," I quietly scolded, then sighed.

Dammit. He was good.

"Where?" he questioned again with a look of exasperation.

"Thomas, listen to me. I need to leave for a bit, but I'll be back."

"Where?" he pressed in a deeper, non-friendly tone. His hand was still locked tightly around my ankle.

"I have to talk to Ethon," I finally sighed.

"Oh, hell no," he said, sitting up. "You are not leaving this house, especially with that demon."

"I have to. I need to find answers only he can give, and if I don't talk to him and make him believe I'm still moving forward with our bonding, bad things will happen to everyone here," I whispered.

"It's too dangerous. Why do you think Alaine wanted you protected at all times? They all know you're going to transform soon. They're watching and waiting."

"That's exactly why I need to go. We've been bonded, so you know he won't hurt me. He wants to protect me too, and you know he can outrun any of the Fallen."

"I will be tortured and killed by Alaine if she ever finds out you left—"

"She won't," I cut in. "I promise. I'll be back before anyone wakes up. Please, Thomas. It's imperative I talk to him. Like a matter of life or death. It's for all of us."

"I don't like this, Emma."

"Thomas, you have to trust me."

"Holy crap. You can't even begin to understand the insurmountable stress you're putting me through right now." He paused and grabbed the sides of his head with his hands. "You better come back, or I am dead. Dead. Dead. Dead," he repeated, rocking back and forth.

"I promise. I'll be back way before sunrise. No one will ever know."

"Fine. If I don't get my wings, it will be because of you. And if you get caught, I will blame you for all eternity."

"Deal, but it won't happen. I'm just going to get some answers and smooth things over to buy us a little more time. That's it."

He let out an exaggerated sigh. "Dammit. I can't believe I'm going to go along with this," he said, shaking his head in disbelief. "Do you have your dagger?"

"Yes," I answered, touching the tip.

"I'm only doing this because I believe in you, but you have to make me *one* promise," he said, thrusting his pointer finger at me.

"What's that?"

"Do *not* seal that bond," he said, his blue eyes were cold and dead serious.

"I promise. No bond sealing." I drew a cross over my heart. "And I will be back soon."

"You better be because I'll be freaking stressed out, not sleeping, watching the windows, waiting for you."

"Thank you, Thomas," I said, hugging him.

He grudgingly tapped my back.

"Yeah, yeah, yeah."

I didn't blame him. He was really putting everything on the line for me. But my mission was to make sure everyone stayed safe.

Against his better judgment, he escorted me down the stairs, sighing stressfully every few seconds. When we reached the bottom he stayed hidden in the darkness and I quietly went the rest of the way to the front door. As soon as my hand touched the knob, I felt him. A rush of tingles and euphoria surged through me. I quietly opened the door, when as I stepped outside, Ethon landed directly in front of the barrier.

His crimson eyes glowed in the darkness as he held out his hand to me. I ran to him, stopping a foot from the barrier.

"You actually came," he said, almost surprised.

"Did you have any doubt?" I questioned, with a grin.

"Maybe," he smiled, his hand still open and waiting.

I placed my hand in his, and he yanked me against him, wrapping his arms tightly around my waist, pressing our bodies together. I gasped as the bond sent a wave of electricity over me.

I heard him chuckle. "Are you ready?"

"Yes," I breathed.

With a flap of his wings, we were in the air, the wind whipping through my hair. The air was cold, and I was glad I had the suit on to keep me warm.

"Emma," he spoke, his voice carried a tinge of urgency.

"Yes?"

"Hold on tight, and don't let go."

"Why? What's the matter?"

"A few of Lucian's horde are following us. It looks like there are only two, but I'll have to lose them or kill them before we start for my place."

"Kill?" I shrieked. "I think losing them will be much easier."

"They will alert others if I don't kill them, and then we will have more to deal with."

"How will you do it?"

"If you trust me, I will use you as a distraction. They won't even know what hit them."

"I don't think I like the sound of that." My voice was shaky.

"You would never leave my arms, and I promise you will be safe."

"Are you sure?" My heart was thumping wildly in my chest.

"Don't you trust me?"

I paused. He hadn't given me a reason not to.

"Yes," I answered.

"Then hold on tight," he said stopping in mid-air. He turned around and started flying fast, head-on with the Fallen.

Every muscle in my body tensed as my grip tightened around him. My fingers almost embedded themselves into his flesh. I quickly started to second guess leaving the barrier. Was this even worth it?

"Just breathe, and witness my power. Maybe then you won't worry if I can protect you." His words both excited and terrified me.

In a matter of seconds we had come to a dead stop, facing off with two overly muscular Fallen. It was dark, but the moon outlined their bulging frames, with sharp metal weapons wielded in their hands.

"Give us the girl," one spoke. His voice was gruff and deep.

"Why do you think I turned around when I could have easily outrun you?" Ethon responded. "If you want her, come and take her."

I closed my eyes as his left hand rested on the small of my back, pressing me tighter to him. "Wrap your arms around my neck," Ethon whispered softly in my ear. I quickly did as he said, and also wrapped my legs around his waist. It would take tons of effort to pry my body from his.

"Well?" the other Fallen snarled.

"She's afraid. You'll have to come and take her from me," he answered. Ethon's arms left me, and for a moment I was terrified. "Like I said...you want her...come and get her."

I felt my body tingle.

"Where the hell did they go?" one of the Fallen hissed.

I opened my eyes and realized we were invisible.

"Whoa," Ethon exhaled. "Hold on, baby. Let's do this." He wrapped his arms tightly around my waist, and with a flap of his wings we twisted like a tornado. He spun so fast, it was almost as if we weren't moving.

He stopped abruptly.

"What happened?" I asked, breathless.

"It's done."

"Where are they?"

"Look down," he replied.

I glanced below and saw two headless bodies plummeting toward the earth.

"Wow. That was fast," I gasped.

"Emma, look at what kind of power we have when we're together. We'll be unstoppable. Imagine what we will do once we've sealed the bond and you transform. There will be no one who can match us." His eyes narrowed and I could see a faint grin rise on his lips. "I just caught a glimpse of our future. It will be amazing." He grabbed the back of my head, his lips crashed down onto mine, then he quickly pulled back. "You and I will rule the Underworld for all eternity. It will be amazing." He looked at me with wonderment.

"Yeah," I breathed, trying to force a smile.

Ruling anything was not what I wanted to do. Actually, it was the furthest thing from my mind. I just wanted to live a simple life – a life without the constant threat of death or war lingering over my head – and to experience every good thing it had to offer.

I did, however, need to take out a few key players if this was going to happen, and little did Ethon know... his father was on my secret hit list. I wouldn't tell him, of course. It was a super-secret list carved onto my heart.

"We're safe now. Let's get to the portal."

"Okay," I breathed, slowly releasing my grip. Still face to face, Ethon held tight to my waist; the moon light glistened on his silky, raven wings as we soared high above the trees. I closed my eyes and held my arms out to my sides, imagining I had my own wings.

His lips found their way to my neck, his tongue softly twisted against my skin sending pulses of heat through my body. I inhaled and my arms grasped for his shoulders as his hand caught the back of my neck, steadying me.

Ethon's crimson eyes were inches from mine, burning deep with passion. I closed my eyes, trying to fight the overwhelming pull of the bond. It was something no normal immortal would ever do. The bond was created for soul mates to find each other, copulate, and begin benefiting completely from its many pleasures.

I just couldn't allow it to take me. Not yet. It was something I had to fight until I came to a solid decision. Only then, when I was completely certain, would I give in. Until such time, I would have to keep treading, holding my head above the fine line of sealing the bond. If I ever lost control and went under, even for a moment, my world would change. Forever.

"You're resisting," he hummed against my neck, making my world spin.

"I have to," I breathed.

"Why?"

"Because it would be too easy to give you everything."

I knew the answer satisfied him when a smile grew on his lips.

"I promised you I wouldn't seal the bond, and I will keep my word. But that doesn't mean we can't have a little fun."

"Alaine will be waking up in a few hours to take Courtney and Caleb to the airport. I'll need to be back in bed before she wakes. If she finds me missing, I won't be allowed to see you again."

"I promise to have you tucked safely in bed before then," he winked.

"*My* bed," I clarified, knowing he was the son of the Deceiver.

He laughed deep from his belly. "Yes, love. In *your* bed... all by your lonesome," he added, playfully nipping my bottom lip. "Since you have a curfew, I guess I should fly faster."

"Most definitely," I giggled, and grasped his neck.

He flapped his wings and shot forward.

I hated the way my feelings whiplashed whenever I was with Ethon. He was fun and wild, and could easily be a bad influence, a total different feeling from those I experienced with Kade.

Both wonderful in their own way, and both of them loved me, but which would I be able to live with for the rest of my life?

A realization hit me... I wouldn't have Kade for the rest of my life. I would only have him for the rest of *his* life. Now in a mortal body, I would have to watch him grow old and eventually die, and I wasn't sure if I could handle the pain.

"Hey," Ethon whispered.

I smiled. "What?"

"Your eyes were distant. Where were you?"

"Just thinking about the future," I answered.

"Well, it must not have been too good," he added.

I narrowed my eyes on him. "You were watching me that closely?"

"You're in my arms. How can I possibly take my eyes off you?"

My cheeks heated.

The bond continued to weaken my defenses, making me vulnerable. I could feel the walls I'd built up against him slowly start to crumble away. With his touch, I was becoming unglued.

Damn bond.

TEN

I T WASN'T MUCH LONGER BEFORE we finally reached the portal. Without slowing down, he dove straight toward the huge tree and did a spin as we entered. I held my scream down to a squeal, which made him laugh.

We went from complete darkness to beautiful, bright blue sky.

He set me down right next to the little lake. As I stepped back, he didn't release his grip.

"Leaving so soon?" he asked, a playful look in his eyes.

I leaned into him, but didn't say a word. He held me, the bond twining and curling itself tightly around us. I closed my eyes and sent my thoughts back to Kade, Alaine, and Samuel. I had to remain strong, because the bond was hard to resist.

Ethon exhaled loudly, then stepped back and let me go.

"I don't know why you try so hard to fight what is supposed to be. It's a natural thing."

"It's not natural. It's magic."

"Call it what you will, but the bond was created perfect. To seek and find two immortal hearts who were destined to conjoin for all eternity. It's as simple as that. You, my dear Emma, are complicating it."

I shook my head. "No. The bond screwed up on me. It gave me two choices."

"And you are torn," he answered.

I sighed, not sure if I should answer. "Yes and no."

His arms crossed over his chest. "Explain."

"Yes, I am torn because the bond chose two men who are my perfect match. And no, because one of those men has become mortal, and will die long before I do."

"I'm glad to see you're being rational. He shouldn't be an option anymore. Kade could never protect you the way I can. You'll be the one babysitting his ass as he grows older and weaker. I mean, it would be weird because eventually he will look old enough to be your grandfather."

"Don't," I snapped. I felt anger rise within me. One – because he was putting Kade down, and two – because he was right. My heart and mind were warring. My life was a continuous freaking nightmare.

"I need to ask you something, and I need you to tell me the truth," I said, looking into his eyes.

"Ask away," he said with a grin.

"Would you be willing to forsake your father for me?"

He hesitated and I could see a look of confusion in his eyes. "You don't have to answer that," I said quickly, trying to move on.

His appearance softened. "Emma, you don't understand. You will *always* have my heart. I will protect you, and you will be my one true love and mate for all eternity. You will be taken care of in the best possible way. If you would just give in to our bond we could finally be together as intended." He stepped forward, taking me into his arms, crushing his mouth over mine. His kiss was firm and eager.

Pulling back he gestured to a spot under the tree. "I'd like to just sit and talk for a little while. It's not often I get to have you all to myself. Come, sit with me." He sat himself down next to the bank of the small lake and pulled me down into his space, setting me right between his legs. My back was resting on his chest as his arms wrapped tightly around me. I could feel his warm breath tickle the back of my ear.

"I need you to know I will love you like you've never been loved before. For the rest of your life you will be satisfied, and I will do whatever is in my power to make you happy." He kissed my cheek then spoke ever so softly into my ear. "Once we've sealed the bond, I would stand up to my father. You will be mine to guard and protect. My bonded. My love."

His words made my heart thump a little faster. I closed my eyes and imagined a life with Ethon, and then a flash of his father's face, and his wicked eyes, came into perfect focus. He would always be there to make sure we were part of his agenda... hidden or not.

Ethon said he would stand up to his father, but I saw how he'd submitted and cowered when his father spoke to him. Even if he didn't want to admit it, his father had the upper hand. He was ruler of the Fallen and the Underworld – he had been for centuries. Did Ethon really think he could stand up to him? Maybe he would once we were fully bonded and I was his for all eternity. Who knew?

I sighed a little too loud.

"Hey," he said, lifting me up and turning me around. I had a sudden bout of Déjà vu as I was drawn into his burning gaze. A few stray strands of raven hair feathered down in front of his flawless face. His strong arms held me tight. "What's the matter?"

"Nothing," I said.

"I know something is wrong. I can feel it."

"There's nothing wrong. I've just been feeling really tired and achy lately." That was the truth.

"It's what happens before your transformation. It sucks the energy out of you, but once you're transformed, you will feel reborn. Rejuvenated. You won't have to worry about feeling sick or tired, unless you are wounded. But you will have me to fix you." His arm tightened around me. "God, you're so beautiful. I can't wait until we seal the bond and you are mine forever."

He held my back and laid me down facing him. He laid over me, propped up on his arms, not touching me. Then, I slowly felt the weight of his body from my feet, to my thighs, to my stomach, and all the way until he was pressed tight against me.

His eyes never left mine, and as hard as I tried, I couldn't pull mine away from his. Our bodies fit perfectly and it sent an intoxicating high rushing from my head to toes. It was a feeling I couldn't deny and was too hard to pull away from. I was frozen under his spell. His crimson eyes burned bright a few inches from me.

"Ethon," I breathed.

"Don't worry. We won't cross the line, but I want to give you some of my energy." He closed his eyes, and then I saw the familiar smoke tendril from the edges. When he opened them they were bright. He then placed his hands on either side of my forehead. As soon as the heat touched me, I gasped, and he pressed his mouth to mine.

At that moment, I was whisked away. I closed my eyes and let the overwhelming sensations take over. It was the most unbelievable feeling. Me and him. Face to face. Body to body. All I wanted was to feel his bare skin against mine.

The bond was pulling us together, trying to make us seal the deal.

Just as I felt our souls reaching out, trying to connect, he pulled away. His eyes were closed tight, but when he opened them, they had dimmed back to normal.

I was breathless, my mind and body in a state of complete calm.

"You look so much better now. Hopefully what I gave you will help you through the next few days. Of course, we might have to do it again. But I don't mind," he smirked.

I'd never felt this close to him and my body took over. Wrapping my legs around him, I rolled him to his back, so I was lying on top of him. I then pressed my lips to his, making him groan.

"Thank you," I said. "I do feel much better."

His smile returned and he wrapped his arms around my back, pulling me snug into his chest. "My energy is yours. All you have to do is let me take care of you."

I assessed myself and I did feel a lot better. The overwhelming exhaustion had lifted and I felt enlivened. His touch was magic, just as Kade's potion was.

His finger lifted to my chin and held it, while his eyes held a question.

"What?" I asked.

"Do you love me, Emma?" Ethon questioned, searching for an answer.

I quickly responded. "Why would you ask me such a question? Love is such a broad word, and overrated. Love is something that shouldn't be spoken of too often, unless you truly, deeply mean it. It should never be thrown around, but should be something felt. You know... action is better than words."

"So... do you?" His brow furrowed.

I stared at him and giggled. He was so damn persistent. I didn't want to answer him because right now I knew the bond was forcing me to love him. So instead, I leaned over and kissed him, hard and quick, leaving us breathless.

"I guess you put your words to action," he chuckled, folding his arms behind his head. Why the hell did he have to look so freaking handsome?

"Like I said... action is much better than words." I winked at him.

He quickly sat up and grabbed me. "Soon, you will be mine. All mine, and for all eternity. And I will spend the rest of my life proving my love."

I nodded and watched his lips rise. His hands slowly slipped down my back and stopped on either side of my hips, then I felt him rock into me. I gasped. My insides burned and twisted with a rush of electricity. Then he pressed his mouth to mine again and I felt myself let out a moan.

His lips left mine and then he laughed.

"Our future will be amazing," he said, then lifted me off of him.

"What are you doing?" I asked, breathless.

"I made you a promise I intend to keep. We weren't going to seal any bonds tonight, remember? In order to keep that promise I have to disconnect from you now, before things get too heated. It's hard to control myself when I'm around you. It's taking every ounce of self-control, and it's killing me."

"Thank you," I said. "I've never had a boyfriend, so this is all new to me."

"Holy shit, that's right. You're a virgin."

"Yep, and I'm proud of it."

"Being a virgin is overrated."

"So says the son of Satan," I smirked, and he let out a bellowed laugh.

"And you shall soon be his daughter-in-law."

"Don't remind me," I huffed.

"Well, you shall find out when we seal the bond, what *real* pleasure is. You will never want for anything else."

"Oh, really?" I narrowed my eyes at him, and he winked.

Dammit. That was sexy.

"Alright, princess, I think it's time for us to go. If we wait any longer, I might have to keep you here and there will be nothing to hold me back from sealing our bond."

"Yes," I said dusting myself off a little rougher than I normally would, trying to snap myself out of this cloud of lust. "Alaine will be up soon, and I still have to sneak into the house."

"Well then, let's get you back."

He stood and extended his large, beautiful black wings out to his sides.

I still wasn't used to those magical hidden wings. It took my breath away every single time, no matter who it was, but especially being from the one I was bonded too.

He held his arms open to me, so I stepped into him.

"Ready?"

"Ready."

He then shot up into the sky, my stomach twisted and turned as he rolled and maneuvered through the portal, and again we went from light to pure darkness. As soon as we exited something crashed into us. I screamed as we plummeted to the ground, but Ethon wrapped his wings around us as we hit.

"Shit," he cursed.

"What happened?" I screamed, still shaken and a little disoriented.

Grabbing my hand, he led me behind a large tree. "If you can become invisible, now is a good time."

I closed my eyes, concentrating, and felt a warm tingle through my body. As soon as I opened them, the world around me was a haze and my body was gone. I placed my hand on Ethon's shoulder.

"What is it?" I asked.

He sniffed the air and then paused. "What the hell?"

"What?" I pressed.

"It smells like Hellhounds."

"Hellhounds? Why would there be Hellhounds here?"

"They were probably raised by Lucian," he said. "I will need to disconnect from you."

"No, wait," I said, holding on tightly. "I don't want you to go. What if we did the same thing we did to the Fallen?"

"I knew I could kill the Fallen, but there are more than one of those creatures out there, and I will not risk your life." He held me in his arms and with a flap of his wings we flew upward. He placed me on a branch of a large spruce tree, where I instantly clung for my life. As he turned I held on.

"Ethon." He turned back to me. "Please be safe."

"I will," he answered and kissed me. He then let go and dropped back down to the ground, blending into the darkness.

Deep, evil, guttural growls and six sets of blazing eyes glowed in the darkness below, bringing back horrifying memories of the Underworld. My heart thrust itself against the walls of my chest, beating so hard I thought I was going to faint. But it wasn't only the creatures I was terrified about. It was knowing that if these creatures were here, the ones who sent them weren't too far away.

The tree shook, almost releasing my grip and knocking me down from my perch.

I held my breath.

A few branches down, a Fallen had landed. He was huge and muscular. I watched him sniff the air, and then raise his head as if he were looking at me. I froze. Every cell in my body was weighted, then I felt a tingle in my right arm as it released from the tree and grasped the handle of my dagger. I didn't want to unsheathe it because I feared it was glowing and would give away my location.

He knew I was here though. He could smell me, and he was only about ten feet below. He crawled around the branches like he weighed nothing, using his wings to balance. Then he stopped directly below me, and his head snapped back. His evil black eyes locked onto me, but I knew he couldn't see me. Could he?

He sniffed again, and before I could unsheathe the dagger, he reached up and grabbed my leg. I screamed and tried to kick away, but when he realized he had me, he tightened his grip. I couldn't let go of the branch because if I did, I would go crashing to the ground, or into his unwelcoming arms. So I held on, struggling to stay on the branch.

"Ethon!" I screamed.

"You're mine, bitch," the Fallen threatened. There was nothing I could do, and I could hear Ethon in a fight for his life against the Hellhounds.

The Fallen placed both hands on my leg and flapped upward. I had to let go or his strength would have ripped my arms from their sockets. I was in the air, upside down, hanging by one leg. I screamed and tried to kick free. Unexpectedly, he released me. I hit a tree and spun, being tossed around like a rag doll, trying to grasp at anything that could break my fall. Branches scratched my hands and my face, but I couldn't get a grip on anyone of them.

I hit the ground and everything went black.

When I opened my eyes, I felt pain and could hear growls in the distance. I was on the ground lying in between a bunch of trees, out in the open. I wondered how long I was out. Hoping I hadn't broken anything, I slowly moved. I didn't feel like anything was broken, but my back and neck were aching. Sitting up, I quickly pressed myself back against the biggest spruce tree. I could hear the Hellhounds and Ethon, but I couldn't see them.

Then I caught a scent in the breeze and it made my body stiffen.

About twenty yards away, the same Fallen who'd grabbed me, dropped down out of the sky. He sniffed the air, looking for me. I needed to get out of here. The thought being captured threatened to freeze my limbs. But I wouldn't allow it. I would fight.

I quietly made my way around the tree, out from his view. My pulse raced as I reached for my dagger and unsheathed it. Thank God I still had it with me.

I figured that if I ran toward the Hellhounds maybe I could lose him. I'd rather be in the middle of the Hellhounds than dragged away to who knows where and have who knows what done to me. At least if I was near Ethon, he would know if I was taken and he could try and rescue me if I was captured.

It was a huge risk, but the only one that made sense at this very moment, so I sucked in a deep breath and took off in his direction. I ran as fast as I could toward the sounds of growling. When I was about fifty yards away, I stopped and turned back. The Fallen wasn't there, but I knew he must have been close by.

There was a crack to the side of me, and when I turned there were two burning red eyes and sharp teeth standing about ten feet away, fixed directly on me.

Glancing down, I noticed I was still invisible. There was no place for me to run. I would have to fight the Hellhound, and readied myself, holding my dagger out in front of me.

Before I could blink, it crouched and pounced. I thrust my blade forward, and covered my face with the other arm, preparing for pain. Instead, I heard a horrifying scream. The Hellhound had leapt over me, attacking the Fallen who had captured me earlier.

The Hellhound sunk its sharp teeth into the Fallen's shoulder, then thrashing its head, it severed his arm. With another whipping movement, the detached limb flew over and hit me in the leg.

I internally screamed and jumped back. *Eww!*

Agonizing cries filled the air as the Hellhound mauled its prey. Another Fallen dropped from the sky with a sword held above his head. As soon as he landed, he thrust his weapon down and severed the Hellhound's head. He then reached down and picked up his Fallen friend, who was on the brink of death.

"Do it," the injured man yelled. He was fatally marred and covered in blood; shredded flesh hung from his severed arm.

His partner helped him to his knees, and then he leaned forward bowing his head. In an instant the other Fallen lifted his sword and beheaded him. His lifeless body toppled over to the ground. The Fallen began to speak a few angelic words, and within seconds his friend's body began to burn. I knew he would be coming for me next.

The only reason they knew I was here was because they could catch my scent. I glanced down at the severed arm at my feet and had a flashback. When I was near a riverbank and being chased by Darkling, I covered myself with mud and they couldn't smell me. But I didn't have mud this time. The only thing I had now was that disgusting severed arm.

I bent down and picked it up, fighting the overwhelming urge to puke. I could feel the burning bile creeping up my chest, but I held it down. The limb disappeared as soon as I touched it, and not being able to see it helped. I was out of options. If I didn't do this, he would find and capture me.

I held my breath, and clasped my eyes shut tight. Then I began to rub the bloody stump all over my exposed skin. Head, face, neck, and hands. I gagged and clasped my lips shut as thick blood trickled down them. The strong smell of iron was almost too much to bear. I dry heaved a few times, then began to breathe from my mouth.

This better freaking work.

The Fallen sniffed the air, trying to catch a scent. I took the arm and tossed it away from me. As soon as it left my hand, it became visible and hit the ground. In a flash, the Fallen shot toward the area. I was safe for now, but didn't know for how much longer.

In the distance, I saw Ethon battling with the Hellhounds and a few Fallen. It seemed like he had everything under control. His advantage was his wings and speed. He was maneuvering quickly from the mouths of the Hellhounds and trying to fight off Fallen which were airborne.

I watched in horror as one leapt up, snapping at his wing, but he twirled out of the way, while blocking an incoming sword at the same time.

I stepped to the side and my foot landed on a branch, which cracked loudly. I gasped and was slammed from behind. A Fallen had run into me, and when he realized it, he wrapped his arms tightly around me, constricting my chest.

"Ethon," I screamed, but as soon as I yelled, the Fallen took to flight. In seconds I was being carried further and further up and away, with all hope of being found, quickly diminishing.

I tried to reach for the dagger but with my arms pinned it required some effort. I finally had it, and with all my might I thrust it deep into the Fallen's thigh. He screamed and grabbed for his wound, letting go of me. I was falling fast, screaming and watching the tree line get closer and closer. I clenched my eyes just as I was about to hit.

In midair, someone grabbed me. Screaming, I attempted to thrust the blade into whoever it was, but he caught my hand.

"Don't," he said in a familiar gruff voice.

"Bane?"

He responded with, "You stink."

It was him alright, and for some odd reason, I felt safe.

"You need to go back and help Ethon. There are too many evil things down there."

"Azzah is assisting. Ethon ordered me to take you back to safety."

That was the most words I'd ever heard Bane speak... ever.

"But they need your help. They can't do it alone."

"They are more than capable of protecting themselves. I cannot return, unless you give me permission."

"Why would you need *my* permission?" I questioned.

"Because you will soon be Ethon's mate, and I have been ordered to protect the line of Lucifer. I take orders from them alone."

"Well, I order you to turn around and help them. Besides, we're still a long way from home."

Bane nodded and slowly turned around.

"You don't like me do you?"

He shrugged his shoulders, confirming what I already felt.

"Why?"

"It's not that I don't like you. I am sorrowful for you."

"Sorrowful?" I questioned.

"Yes, and don't ask me to tell you why," he replied.

"What if I ordered you to tell me?" His eyes narrowed and I swore he growled at me a bit. "Or not," I quickly added.

He huffed. "If I tell you, I could be severely punished or killed."

"I promise to God, or to Lucifer – whatever fancies you – that I will not speak a word to anyone. There is no one to tell anyway. Besides, I need to know things before I make my final decision."

"You made a deal with Lucifer. You have no choice," he said roughly.

"We'll see about that. I need to know, Bane. Why are you sad for me?"

He shook his head them paused for a moment.

"There are two sides to him, and right now you have only experienced his good side. But what you and the others don't know is there is a very dark and evil side to him, which is almost identical to his father.

"He has killed countless Fallen and mortals alike. If they look at him the wrong way, they die."

"And you're scared of him?" I asked. He didn't answer, but I could see it in his eyes. "How can someone so big and powerful be scared of him?"

"Because he has much more power than anyone thinks. There are secrets only a select few know, and we have been sworn to silence. But since you are going to become one of them, I think it's time you know what you're bonding into."

"Why are you telling me all of this?" I asked. He, of all people, was the last person I ever thought would share any information with me.

"Because I see how innocent you are. You remind me of my daughter."

"You have a daughter?"

"I had a daughter, but not anymore," he said sadly.

"What happened to her?"

"When I was chosen for service, they murdered my family so I could serve without barriers. They did the same to all Lucifer's personal guards."

My heart broke, and I felt my eyes well with pain for him.

"I'm so sorry. I didn't know," I breathed.

He shook his head. "It was a long time ago. My heart has grown calloused, and I've learned to become numb to everything around me. With my work you have to be hard, or you die."

"I wish there were something I could do," I breathed, seeing Bane for the first time in a whole new light. Yes, he had a very rough exterior, but he was hurt inside. I couldn't imagine the pain he had to endure when his family was murdered. I wondered if he had to watch. Just the thought of it made me sick inside. No wonder they were so submissive to Lucifer. He'd stripped them of everything, and made them slaves.

That was the same thing he had done to me, only not completely yet. He never gave me a choice, and knew what I would do to save those I loved. He knew I'd submit if they were involved. But I had a sinking feeling that even though I made the pact, their lives would still be in danger. He just better keep his end of the bargain, or so help me God.

"It's too late for me," he said with a bit of sadness in his voice. "I am dammed. A slave for all eternity."

I didn't know what else to tell him. My heart broke with his words. We were quickly approaching Ethon and I knew because I could feel him.

"Wait," I said, placing my hand on Bane's chest. He stopped in mid-air. "I want to know Ethon's secret."

He closed his eyes then sighed. "You have to swear to me you will never tell a living soul."

"I swear," I said with confidence.

He exhaled loudly. "Ethon is Lucifer's *true* son."

Gasping, I shook my head. "I thought Lucifer's brother was his father, and after he was caught and killed, Lucifer took him in?"

Bane shook his head. "That's what they want everyone to believe, but Lucifer was the one who impregnated Ethon's birth mother. Then Lucian found out. If Lucifer had been found guilty, he would have been stripped of all authority and executed. Lucifer blamed his brother and made him plead guilty to his transgression. He had no choice. Lucifer threatened to kill his bonded in front of him. So, when Lucian came to Lucifer, he charged his brother. His brother was taken and murdered for a transgression he never committed."

"*That* is seriously screwed up. How could he live with himself? He blamed and killed his brother for something he did."

"Bottom line, Ethon is Lucifer's son and Prince of the Underworld. It is Lucifer's blood that flows through him, which is why he has more power than any other Nephilim, and is also stronger and faster than any of the Fallen around him. He was trained by the Fallen's best warriors, and thus, nearly undefeatable."

"Holy crap," was all I could say. His words painted Ethon to be a monster in training, and made me want to get back into the safety and protection of Alaine's home. "I think I've changed my mind. Could you please take me back home?"

"Of course," he said, then turned around and started back. "There is someone following us," he said, and then held on tighter to me.

I turned back and didn't see anything.

"If you can, you need to go invisible."

I nodded then closed my eyes and concentrated, and soon felt the tingle. I grabbed Bane's arm and he disappeared.

"They can't see us now," I whispered.

"How are you doing that?" he asked.

"It's one of the powers of my suit. If I'm invisible, so is anything or anyone I'm touching."

"I think we might be able to shake whatever is out there. I'm going to fly low. Just hold on."

"How do you know something's out there?" I asked.

"After centuries of war, you know when your enemy is near. It becomes instinct."

"Okay," I exhaled, holding on a little tighter.

Centuries? Every time they used the word according to their age, it rattled me. How could anyone live for centuries, especially under Lucifer's rule? It was mind blowing.

I was cradled in his arms, and instinctively wrapped my arms around his neck for extra grip. His eyes snapped to me, and I quickly let go.

"No, it's okay," he answered. "I'm just not used to anyone's touch. You took me by surprise."

"I'm sorry," I said.

"Don't be. You should hold on because I will have to maneuver to try and lose whatever is out there."

He flew a bit faster. Not nearly as quick as Ethon, but much faster than he was before.

A loud screeching sound suddenly alerted us something was there. Then swooping out of the sky, a huge dark creature with a wingspan, double Bane's, came flying toward us.

"Shit," he cursed, diving down toward the trees. He headed for the largest one and landed on a thick bough, then sniffed the air. We became visible.

"What is it?" I gasped, not being able to make out what it was.

"Gryphon."

"A what?"

"Another creature from the Underworld used to bring death and destruction. But they've never been sent out into the mortal world."

"Until now," I said, holding on tighter to him. "Can it see us?"

"I don't know. It has the head and wings of an eagle, and eagles have exceptional vision. It also has the body, tail, and legs of a lion, but there are eagle's talons as its front feet. Those are its greatest weapon, and what we need to stay away from. It can rip anything to shreds, including wings."

"Who would be sending these creatures?"

"It has to be Lucian. He knows you are going to transform soon, and will do anything to try and capture you before you seal your bond with Lucifer's son."

"Maybe I should be caught. Then I wouldn't have to seal any bonds."

"No. Being with Lucian will be just as dangerous as being with Lucifer. He's wild and has no restraint. There are no rules that bind him, and he has no conscience. All he cares about is revenge and ruling the Underworld, and will do whatever it takes to make that happen. I need to get you back to the house and into the barrier."

"I know you've probably heard this before, but you will need to hold on tight, like your life depends on it. I don't think this will be a simple flight home."

He set me down on the branch, and I faced him. He was so much taller than me and his huge muscles bulged from under his shirt. I didn't think I would be able to wrap my legs around his waist, but I would try if I had to.

"You ready?" he asked in his deep voice.

"I'm ready," I whispered. "How much further are we from the house?"

"A few miles."

"Oh God."

"You should be praying to him about now. We could use all the help we can get."

"What if we stay low, like down on the ground?"

"There are Hellhounds all over these woods. They've released at least a dozen, and who knows what else."

"Alright. Well, I guess one big lion bird is better than a dozen Hellhounds," I said, my voice shaking.

"Let's hope," he exhaled.

I tiptoed to reach my arms around his neck, but he put his large hands on either side of my waist and lifted me up, then locked his left arm around me. His right held his sword.

"Can you make us invisible? We need every advantage."

I closed my eyes again, willing invisibility, and when I opened them, we were gone, and I could only see his outline.

"Hold on," he demanded, "And try not to scream."

"Okay."

We shot into the sky, but Bane stayed low to the trees. He tried to a zig-zag to throw off our scent. Well, that was my best guess, and I wouldn't question it. Whatever he was doing was trying to save our lives.

There was another loud, ear piercing screech. I turned to see the enormous black figure soaring right toward us. It was fast, and I could see its sharp talons out ready to strike.

Bane shot straight up, and even though we were invisible, the gryphon followed us.

"It can see us?" I panicked.

"Yes."

The creature was huge, and Bane was right. Its body looked like a gigantic lion, but the rest was an eagle. It was completely appalling, and reminded me of the creature in hell, the one that burned Kade. Its wingspan was between thirty to forty-feet long, and its beak was razor sharp.

I'd heard an eagle call before, but the sound this creature made was not even close to that. It was more of a horrifying death scream.

"Can it blow fire?"

"No," he answered, concentrating.

I wasn't going to ask him anymore questions.

Bane banked left and I tightened my grip on him. As I glanced down, I saw the Gryphon still heading toward us, fast.

He tucked his wings behind his back and we began to fall hard and fast. I wanted to scream, but managed to hold it in. The weightless feeling was torturous, and felt like it was never going to end.

He finally unfolded his wings and we evened out, soaring right above the tree line. Because we were low he wasn't able to see what was above him. He quickly did a roll, and as he did, I let out a yelp.

The Gryphon was right above us and came crashing down, knocking right into Bane's right wing, sending him spiraling into a tree. Bane released his grip on me and caught one of the branches and pulled us up. My grip was so tight, he didn't need to hold onto me.

We heard loud growls in the distance, heading in our direction. The Gryphon screamed right above, soaring in a large circle, waiting for us to come out. It was also signaling the Hellhounds to our location.

The Gryphon was much too large to come down into this area. The trees were too tight and pressed together.

"What do we do now?" I asked.

"We can't stay here much longer. We have about a mile left before we reach the barrier."

A mile could have been a thousand miles, especially with creatures and Fallen surrounding us.

"What do you want to do?" he asked.

"You're asking me?" I shrieked.

"Yes. You made it through the levels of the Underworld and survived. You have what it takes to survive within you. Do you have any suggestions?"

I thought about it. "Does the Gryphon have any weaknesses?"

"Its chest, but you'd have to pass its razor sharp beak and talons first."

"What if you threw me? You could toss me hard, directly at it, and I would hold my dagger out in front of me like an arrow. It probably would never expect us do to anything like that. Those things are probably used to chasing and ripping things apart. But if we attack it unexpectedly, I think we could do it. I have this super suit which has kept me protected, and this dagger is magical. I know if it reaches its mark, it will get the job done."

Bane looked at me with narrowed eyes, and I couldn't read his expression.

"What?"

"You are something," he said, shaking his head. "I don't think anyone would have thought of meeting a Gryphon head on in an attack. What you are saying makes sense. It would never expect it because it has never had its prey attack. Maybe on a few rare occasions, but it knew when an attack was coming." He looked like he was seriously considering it, but then shook his head. "No. It's much too risky. We have to consider everything. What if you aren't thrown fast enough, or miss the mark, or get injured? I don't want to take a chance."

"But we can't hang in this tree forever. If we go now, and try, we could be on our way to the house in no time. I think it's worth a shot, and I trust you. I think you should trust me. I have a feeling it will work."

Again, he paused and I could see him battling within himself.

"Alright," he finally agreed. "But only because I need to get you back to the barrier."

"Good," I said, my stomach began twisting.

"We will fly straight up, as high as we can before it gets too close. It will be coming up from below us. That's when I'll quickly turn and throw you at it. Just make sure you don't drop that dagger. Keep a strong grip on it and aim straight for the chest."

"Sounds easy enough."

"Let's hope it is easy."

I took hold of my dagger, and he sheathed his sword and held onto me.

"You can do this," he said.

"So can you," I answered.

He called his wings and folded them behind his back. He took in a deep breath, and jumped, his wings flapped once, carrying us up quickly. I glanced around but didn't see a thing, then my skin crawled as I heard the loud screech of the Gryphon. It was already above us.

Plan A was out the window, and I wasn't sure of plan B. Instead of going straight up, Bane flew at an upward diagonal, heading toward the house. The Gryphon screeched again as it headed in a course for collision.

I closed my eyes and concentrated, making us invisible. I knew it could still see us, but maybe if it saw us change it would throw it off. And that's exactly what happened. As we disappeared, the Gryphon paused and flapped backward for just a moment. As its eyes adjusted again, it screeched and continued directly after us.

Turning invisible did throw it off, but I needed to be sure.

As it barreled toward us, I willed visibility, and its course remained straight. But as soon as I willed invisibility, the Gryphon paused for a brief moment. It was confused. Its head shifted slightly to the side, its eyes trying to adjust to the change. After a few blinks, its eyes refocused on us again.

"I have a new plan," I told Bane.

"What?" he asked.

"I am going to count to three, and when I say three, you turn and throw me."

"No," he replied.

"Bane, trust me. Just throw me on three, and aim me straight for its chest."

He exhaled loudly. "I hope you know what you're doing."

"I do. I promise." I just hoped it would work again. It seemed like whenever we were visible and disappeared, the Gryphons eyes needed to adjust. I knew eagles could see seven times better than humans, and I wondered how much better this creature could see. It was obviously way more than seven times if it could see something invisible.

"One," I said, grasping tightly to my dagger.

"Two." My heart and pulse began to race, and as I looked at the horrifying creature chasing us, my mind began to second guess. No. I couldn't wimp out now. I willed visibility and held out my dagger ahead of me, while Bane adjusted his grip to toss me.

"Three!" I shouted.

As soon as Bane started to turn I willed invisibility.

The Gryphon stopped and I was thrust forward like a rocket, the wind whipped in my face. I held out the dagger, aimed at its chest, but then the Gryphon did something I hadn't expected.

It dipped.

No! I struck its wing and was tossed in the air, but before I fell, I pushed the dagger into its side. It screamed, dropping quickly, which allowed me to fall directly onto its back. I withdrew my dagger and pushed it into its skull. Bone splintered as the blade entered, going straight through like butter. The Gryphon screeched and thrashed its head wildly, but I held onto the dagger, slipping down to its side. The dagger was coming free, and I was now hanging at its front. It was frantic, thrusting its talons, but I was in a position where it could barely touch me.

The dagger was coming free, and as I was slipping I noticed the Gryphon raise its front leg. I pushed off of it, using it as leverage, completely dislodging the blade from its skull.

As soon as its leg dropped, I fell but managed to plunge the dagger into the Gryphon's chest. It clawed at me, its talons hooking into my back and tearing. I screamed in excruciating pain, pulling the blade and holding it in my grasp as I kicked backward away from it.

The Gryphon was dying, sustaining major injuries to its brain and heart, but in its last moments, it dove after me. Its sharp beak and talons ready to tear me apart before its end.

Then, out of nowhere, it was hit from the side, and tumbled away from me. Bane had come to my rescue. I watched the Gryphon's wings tangle as it spiraled downward, crashing into the trees which were instantly leveled as it hit and tumbled to the ground below.

Bane flew back and caught me before I hit. As soon as he grabbed me, he hugged me close. "Shit, you did it. I can't believe you did it."

"I told you to trust me." I smiled, and then cringed as the pain in my back felt like it was on fire.

"You're hurt."

"I'll be fine," I said. "I just need to get back to the house."

He nodded and flew as fast as he could. It wasn't as far as I thought it was, and as soon as the house came into view, I was instantly relieved.

A loud caw right to the side of us scared the crap out of me. As I turned my gaze, I saw Ash flying right next to us.

"Ash," I yelled, hoping Lucifer was watching. "Go help Ethon. He's battling Lucian's Fallen, and Hellhounds which have been set free."

It was as if the bird understood because it immediately banked right and flew behind us, in the direction of Ethon.

"I hate that bird," Bane growled.

"I hate its master," I sighed, then winced.

Bane shook his head.

As we reached the house, he set me down in front of the barrier.

"Thank you for saving me," I said, hugging him.

He stood stock still.

"Thank you." He bowed his head. "Now, hurry and get inside, and remember... not a word."

I nodded then turned and ran for the front door. Relief blanketed me as soon as I touched the knob. I twisted and pushed it open, bumping into someone.

I gasped and threw my hand over my mouth.

"Emma?"

"Kade?" I cried and instantly fell into his arms.

"Holy crap. Are you okay?" he said, his eyes wide with horror.

"Yes. I'm fine. How did you know I'd be here?"

Kade turned his head and I saw Thomas peek around the corner and wave, but when he saw me his eyes went wide with horror.

"We need to go to that secret place. Now."

I took a step and collapsed to my knees. The pain in my back was excruciating.

"You're hurt?"

"Just a scratch on my back," I exhaled.

Kade lifted me into his arms and carried me up the stairs and down the hallway. Thomas stayed back near the room just in case.

When we entered the secret passage, we quickly made our way down to the safe room. He turned on the light and set me down on a chair before securing the door. Then he helped me stand and walked me over to the sink, and grabbed a towel. Wetting the corner, he began wiping the dry blood off my face and hands.

"How did this happen?" he asked.

"We were attacked by Fallen and Hellhounds."

"Hellhounds?"

"Yes. We think Lucian let them out. There are at least a dozen running around outside. And there was a Gryphon."

Kade stopped and looked at me. "A Gryphon? Do you even know what a Gryphon is?"

"Yes. The eagle-lion monster. I know it well because it almost killed me and Bane. But don't worry, I killed it first."

"First of all, the Gryphon are not allowed into the mortal world. Second, if it was a Gryphon how the hell did you kill it?"

"I know Gryphon aren't allowed into the mortal world, but there was one chasing us on our way back here. Its talons sliced right through my super suit. I turned my back to Kade.

"Shit, Emma. That's deep. How are you even standing? Come." He led me to the bed and helped zip the suit down. I was only wearing a cami and underwear underneath, so I kept the bottom part of the suit in place. He helped me lay on my stomach and situated a pillow under my head before going to the cupboard to retrieve the vial of healing potion.

"This might sting a bit at first, but the pain will quickly subside."

"It stings right now. Just do it," I said, pinching my eyes closed in anticipation of the pain to follow.

He unscrewed the vial and I felt the liquid drip over my back. It stung ten times worse than I'd remembered. Holding my breath, I gripped the side of the bed and waited until the pain subsided.

"It's already starting to mend," he said.

"Thank you." I exhaled the breath I had been holding. "It does feel better. I think I need to get back to my room and take a shower."

"Yeah, that would be a good idea." He chuckled.

"Thank you for fixing me. I'll tell you about the Gryphon after."

"Deal," he grinned.

"Will you stay with me tonight?"

"If you want me to."

"I do."

When we got there, Thomas was waiting inside, biting his nails.

"She wants me to stay with her tonight," Kade advised him.

"What about Alaine?"

"I'll deal with Alaine," I responded. "I need him. Please. And don't worry... we aren't going to do anything."

"Fine, but I'm staying in your room," Thomas replied, heading for the door.

"That's cool. Thanks bro. I appreciate it."

I took my pajamas and went into the bathroom to shower and change. When I clicked on the light and looked at the reflection of myself in the mirror, I gasped, scaring myself. There was blood smeared all over my face, even with Kade's attempt to try and wipe it off, I looked like some kind of psycho murderer who rolled in my victim's blood. I tried to turn and see the injuries on my back, but couldn't really see anything.

As soon as I was released from the super suit, my body began to ache. I picked it up and saw two large slash marks in the back. One about ten inches, the other a little longer. I sighed, rolled it up, and threw it in the hamper.

I quickly turned on the shower, making the water extra hot. I stood under the falling water and let the dried blood rinse from me. The smell became overwhelming, so I filled my hand with shampoo and lathered my hair. I scrubbed and scrubbed, every inch of my body until it felt raw and there were no signs of blood. I washed my hair three times, and then conditioned it to make sure I was free from contamination.

When I stepped out and dried myself off, I glanced into the mirror again. This time I recognized the girl looking back at me, but just barely. I blinked and watched a tear trickle down my face. My human past had become a memory. I still had connections to it through Jeremy and Lia, but it would never be the same. Not without my parents.

Yes, Samuel and Alaine were my true parents, but would I get to live the rest of my life getting to know them? Or would I have to seal the bond with Ethon, effectively taking me away from everything and everyone I knew. I didn't think Lucifer would allow me to keep relations with them because they were a threat.

I wiped away the few tears which had escaped my eyes and quickly slipped into my pajamas. Then I brushed my hair and teeth and opened the door.

When I stepped out of the bathroom, Kade was lying on the floor. The side lamp was on, barely lighting his beautiful face. He was on his side, with his head resting on one arm, looking through my scrapbook.

"Hey beautiful," he said, looking up as I stepped out. I blushed, not feeling beautiful at all. "I hope it's okay to be looking at this."

"Of course it is," I grinned. "And you don't have to stay on the floor. You can stay up here with me," I said patting the bed. "I need your arms again, and you did say that your hugs were free."

"I did, and yes, they are... anytime of the day or night." He gently closed the book and slid it back under the bed, before jumping up and walking toward me.

I placed my hand on his chest, stopping him a foot away. "Wait. I'm sorry. My brain is acting like a ping pong; my emotions are all so mixed up. And none of this is fair to you. I feel like I'm taking advantage of your good nature.

Kade grabbed my hand from his chest and kissed it, pulling me into a hug. He shushed me and swayed us back and forth.

"I'm terrified of my future, and what I could be leaving behind," I said.

Stupid automatic tears began to well in my eyes, and stream down my face.

"I have been too. As soon as I became mortal, I began worrying about you, about us. I wish I could go back and set everything straight, but all I can do is be here for you. If you need a hug, then I will give it to you. If you need a kiss, hey, those are free too, but strictly for you alone."

"I'll take it," I whispered.

He gently placed his hands on either side of my face, and leaned down, pressing his warm lips on mine. I instantly became dizzy, and then he pulled back.

"Thank you," I breathed.

"It's always a pleasure," he said, leaning over and kissing my forehead. "You need to get some sleep, but I can't put the sleeper on you.

"I think I could fall asleep in your arms," I said.

He led me over to the bed and tucked me in, then he laid on top of the covers. I backed up into him, spooning, and rested my head on his arm. When the other arm came over top, his scent enveloped me. I took in a deep breath and exhaled.

"I could get used to this," I breathed.

"So could I," he added, sounding a little sad.

I didn't know what he was feeling, and I couldn't imagine. He didn't know if he was going to lose me, but I also had the exact same fear. Would I lose the only one who made me feel whole? The one who had protected and watched over me, and was there since the beginning of this crazy new journey? I couldn't imagine my life without him in it.

Our future was unclear; fate had the upper hand and wasn't giving out any hints as to what its plans were. We had no choice but to ride with it.

Wrapped in the warmth of Kade's arms, I listened to the sound of his steady breath, the rising and falling of his chest on my back, and the faint thumps of his heartbeat. I felt the tensions relax and the stress melt away as his closeness slowly lulled me into a deep sleep.

ELEVEN

WHEN I WOKE, I WAS surprised to feel Kade's arm still wrapped around me. I didn't think he'd stay with me for the whole night, especially with Alaine checking up on me all the time.

I rolled over to him, and his eyes were open and bright. I threw my arms around his neck and kissed him all over his face.

"Whoa. What's that for?" he said, chuckling.

"I'm surprised to see you here."

His smile widened. "You were moving around a lot in your sleep."

"I had another dream, and when we kissed, it was magical and healing."

"Does my face need healing?" he questioned, rubbing his cheeks. "Or do I need to shave?"

"Nope, you're perfect," I said.

The sides of his mouth turned up, and his radiant smile brought happiness to the beginning of another new day.

"What time is it?" I asked. The sun was trying to peek in from the sides of the shades.

"A little after ten."

"Holy crap!" I said, sitting up. "Did Alaine come in to check?"

"She did, right before she left to take Courtney and Caleb to the airport."

"Was she surprised to see you?"

"Yep," he chuckled. "But after a few awkward moments of silence, she saw you were safe and sleeping and she was fine."

"I'm sad I didn't get a chance to say goodbye to Courtney and Caleb."

"They weren't fully awake anyway, and didn't say much."

"I hope they'll be alright," I sighed.

"They'll be fine. Alaine has made sure they will be under full guard while they are away."

"That's good to know," I said, falling back into his arms, pressing the side of my face into his chest. The sound of his beating heart brought me so much comfort.

"Are you going to tell me more about this magical kissing dream?" he asked.

"Nope," I teased. "But I do want you to know one thing."

"Tell me," he grinned, throwing an arm behind his head.

"I want you to know that—"

We were rudely interrupted by a loud knock on the door. I wouldn't doubt if it was Malachi.

"Come in," I yelled. Thomas pushed the door open covering his eyes.

"You can look, crazy," I smirked.

He dropped his hand. "Okay, cool. I just came to give you an update. Someone has released beasts from the Underworld. We aren't sure if they are immune to the barrier like the Darkling are yet, but we need to be prepared. If anything, they will strike during the night."

I nodded. "Yes, last night we came across Hellhounds and a Gryphon."

"Gryphon?" he choked. "Are you sure?"

"Yes, the ginormous eagle-lion creature with a sharp beak and deadly talons."

"Holy crap. How the hell did you make it back alive?"

"I killed it." I shrugged.

"Don't shit me, Emma." Thomas narrowed his eyes at me.

"I'm serious. Ask Bane. He might not talk to you, but if you ask him, he can always nod."

"How the hell did you do it? I can't remember anyone who went up against a Gryphon and lived to tell about it. And these are immortals I'm talking about." He paused. "Not saying your lame or anything, you just aren't—"

"I know," I smiled. "It's alright."

"So?" he pressed.

"I noticed that every time I went from visible and to invisible it would pause and get confused. So, I told Bane to throw me at it when I changed mid-flight. It almost didn't work, but I managed to sink the dagger into its head and then into its heart. I have scars on my back to prove it."

"You are simply amazing," Thomas said bowing down to me.

"Don't. It's embarrassing," I giggled.

"You must teach me your ways oh wise one," he said in a deep voice.

"All you need is a super-suit and a magic dagger."

"I guess there is no hope for me then," he sighed.

"Thomas, is there any other reason why you came in?" Kade questioned.

His eyes narrowed in thought. "Oh, yes! Alaine is back and she wants everyone to meet downstairs. Miss Lily has a brunch spread and the rest of the group is already there. She wants to discuss upcoming plans and these new threats."

"Alright, we'll be down in a minute," Kade answered.

"Cool. I'll see you guys." Before he left, he turned and bowed down to me again, so I tossed a pillow at him. It missed as he quickly slipped back out the door.

When the door shut and we were alone again, reality began to sink in.

"Do you think they will attack soon?" I asked Kade.

"I don't know. If they are sending out creatures from the Underworld, I suspect an attack soon."

"I have less than a week before my transformation."

His fingers grazed my face. "And you will be magnificent. I cannot wait to see what you finally become."

I sighed. "But I'm supposed to be bonded with Ethon during my transformation. I want you to be with me and help me through it. You've been with me since the beginning of this crazy journey, and I really wanted you with me until the end."

"If it is within my power to be with you, I will. That is my word."

I knew his words were heartfelt but they brought me little comfort. We both knew he wouldn't be there; Ethon would be, and probably his murderous father.

My heart ached and twisted at the thought.

There had to be a way.

We both got ready and made our way down the stairs. Glancing out the windows, I looked across the driveway into the thick spruce trees, and a shiver shot down my spine. The feeling of wicked eyes watching us, made my skin crawl.

I wondered if Ethon and Azzah had defeated the Fallen and Hellhounds. There had been no signs of him, and I hadn't felt his presence since I left. I wondered if he had been injured. I highly doubted it after watching him in action. Besides he had Bane, Azzah, and Ash with him.

After what Bane told me, I wondered if I should be concerned for him at all. My whole outlook of Ethon had been tinged with even more doubt. He had an evil side.

But the bond also made me remember his gentle touch, his beautiful black wings, his handsome face, and his burning crimson eyes. The times when he was with me had felt so sincere. During those moments I believed he would never hurt me, and his promises to take care of me and protect me were heartfelt. It was almost impossible to know what to believe anymore.

I sighed to myself as my foot hit the last step.

"Don't worry. We'll figure it all out," Kade whispered, grabbing hold of my hand.

"I hope so," I sighed.

Time was ticking down too quickly, and so was my luck.

As we made our way down the hall, the wonderful aroma of food teased me, making my mouth water. When we entered the kitchen, Miss Lily greeted us.

"Good morning," she chimed, with her normal cheery smile. "Buffet is in the dining room."

"Thank you, Miss Lily," I said, and Kade repeated.

Everyone was already seated around the table with plates of food piled high. They were talking and laughing and it made me happy. For a moment everything seemed right with the world. We were encased within the barrier, temporarily protected from the darkest evil creatures lurking about in the shadows.

Alaine entered from the back door, and I assumed she had come from the cottage. Hopefully Samuel had returned with some good news. I studied her face, but it didn't seem like it was bearing anything good. She looked weary, and I noticed dark circles under her eyes for the first time.

It wasn't until that moment I put myself in her shoes. For years she kept me safe, staying away so I could live a normal life. Then all of a sudden, life carried me back to her, and was now threatening to take me away again. The stress of it all must be ripping her apart.

Her eyes caught mine and a faint smile rose on her lips. Making her way over to me, she wrapped me in her arms.

"How are you, sweetheart?" she asked.

I'd forgotten to ask Kade is she knew about my escape. I was assuming he didn't say anything so I answered vaguely. "I'm good."

"Good," she answered.

"Is Samuel back?" I asked.

She shook her head. "No, not yet. I expect he should be back soon. Go ahead get some food. You need to keep your strength up, especially over these next few days. We will discuss our plans once everyone has finished eating"

"Alright," I agreed.

She released me from her embrace and proceeded into the kitchen. Kade and I took our plates and headed toward the food. I took a small amount of eggs, a few slices of bacon, and a biscuit drowned in homestyle gravy. Kade opted for the fried chicken, corn, biscuits, and gravy.

All the rest of the Guardians welcomed us as we took our usual seats at the opposite end of the table.

"Hey, Emma," Malachi waved, with a mound full of food in front of him. It looked like he had both breakfast and lunch.

"Hey, Malachi," I responded with a smile.

The rest of them were already piling food in their mouths. Dom waved and tried to speak, but his mouth was too full.

"Jeez, Dom," Alex stated. "Slow down."

Miss Lily entered the room with more napkins. "You let him be. He's a growing Guardian. Look at these muscles," she said tapping his biceps. "He needs to feed these pythons."

Dom swallowed down his food. "Damn right," he chimed, throwing in a quick flex. "Miss Lily knows where it's at." He held out his fist, she pounded it, and then left the room. "She's got it going on."

After brunch, Miss Lily and Henry cleared the tables.

Henry patted me gently on the shoulder before he took my plate. "It's good to see you, Emma," he said softly.

"It's good to see you too, Henry. How is your sister?"

"She's doing very well, thank you," he answered.

"I'm glad."

"You stay safe and eat up. You need your strength."

"I will." I turned and he winked, placing a chocolate chip cookie down next to me.

"Why does she get a cookie?" Dom yelled from across the table.

"Because she's extraordinary and you're not," Alex answered, smacking Dom on the back.

"Hey, I'm special too," he said in a cry-baby voice, pretending to wipe away tears.

"You're *special* alright..." Malachi grunted sarcastically.

Dom hurled a biscuit at his head.

"Yes, you are special, my dear." Miss Lily came and placed a large platter of cookies in front of him.

"I knew you loved me," Dom said, standing and hugging her.

Miss Lily laughed and exited the room once again.

They all dove for the plate but Dom threw his body over it. "Hey, let's not get crazy." He stood up with the plate and walked around, placing one cookie in front of each of them.

"You're such an ass," Alex huffed.

"What did you say?" Dom said swiping back his cookie.

"Hey," Alex grumbled.

Alaine stood up. "Alright, we need to discuss important issues."

Dom took his seat and threw Kade and Malachi a cookie.

"Do you want one, Alaine?" he asked, ready to toss one her way.

"No thank you. I'm good," she said, holding up a hand and walking to the front of the table. "There has been a lot of movement in our surrounding area. I've received word from Bane that creatures from the Underworld have been released."

I turned to Kade, and he grabbed my hand under the table. At least she knew; that was the main thing, and I didn't have to say anything. If I did, she'd know I went out unprotected and I'd be even more heavily guarded. I knew it was for my own good, but she didn't have to worry about me leaving. I was staying inside from now on.

"So what kinds of creatures are we talking about?" Dom asked, crunching on a cookie.

"There have been multiple sightings of Hellhounds, and the body of a dead Gryphon. It was found about a half mile from here in the forest. Bane also mentioned seeing a few Grimlock."

"Grimlock?" I gasped. Those creatures terrified me. If we hadn't had backup in the Underworld, Samuel and I would have been dead at that Grimlock gate. They had already captured and injured both of us, and we were only alive because of Dom, Malachi, and Danyel.

"Yes, but I'm only going on hearsay, and what others have witnessed. I haven't seen any of these creatures myself, and am hoping we won't have to."

"So, in other words... all Hell has broken lose," Dom stated flatly.

"Yes," Alaine answered. "The barrier is set up to keep the Fallen out, but we aren't sure how it will affect the rest of these creatures. At the moment someone is holding them back and it might be because they are still gathering others.

"Whether it is Lucian or Lucifer, we need to be ready. It's coming down to the end, and we need to make sure Emma is safe. Her safety is our top priority. I doubt they will attack us during the day because it will take time for their eyes to adapt to the light. But I have a feeling that soon, when darkness falls, we will have a battle on our hands. Until then, I need all of you to stay within the barrier." She glanced around the room with a look of adoration. "I'm so proud of each and every one of you. I hope you all get your wings for this. You have proven yourselves time and time again."

"What about Emma?" Malachi asked. "If those creatures were sent by Lucian, they will be coming for her. Shouldn't she be taken to safety, or at the very minimum hide in the safe room?"

"Yes, Malachi. Our plans to leave and take her to a safe-house have been canceled. It's too dangerous to take her outside of the barrier now, especially with the new threats. To be certain of her safety, Emma will stay in the safe room during the night, and I will allow Kade to stay with her."

Both our heads snapped up to her.

"I trust you both, and know Kade's intentions."

"Thank you," he said. "You know her safety is my priority."

"I know," Alaine answered. "This is why I am delegating it to you." She turned toward the others. "I want you all to rest today and make sure your weapons are ready. I'm not sure if they will attack tonight, but if they do, I want to be prepared. I will be sending Henry and Miss Lily on an extended vacation, until this is all over."

James was the only quiet one, and I'd forgotten he was even in the room until he spoke. "We all need to be on top of everything. There is no room for mistakes. We will stand guard around the property but inside of the barrier. The guard posts will be held until the sun rises."

"I call back of house," Dom said, raising his hand.

"Why? So you can be close to the kitchen?" Malachi smirked.

"Dude, you do have brains in that huge noggin of yours," Dom snickered.

"Yeah, and if you keep jabbering, I'm gonna use my huge fist to knock in your huge noggin."

"Oh, someone's mighty feisty today," Alex said, slapping Malachi on the back.

Malachi turned and glared at him, "I'm prepared... for anything," he rumbled back.

"We're all prepared," Dom added. He then stood and threw his fist in the air. "We may be outnumbered, but we are mighty, and ready to kick some ass!"

"Yeah!" the rest of the Guardian's yelled in agreement.

Whoever sent them knew what they were doing. They were an awesome team. I looked around at each of their faces, gleaming with confidence and positivity. We had the best team of Guardians in any world. I knew it because through each obstacle we'd endured, they all still remained.

My thoughts immediately went to Samuel. I prayed he was alright out there on his own. I wondered if he would be able to find some needed answers. Time was ticking, slowly running down to either our victory or demise.

The day went by much too fast while the Guardians prepared themselves for battle. War was coming, and it was coming soon. An annoying buzz of doom lingered in the air. I knew what we were up against. Our enemy was strong, and we were fiercely outnumbered. If the creatures of the Underworld could break through the barrier, I didn't see any of us surviving. Not without help.

Would Lucifer keep his end of the deal and come to our aid when we needed him?

All we could do was wait and see. My hope was dangling by the smallest of threads. Any kind of intense pressure would easily break it in two. It was fragile, but for now, it was intact. There was nothing I could do to make it stronger. My fate was balancing precariously on those around me. And when it came down to the end, I would do my part, whatever that may be.

War was inevitable. My greatest hope and prayer, was that we all survived.

TWELVE

PREPARED FOR THE NIGHT, I glanced out my window. The sun was lingering on the horizon, and I soaked in the beautiful colors it created against the darkening sky. It was as if the hand of God had created a master piece right in front of my eyes.

A single tear tickled my cheek, and I quickly swiped it away. I didn't know how many more sunsets I would be able to watch, but at least I had this one. I made sure I took it all in. As the end drew near, I didn't want to sleep. I wanted to be awake and aware of everything around me – to make every moment count like it was my last.

I was waiting for Kade to arrive and take me to the safe room. My super suit and dagger were in my duffle bag, and I was dressed in black sweatpants and my grey hoodie. I traced my finger across the black words over my left chest, wondering if in less than a week I would possess the same magical hidden wings as Ethon. No other Nephilim had the gift of wings, not even Alaine. But I couldn't dwell too much on something so doubtful. I had enough to deal with in the present.

A soft knock at the door made my stomach flutter with butterflies. I walked just a little too fast to open it.

Kade held out his hand to me.

"Are you ready?" His charming crooked grin made me warm inside, and I watched on as he raked his fingers through his thick brown hair. I placed my hand into his and he pulled me against his body. Pressed tightly together, he leaned over. I thought he was going to kiss me so I closed my eyes, only to hear the door shut behind us.

That was embarrassing.

I quickly opened my eyes and his angelic face was an inch away, his sweet breath tickled my nose. Gently clasping his hand behind the back of my neck, he leaned closer and kissed me. When he pulled away, I was left dizzy.

"I'm ready," I exhaled. He took the duffle from my hand and we began to walk down the hall toward the bathroom that had the secret door.

"How many secret doors are there in this place?" I asked.

"Three. One on each floor. There is a room right below us on the opposite side of the hall, and the last one is on the first floor, behind the grandfather clock in the foyer."

"Wow. I would have never known."

"Yeah, Alaine wanted to build a few more, but her late husband already thought she was crazy for even thinking of making secret doors which led to a safe room in the middle of the house. She had a lot of convincing to do, but he finally gave in. I'm glad she did it."

"Me too." I smiled thinking about how Alaine had planned everything out from the beginning, even though she didn't know what the future held. She was a prepper.

Familiar thundering growls and barks erupted outside, just as we were making our way to the last room. The darkness had awakened the creatures.

As we entered the bathroom, I disconnected from Kade and made my way to the window.

"Emma," he called after me.

"Just keep the light off. I have to see what's out there."

I slowly pulled the curtain from the window, and saw fiery red eyes slowly emerging from the forest.

Hellhounds. There were at least a dozen of them; more than any of us had anticipated.

"Emma," Kade called, pulling the secret door open.

"Wait, please," I whispered, frozen.

Malachi stood just inside the barrier, about twenty feet away from one of the beasts. His sword was drawn, and he was crouched, ready to take it on. There were too many Hellhounds for the few we had, even with all six of them fighting.

As I glanced to the right, I saw Thomas, and beyond Malachi to the left was Alex.

The Hellhound in front of Malachi stopped. Kade stood behind me and pulled back the curtain a bit more so he could see. His chest pressed against my back, so I leaned into him for support.

"What happens if they come through the barrier?" I said, my voice quavering.

"Then we run for the safe room," he said, taking hold of my hand.

We watched helplessly, incapable of offering any help.

My breath seized as the beast crouched. It pounced toward Malachi, who stepped forward to meet it, his sword raised above his head. But as soon as the beast hit the barrier, it slammed to a complete stop and dropped to the ground. Sparks flew everywhere and the Hellhound yelped in pain.

"Oh my God. It worked," I exhaled loudly. The barrier actually kept the Hellhounds out too. I wondered why it worked on Hellhounds and not the Darkling.

"Now we know they'll be fine, so it's time I get you inside before Alaine finds us standing here. There are monitors in the safe room where you can watch what's going on outside."

"Okay," I agreed. Our hands were still locked together as he led me into the secret passageway. As soon as we were inside he clicked on a flashlight and handed it to me, then closed and locked the door behind us.

While we were walking to our safety, I started to feel horrible; I was abandoning the others. But I knew there was really nothing I could do to help. If I were out there, they would probably be worried about saving me, which would be more of a hindrance than good.

Once we reached the safe room and Kade locked the doors, I began to feel a bit claustrophobic. I walked over and sat on the bed.

"What happens if the Fallen break through, and find this secret room? We won't have a way to escape, and this safe room will become our tomb." My mind started to go haywire again, thinking up every negative scenario.

Kade grinned and made his way to me. He sat down on my side and took my hand. "Don't worry. They all know what they're doing out there. This is just for safety measures. Plus, there is another way out," he said pointing under the bed. "It's a downward drop of about a hundred feet that will take us into an underground tunnel that leads to the garage. It's a last resort."

"It's good to know we have an option."

Kade walked over to a cabinet on the wall, just above a small desk. When he pulled open the cabinet, inside were five small monitors which he clicked on.

Each screen was split, with two different views from different areas around the house. My eyes locked onto the first screen, looking out from the front of the house. Malachi was in the left corner of the screen but beyond him were three huge beasts, Hellhounds, stalking the perimeter trying to find a way in. Behind them I saw a set of black wings quickly fly past, and I could swear I saw red eyes flash. My heart dropped.

Was it Ethon?

I hadn't seen, felt, or spoken to him since Bane dropped me off that night at the barrier. From what Alaine and the others had said, he and the goons hadn't been in the tower. I didn't even know if he was alright, or had been injured. Alaine said she spoke to Bane about Lucian setting the Underworld creatures free outside, but directly after he gave the information, he left as well.

Maybe they were in danger and needed to find another place to hide since Lucian's Fallen and his creatures were out there now. They weren't protected by any barrier, and would be easy targets. It could have been Ethon doing a fly-by just to check and make sure the barrier was still intact. Or maybe he was making sure I was safe.

But then again, maybe it wasn't him. It could have just been one of Lucian's Fallen. Hopefully it wasn't Samuel. He couldn't come on to the property and would be a sitting duck outside the barrier. I searched the other screens for any signs of a winged, but the skies were dark and empty. I still worried about Ethon. The bond wouldn't allow me not to.

My mind started to run through even more scenarios, and this time I wondered if Bane had been telling me the truth. Up until the time he was sent by Ethon to take me to safety, he didn't like me, and it was very obvious. Had he been trying to drive a wedge between us? It was too hard to judge the Fallen. For centuries they had been deceivers. I had no clue what to think anymore.

The only time Ethon lashed out was when I had hurt him by mentioning Kade. We were bonded, so it was understandable. But Kade was also a factor. A huge factor. I couldn't just forget him and brush him off to the side like he didn't exist.

"Hey," Kade said, stepping in front of me, breaking my eye contact with the monitors and momentarily silencing my crazy mind.

I looked up into his beautiful eyes.

"You were in deep thought again. What's bothering you?"

"How do you always know when something's bothering me?" I questioned, gawking at him.

"Your brow was furrowed and your lips were turned down. I can read you like a book," he replied.

"How?" I asked.

"You're pretty easy," he noted, shrugging his shoulders.

"Well, I think you're pretty easy too," I countered.

"Alright then," he said, stepping forward until he was about a foot away. He knelt down in front of me until we were eye to eye, and then placed his hands over mine.

His touch sent waves of pleasure through me.

Speaking in a very sexy, very slow voice. "What am I thinking right now?"

His hazel eyes locked onto mine and captured me. I swallowed hard, "That you want to—to..." I paused, my mind went blank.

"That I want to – *what?*" he asked, leaning forward.

"That—"

I tilted my head to one side, studying the expression on his face. If I was reading him correctly, the feeling was mutual.

I placed my hands on either side of his face pulling his sinfully beautiful mouth to mine. His protective arms coiled around me, his sweet mouth eagerly slid against mine as his velvety tongue entered my lips. Desire tingled through my insides When we finally parted he trailed warm kisses along the underside of my neck before resting his forehead against mine.

His breath was heavy. "I guess I am pretty easy to read."

"Very easy," I said breathless.

"Just for your information, I've never been easy to read until I met you," he confessed.

Kade's hand brushed down my cheek and landed on my chin. "I still vividly remember the first day I laid eyes on you. As soon as I walked into the hospital, I was incredibly nervous, when I asked the nurse which room you were in. It was the first time, after guarding you for over a year, I was going to finally meet you in person. I'd never previously met any other mortal I had guarded. You were the very first, and I never, in a million years, expected my bond to be attached to you."

I smiled, remembering. "You must have been just as shocked as I was."

"Shocked is an understatement," he laughed. "When I walked down that hall, twenty feet from your door, I was slammed with a wall of feelings I couldn't explain. It was as if I was being electrocuted, and the buzz continued to surge through my body. I had difficulty breathing, and although it was confusing, I knew it must have been the bond."

"Didn't we touch when you saved me from the car, the night of the crash?"

"If it did happen, I wasn't aware. That night was a blur and a complete nightmare. My adrenaline was pumping, and my whole focus was set on keeping the car from crushing you. It killed me inside that I was helpless to save your parents. You were screaming and in pain, so I had to put the sleeper on you and then quickly escape as help arrived."

"I'm sorry you had to go through that, and I cannot thank you enough."

"If it was to keep you safe, I'd do it all over again... in a heartbeat."

My eyes threatened to tear, but I refused to be sad. There was too much of it right now, so I refocused on the good.

"How did you know it was the bond?" I asked.

"What do you mean?"

"You said after you experienced all those feelings, you knew it was the bond. How did you know?"

"I've had several friends who found their mates, and the feelings they described when the bond connected them were the exact same I was feeling at that very moment. When I came around the corner and saw the same flustered, bewildered look on your face, I knew you were the one.

"But back then, all I could see was a girl who was lost, confused, and agonizing over the death of her parents. You were so innocent, and I wanted so much to help take the pain away. That look has faded, and is much different than the one I'm looking at right now. I can still see your pain, but I also see your strength, selflessness, and honesty. I see a girl who would do anything in her power to protect those she loves. But she is also confused by the bond."

He leaned in closer. "I know the bond won't allow you to hate Ethon, and I can see how torn you are between him and the other who loves you unconditionally."

Tears burned and pooled in my eyes then cascaded down my cheeks.

"You do know me," I breathed. I fell into his arms, and he secured them around me.

"Of course I do. You started off as my assignment, but stole my heart. You've been so strong these past months, trying to hold everything and everyone together, but I can see your internal struggle. You don't always have to be strong. If you ever feel like you're falling, just tell me, and I'll be there to catch you."

"You have always been here for me, and I can't imagine my future without you in it," I said, truthfully.

Kade sighed and hugged me tighter. "I wish things were different. Every day I awake to deal with the reality that it was my decision which put us in this position. I cannot express to you how truly sorry I am."

I pulled back from him and wiped my face dry, then noticed his eyes were filled with sadness. "Kade, you don't ever have to apologize, or regret your decisions. We can make our own choices and choose our own paths, but our fate is already sealed. There is nothing we can do or say to change it."

His eyes softened. "You are wise beyond your years, Emma Wise."

"I'm not wise. I'm just living and learning, trying to survive. One thing I have learned is, right when you think you have life all figured out, it will throw a curve, and you either have to bend and adjust to it, or break."

"You've done an amazing job of adjusting," he said softly.

I sighed and shook my head. "I haven't adjusted. I'm still in the process of bending."

"I think we all are," he admitted.

The house shook, so Kade turned his head to glance back the monitors.

"Oh shit!" he cursed, standing up off the floor and heading toward the screens.

"What?" I asked, pushing off the bed. I stood next to him.

A surge of fear had every hair on my body standing on end. I began to hyperventilate as one of the spotlights landed on a large horrifying creature, with unforgettable white pasty eyes, just outside the barrier.

I grabbed Kade's hand and held it tight.

"What the hell is that?" he asked. Its white eyes illuminated like a cats once the light hit them.

"A Grimlock," I exhaled. "Those are the creatures that almost killed me and Samuel."

Kade's head turned toward me. "I won't let them touch you. Not while you're with me," he said.

I nodded, and our eyes fixed back on the monitors. I watched in terror as the Grimlock began to swirl its deadly weapon round and round. I held my breath, hoping and praying the barrier would hold. Faster and faster the Grimlock swung its weapon until it was nearly invisible, and then it set it free.

I gasped and squeezed Kade's hand as the morning star flew forward at an unbelievable speed, then stopped dead in mid-air, crashing into the barrier. As soon as it hit, it bounced back, sending sparks from the impact raining down below, illuminating the Hellhounds who were frantically trying to find a way in.

The barrier held, but a small glowing crack slowly appeared and took a while to mend.

Could the barrier be broken?

"Did you see that?" I gasped.

"Yes," Kade answered.

"Do you think they can break through the barrier?"

"I don't know but it seems likely," he answered, his eyes still locked on the monitors.

Another Grimlock came charging forward from the left side, swinging his deadly morning star. When the beast released its weapon, it again crashed into the barrier. The foundation of the house shook, and even more sparks rained down. It looked like a firework show, but this show was far from entertaining as it lit the horrors below.

The barrier held, but again, there was an even longer crack which extended upward toward the center with another two cracks branching off to the sides, making it look like a fork. My heart sunk until it slowly began to mend and disappear.

"They're checking the integrity of the barrier," Kade said.

"But the Grimlocks are blind," I noted.

"Oh, believe me, there are others watching and directing. The Grimlocks and Hellhounds are merely pawns, but somewhere in the darkness, Lucian is watching."

"Do you think the strength of their hits is weakening the barrier?"

"I don't know, but it looks like if it sustains too many all at once, it could weaken it enough for them to break through."

His words confirmed what I was feeling. "I wish this would all be over soon," I sighed.

He turned to me. "Me too," he said softly.

I yawned and felt drained.

"You need sleep," he said, turning toward me.

"So do you. Will you stay with me?" I asked.

"Of course."

He walked me over to the bed and yanked the blanket down. I crawled in and as he pulled it back up back up, I grabbed his hand.

"Wait," I begged. "I need you right now. I don't know how much time we have left, but I want to make every second count. Having you close, holding me, helps everything around me melt away."

He paused and a grin formed on his face. "I told you, whatever I have to give is yours."

I patted the empty spot on the bed, and instead of lying on top of the blanket like he usually did, he crawled in next to me. I rolled toward him and he wrapped me in his arms, our bodies pressed tightly together.

"This is exactly what I needed," I whispered, enclosed within his arms. And as always, every stress beyond his arms dwindled away, like dust in the wind.

I felt his warm lips rest on my forehead. "I wish I could seal the bond, and make this whole thing go away," he whispered.

"I do too," I breathed. "We have hope."

"Yes," he said quietly. "And until the end, I will hold tightly to that hope."

"So will I."

Encased in his arms with the rising and falling of his chest with each breath, it was as if he had put the sleeper on me. In no time I faded into a deep slumber.

THIRTEEN

W HEN I WOKE, KADE WASN'T next to me, and the room was empty. I sat up and noticed a small note on his pillow.

Went outside to get us some food, and to talk to the others. You're safe here. I'll be right back. I promise.

-Kade

His handwriting was so elegant. A smile rose on my lips as I picked up the small piece of paper. I glanced at the monitors and they were empty. As I was about to turn away, one of the Fallen, with black wings stopped directly in front of one of them. He stopped hovering beyond the barrier, but looking directly at the camera.

My heart sank.

"Ethon," I whispered, glad to see he was still alive. His crimson eyes looked sad, and then he did something unexpected. He placed his hand over his heart and extended it toward the camera... toward me... like he knew I was watching.

How could he know? Maybe he was guessing.

His head snapped back like he heard something. He turned back to the camera, threw a quick kiss, then shot off over the forest, so fast it was like he'd vanished. My heart ached for him, and I couldn't make it stop.

I needed to get out of this room. I felt like I was suffocating.

I took my duffle and left the room, running down the twisted hallway until I reached the hidden door we'd come through. Breaching the door I heard voices.

Before I reached the stairs I quickly threw my duffle in my bedroom, then spotted the group standing in the foyer.

"Hey, Emma!" Alex shouted

"Hey! I thought you guys would be sleeping." I walked down the stairs into Kade's awaiting arms.

"We were about to get something to eat first."

Dom walked in with an apron over his fighting clothes, looking absolutely ridiculous.

"Wow, this room smells very sweet," he said joining the group with his usual large smile.

I narrowed my eyes at him. What was he talking about? I sniffed the air and could only smell, wait... was that breakfast I was smelling?

James jumped in to explain. "Emma's transformation is near, and her immortal scent is becoming stronger."

"Well, it's no wonder they're coming after her. Her scent is very appealing. Nothing like I've smelled before," Dom noted.

"Hey," Kade barked, giving him an eye, while pulling me in close. "Watch it."

"He's telling the truth, dude," Thomas added. "Her scent is very alluring."

"Alright guys, remember it's my daughter you're all talking about," Alaine said, stepping into the room.

I was glad for her sudden appearance because it took the attention off of me.

"Let's go get something to eat, then you all need to get some rest," she instructed.

Dom led the group toward the kitchen, where we found Malachi in an apron as well.

"That smells good," I chimed. "And those aprons suit you both."

"Yeah, Miss Lily's got nothin' on me," Malachi grinned, flipping a pancake up in the air and catching it perfectly in the pan.

"And, she's got nothin' on me either," Dom added, walking up to the stove to flip an omelet. Half the egg stuck in the pan, and the other half went flying sideways, hitting Malachi in the chest.

"What the hell, man?" Malachi growled. A mixture of cooked and raw egg dripped down his apron; his brows instantly furrowed and his lips pursed.

"Hey Mal, looks like I got somethin' on you," Dom said, pointing to his apron. He looked at us with a sly grin.

"You're lucky that crap didn't get on my shirt," he snapped.

I totally thought Malachi was going to smack Dom, but he didn't. He grit his teeth together, walked to the sink, and began wiping the egg from the apron.

"I don't want *that* egg," Kade said.

"Oh come on. It's perfectly scrambled now," Dom replied, wiggling his brow.

"Let's go, Emma," Kade said, grabbing my hand. "I think I feel like pancakes today. What about you?"

"Yep. Pancakes sound good to me," I laughed.

"Ha!" Malachi snarked.

"Traitors," Dom huffed, under his breath.

We all grabbed platters of food and brought them into the dining room with us. Sitting around the table, Dom and Malachi brought up the rear with pitchers of juice and coffee. When we were all seated and dug in,

Alex started the group conversation.

"Did you see how close they came to breaking the barrier?"

"There's still a lot of hold in her," James answered, sipping on some coffee. "And it'll take a lot more to bring her down."

"Yeah, it looks like the barrier is mending itself," Malachi added.

"Yes," James continued. "But what we don't know is if the areas which sustained the most damage are still integral. We all saw the large cracks across the barrier after it was hit. I'm hoping it will continue to hold, but we will know when it does not."

"If it does come down, maybe Emma should be out there fighting with us," Alex added.

Every eye in the room narrowed on him.

"Dude, she's the reason why we're here. We are supposed to *protect* her," Thomas chided.

"But from what everyone keeps telling me, she seems like she's just as good a warrior, or even better, than we are. She can be invisible *and* has a magical suit, amulet, and dagger which can penetrate almost anything. How can anyone or anything match that?" Alex explained.

"He does have a point," Dom added. "But we all know the warrior princess cannot leave the safe room until her transformation is over. It's way too risky. If she's caught, then the whole reason we're here is for nothing. Besides, she only has two days left."

"Yeah, and we all know what that means. If she doesn't you-know-what, with you-know-who, Lucifer will be able to collect her, no matter where she is because of the oath she made. And once they do you-know-what, everything will change. She won't care about us anymore," Alex said, pointing out things I never realized before, which made me a bit frantic inside.

"What are you talking about? I will always care about all of you," I stated, a bit offended by his statement.

"You don't know the power of the bond," Dom interjected. "Once it's been sealed, your life will not be your own. Your whole outlook on life and love will completely change. The bond will bind and seal your hearts and minds together, each wanting, craving, and yearning to spend the rest of eternity, perusing the happiness and fulfillment of the other. Everyone and everything else will become secondary."

"Damn, that was a mouthful coming from you," Malachi sneered.

"Well, I'm sorry you've never discovered true love, Mal. Sometimes the bond isn't for everyone," Dom simpered.

Malachi growled at him with narrowed eyes.

"Dude," Alex interjected, his eyes darting to Kade. "I'm so sorry. That really freaking sucks."

Thomas smacked Alex on the shoulder and shook his head.

"What? I *am* sorry. Kade and Emma should have been together," Alex reasoned.

"Yes, we should have. I know it's my fault," Kade said sadly. "It's something I have to deal with for the rest of my life."

"Well at least you're mortal now, so it won't be too long." Alex spoke without thinking.

Thomas and Malachi, on either side of Alex, turned and glared at him. Thomas whacked his arm, and Malachi smacked him in the head.

"Ouch! What was that for? I was just saying it would have been much worse if he were an immortal and had to live with the guilt for all eternity."

"You should have kept it to yourself instead of blurting it out," Thomas scolded. "You're just making everything worse."

Alex turned to Kade. "I'm really sorry. I never meant to hurt you more."

"I know," Kade replied. "And you are right. An eternity of hurt and regret is much too long."

"Have you found out anything yet, Alaine?" James asked.

Alaine's eyes landed on mine. Her expression made my stomach turn. "I haven't yet, but we are still searching." The tone in her voice told me that even her hope was diminishing. If there was no way out of the oath, I would have to seal the bond with Ethon.

Kade's hand found mine. "Hey, we still have a couple days. Don't give up just yet," he whispered.

I nodded and when I looked into his eyes, I saw hope renewed. He had enough of it for all of us, knowing full well, time was fighting against us.

"Do you think if they continue like they have, they'll be able to break through tonight?" I asked him.

"I don't know," he answered. "It's hard to tell."

"We just need to make sure everyone is rested up. We need you all on top of your game, alert and prepared," Alaine added.

"I'm going to bed right after breakfast," Alex said, stretching.

"I am too," Thomas agreed.

"So, Emma. Tomorrow night is your transformation," James said. "We haven't heard of or seen Ethon in a few days. Maybe there is hope," he stated.

"I hope so," I exhaled.

"Have you found anything, Alaine?" Thomas asked.

Her eyes saddened. "I haven't, but I won't give up."

"We're all here for you, Emma," James said.

"I know. Thank you." I looked at Alaine. "Any word from Samuel?"

"No. But I'm sure he's fine and we will see him very soon," she answered.

I nodded. "That's good. I can't wait to see him again."

She looked up at me with love and sadness in her eyes. "Me too."

Everyone helped clean and clear the breakfast table.

"So are you guys headed back to the safe room?" Dom asked.

"I don't know. There's still a lot of daylight left," I noted.

"Why don't we all go to Kade's room and play some cards."

"Sounds good to me." I shrugged, glancing at Kade with pleading eyes.

"She'll be surrounded by all of us. It'll be the safest room for her." Dom said. "James, Alaine, wanna join us?"

"No thanks, but thank you for the offer." Alaine said, with a smile. "I need to check on a few more things in my office."

"No, thank you. I am going to get some shut eye," James said.

"That sounds so boring. You can sleep when you're dead," Dom chuckled.

"You all have fun," James smiled, then exited the room.

We headed toward Kade's room, and after an hour of cards, we all ended up falling asleep. Kade and I were on the bed, and the rest of them were sprawled out on the ground. The transformation was really draining me because I slept through their horrible symphony of snoring.

FOURTEEN

THE HOUSE SUDDENLY SHOOK VIOLENTLY, like we were in the middle of a major earthquake, jolting everyone from sleep.

"Shit," Kade cursed glancing outside. My heart sunk watching the sky darken as the sun set.

"Get up boys," Dom yelled.

A loud boom shook the house again. From Kade's window there wasn't much happening, but as soon as we opened his door and looked out the front windows... All Hell had broken loose.

We watched in horror as three Grimlock stood side by side, bashing the same area of the barrier. Every blow felt like a bomb was going off. The barrier's cracks extended longer than they had before, webbing out across the whole front of it.

There was a lot of movement outside, and as my eyes started to focus, I saw Darkling inside the barrier, crawling around the house, but they weren't trying to get in.

Not yet.

"It's not gonna hold much longer!" Malachi yelled.

"Well boys, this is our time to shine," Dom called his brothers to arms.

Everything that followed happened so fast.

I watched in complete horror as one of the Grimlock offered his blow, shattering what was left of the barrier. Brilliant white and blue sparks rained down around the perimeter as our protection finally gave, and disintegrated around us.

It was the beginning of the end.

The front door exploded like a bomb. Like a rocket, Lucian came crashing through the side wall like it was made of straw, tumbling into the foyer directly below us.

He stood, tall and muscular, slowly dusting himself off. His eyes were pitch black, just like his heart. His white hair wasn't drawn back like how I remembered. It was long, stringy, and hung down to his shoulders making him look even more brutal.

Lucian held his arms out to his sides, calling his majestic, raven-black wings, and they immediately appeared behind his back.

His head snapped up toward us, and a wicked grin swept across his face, sending a menacing, hair-raising chill down my spine.

Chaos and terror erupted all around us as Darkling and Fallen forced their way in, shattering all the windows as they crashed through.

But something happened. Something no one, including Lucian, could have expected. A half a dozen Hellhounds charge through the opening, and began attacking the Darkling. Screams of agony erupted as the ravage red eyes and razor sharp teeth pounced on their stinky prey and began ripping them to shreds.

"No!" Lucian roared, as the Hellhounds took out half his army in a short amount of time.

He cursed at the top of his lungs, then began to speak in a loud angelic voice which reverberated of the walls all around us.

The Hellhounds started to yelp in pain and then dropped to the ground. In seconds they were lifeless; their bodies torched and turned to ash.

Lucian killed half the power he came with and we didn't have to lift a finger.

Rage burned bright in his eyes.

Ethon was nowhere to be seen, and neither was Lucifer. I had a crushing feeling they would abandon us and leave us to die. How easy it would be to have one enemy take out the other.

With a wave of his hand, Lucian sent his Fallen forward.

Our Guardians didn't hesitate. Every one of them readied their weapons and charged forward without fear or trepidation, knowing full well they were brutally outnumbered.

I watched Alaine rush out from the hallway. She had been ready, dressed in her black combat outfit with her sword in hand. Her hair was pulled back, her eyes narrowed, and her face hard-set as she immediately engaged with one of the Fallen. His tall muscular frame towered over hers by at least two feet.

I gasped in horror as he lifted his gargantuan sword over his head, quickly thrusting it down at her. Alaine twirled to the side, barely missing it.

I exhaled. That was too close.

The Fallen raised his weapon again and attempted a second strike, but Alaine disappeared. I watched her reappear directly behind him, quickly pushing her blade into his back. He immediately swung around, knocking her backwards.

I knew whenever she disappeared, it drained her. I prayed to God that she would have enough strength to survive.

Kade grabbed me by the arms and yanked me backward down the hallway.

"No!" I yelled, trying to break free, but he held me tight. In an instant, he threw me over his shoulder and I was being carried quickly toward my bedroom. "We can't leave them," I cried.

"We have to. They are fighting for you, Emma. For your safety," he implored, carrying me away.

"*No!*" I screamed.

I watched in horror as Malachi and Dominic jumped from the second balcony, directly into the middle of danger below. Swords clashed and echoed through the house as they fought bravely, but they were surrounded and would be quickly outnumbered.

I screamed as the Fallen closed in on them. Kade ran down the hall, kicked open my door, dropped me to my feet and locked the door behind us. He ran and pulled the chair from the desk and secured the door with it.

"Get your garment on. Now!" he urged.

There was a charge in his eyes, and the seriousness of his voice had me grabbing the duffle and bolting for the closet. I threw open the door and immediately threw off my jeans and T-shirt as I entered. I pulled the garment from my duffle, trying to unzip it, but my body was trembling much too fiercely.

A loud boom on the door shook the entire room.

"Shit. Hurry, Emma!" Kade yelled.

I finally unzipped the suit and quickly slipped it on, then grabbed the dagger and fastened it to my waist.

Another thundering boom against the door sent a jolt of fear through me. If Kade wasn't pushing the door shut, it already would have flown off the hinges. There was no way he could hold it shut for much longer, if whoever or whatever kept trying to bash it in. I rushed to his side and threw my weight against the door.

"Do you have your dagger?" he asked.

"Yes," I said, unsheathing it.

"Whatever happens, fight. You need to stay alive. We are all here to protect you. If you die, then all of this was all for nothing. Do you hear me? It doesn't matter *who* is in trouble around you, take care of yourself first," he said, his eyes were narrowed on me, filled with overwhelming concern.

"I understand." I twisted myself, moving to the front of him, placing both hands on either side of him, still pushing against the door. I pressed my body tightly against his, and then, I kissed him.

"I love you," I breathed.

"And I love you," he whispered. "So much so that it aches. I would willingly give my life for you."

"I know you would. But I need you. So, you have to stay alive."

A grin graced his beautiful lips. "I'll try."

"You'll need to do better than that," I said, and he smiled.

The next blast felt like an explosion, and sent the top hinge of the door flying off.

"Emma, each of us needs to take a side. You go right, so when the door opens you'll be protected. Once whatever is out there comes through, you stay put and let me deal with it."

"Okay," I answered without thought, my heart and pulse racing.

"You should go invisible now."

"Wait," I answered. "We can both be invisible. I just need to touch you."

He pondered the offer, then he grabbed my waist. "Alright, let's do this. But when I attack, you let go and stay hidden."

"Alright," I said, knowing full well if I could help him, I would.

He pivoted with me in his arms, and pushed us to the right side of the door. I called upon my invisibility, and we immediately disappeared.

"Whoa," he whispered.

"What?"

"This is my first time," he said, still holding me tight.

"It is?" I questioned. "I thought—" Then I realized it had been Ethon I was with.

"Nope, invisible virgin here."

"Well, not a virgin anymore," I noted.

"That's true," he said. "Are you ready?"

"Ready," I answered.

He moved me to the side, and I kept my hands on him, running them up his back and placing them on his shoulders.

"Are *you* ready?" I asked.

"As ready as I'll ever be," he said.

The door burst open, flying off the last hinge, tumbling and slamming into the opposite wall. A rumbling growl filled the room, rattling my knees with fear. A huge leg attached to a large torso stomped inside.

My breath seized.

I was expecting one of the Fallen, but this was no Fallen.

It was a Grimlock.

Fear encompassed me, knowing they used their smell as their sight. Being invisible didn't matter anymore. The Grimlock would be able to pinpoint us no matter where we were.

Kade stayed still, waiting for the creature to enter. I wanted to tell him he shouldn't wait, but didn't want to risk making noise.

I wondered if he knew, but I couldn't take a chance. I had to move before the Grimlock entered the room.

Jumping in front of Kade, I lifted my dagger and thrust it deep into the Grimlock's chest. The Grimlock roared, and swung its large arm at me, sending me flying backward, crashing against my desk. As soon as I let go of Kade, he became visible.

The blade was still embedded in the creature's chest, but it wasn't going down. The Grimlock lifted his huge spiked weapon and swung it directly at Kade.

Kade dove, just under the blade, and used his sword to slash its leg.

"The neck. Aim for its neck!" I yelled.

Kade quickly raised his blade, but before he could complete his swing, the Grimlock raised his leg, kicking him backward. He flew back, crashing and hitting the side of my bed.

"Kade," I screamed.

"I'm okay," he assured.

The Grimlock became enraged, and barged in, stomping toward Kade. His lethal weapon swung back and forth heading directly at him. He didn't have protection, and the bed was keeping him from moving backward.

Without hesitation, I shot up. Using the bed to propel me forward, I timed my move. As soon as the beast was mid-swing, I jumped on the bed and thrust myself forward, feet first, aiming at the dagger. As soon as my feet hit the blade, it pushed it deep into its chest.

It halted, its hand frantically grasped at its chest, but there was nothing for it to hold on to. It crashed down onto its knees, then after a loud gurgling exhale, its eyes rolled back and it dropped forward.

Kade shot up. "Emma," he exhaled.

"I had to. I'm sorry," I said.

"Don't be sorry," he said, hugging me tight. "You saved us. I'm just thankful you didn't get hurt."

"Come on, we have to get you to the safe room."

He grabbed my hand and pulled me out of the room.

As we turned into the hallway, it was blocked. Dom was fighting two Fallen, and I was overjoyed to see he was still alive.

"Second floor should be free," Dom yelled, right after he did an awesome flying twist, using both of his sharp blades to behead one of the Fallen.

"Thanks, man," Kade yelled back.

"Emma, I can see you," he called out while dodging another blade swung at his head.

"Not the face," he shouted, pushing the Fallen back into one of the rooms. "No one comes near this face. It's my money maker!"

I held onto Kade's hand and giggled, calling upon my invisibility. We instantly disappeared and I was surprised at how fast and easy it was becoming. Maybe invisibility would be my gift too.

But I wondered why I didn't get tired like Alaine did after she went invisible. Maybe it was the suit.

FIFTEEN

WE BOTH STARTED DOWN THE stairs to the second level. When we reached the balcony I stopped Kade. Below us was devastation and death. There were two Grimlock inside, swinging their weapons, absolutely destroying Alaine's home.

Two more Grimlock lay lifeless on the ground. One of them was headless, and the other was on its back with its large tongue hanging to the side of its mouth. It had an obvious wound to its chest.

The battle was raging. Guardians against Fallen, and it seemed as if our guys were holding their own.

My heart twisted as I saw Samuel, fighting side by side with Alaine. They moved so naturally together, like each of them knew what the other's next move would be. Samuel used his wings as his weapon, and was slaughtering Fallen after Fallen. Alaine let him lead, but fought just as hard and just as bravely.

"Lucifer's Fallen aren't as skilled as most, probably because they haven't been in battle for a while. They seem sluggish," Kade noted.

"That's good," I exhaled. "It works to our advantage."

James, Thomas, and Alex were fighting on the lowest level, close to Alaine and Samuel. They all looked drained.

"Emma," Kade said, tugging at my hand.

"Wait. Where's Malachi?" I asked, concerned. I quickly scouted all of the lifeless bodies on the ground, but didn't spot his.

"Maybe he chased one outside. There seems to be a lot of commotion going on out there."

"I hope so."

Then I watched as Lucian stalked toward the Guardians. The one nearest him was Alex.

"Kade," I wailed, almost letting go of him. "Alex is in danger!"

He held me back, probably thinking I would jump to his aid.

Alex did not see Lucian coming. He was too engaged with another Fallen to notice.

"Alex!" I screamed. "Alex, behind you!"

Alex paused for a split second, and when he turned around, Lucian was already right behind him, his black eyes locked onto his target. Lucian lifted his arm and shoved his sword right into Alex's midsection.

"No!" I screamed.

Thomas rushed to his aid, and drop kicked Lucian backward, just enough to free the blade from Alex's stomach. He grabbed

Alex's arm and swung him away, while thrusting out his blade, decapitating an oncoming Fallen. Alex dropped to his knees, his sword fell from his hands as he leaned forward examining his wound.

"Shit!" he bellowed.

Thomas fought bravely next to him, keeping the others away.

"We need to save him," I cried.

"You are the one who needs to be saved. We need to go. The others will take care of him."

"He's dying," I wailed, watching Alex try to get up, but he collapsed.

"Lucifer failed us, and so did Ethon," I sobbed, watching helplessly as more Fallen and another Grimlock crashed through the house.

"Emma. We need to go. *Now*," he urged.

"They're gonna die. They're all gonna die because of me."

"That's not true."

"It is true, and I can't stand here and let it happen. It's not fair. They shouldn't have to die for me."

"That's what Guardians do. They watch over those they've been assigned. It's their duty to fight, and even die to protect those appointed to them. It's what we were created for."

"It's not fair," I said, falling into his arms.

A thunderous boom shook the whole house. The large chandelier above the foyer came crashing down, along with the beautiful stained glass skylight. Crystal shards and glass exploded all across the floor.

A loud screeching caw echoed around us, and as I looked up, I saw Ash circling outside. A shot of adrenaline and hope surged through my veins.

In the confusion, Thomas picked Alex up and hurriedly carried him down the hall toward Alaine's room.

Through the gaping hole in the ceiling, a black, smoky mist slowly crept in. It rapidly began to swirl like a whirlwind and then took form. Everyone in the room, angels and beasts alike, paused and watched in utter awe as Lucifer stood in their midst.

Huge raven wings spread out and folded across his back. His body had transformed from normal to almost beast-like. Muscles and veins bulged from his bare chest and arms. In one hand he held a very long, very sharp sword. The other was empty, but his fist was tightly balled shut. His eyes were blood red, flickering with flames of rage and destruction, and they were narrowed on Lucian.

"Lucifer," Lucian scoffed. "I'm shocked to see you here. Were you invited or did you merely crash the party?"

"Disloyal traitor," Lucifer growled, his words thundered through the house, shaking the ground and sending debris falling from above.

Lucian smirked. "I knew one day we would run in to each other. I just didn't think it would be here."

"The girl is mine. She is bonded to my son," Lucifer snarled.

"I see you are still living up to your name, Deceiver. The girl is not immortal, therefore cannot be bonded. She is Nephilim, and she is mine."

Two beings from the beginning of time stood confronting one another. Once allies, now archenemies. The two squared off; Lucian slowly unfurled his wings, knowing what was to come. This would be the battle of all battles.

I could see it in Lucifer's eyes. The century old feud was about to be dealt with head on. He was face to face with the very one to whom he entrusted his Fallen army. The one he put in charge of all of his executions, including his own brother. The one whose pride overcame him, making him think he could do a much better job of ruling the Underworld.

"You will die before this day is done," Lucifer threatened.

"Not if I kill you first," Lucian answered.

Lucifer flew at Lucian, their swords collided and sparks rained down around them. Each engaged moving effortlessly around the other, using their wings and swords as weapons. Lucifer took to the air spinning, his wings outspread. Lucian managed to avoid the deadly attack, but four unsuspecting Fallen did not. Two of them were instantly decapitated, one was sliced in half, and the other lost an arm.

When he stopped, Lucian attacked. With a flap of his wings he shot forward, his blade missing Lucifer by inches. As the momentum carried him forward, he wrapped his arm around Lucifer's legs, yanking him downward. Both went crashing and tumbling in a massive heap. Black feathers filled the air around them, gracefully and silently floating down.

Lucifer kicked Lucian in the gut, throwing him backward, but Lucian spread his wings and stopped the momentum. With a loud swoosh, Lucifer flew at him one more time, and swords crashed together repeatedly.

By this time, most of the room had emptied out.

They looked as if they were dancing, but this dance was deadly and as old as they were, they were moving unbelievably fast. Their strikes were so hard, it was almost ear piercing. Each attack was given with a centuries worth of hate, resentment, and revenge.

Everyone watched these two ancient warriors engage from a safe distance. Even the blind Grimlock made their way outside to avoid the bloodthirsty battle unfolding before them.

Then a team of Lucifer's Fallen descended from the hole in the ceiling. I saw the remainder land around the perimeter outside, some engaging immediately with Lucian's Fallen.

Alaine had disappeared, probably to help Alex, and Samuel had made his way up the stairs to the third level. I still didn't see Malachi, and hoped he was alright.

Lucifer kept his part of the deal, but it was something he already wanted from the beginning. He was waiting for his moment to confront Lucian, and we were simply the means for him to do so.

The battle was raging, and war was all around us.

"Emma, let's go," Kade said.

I gasped as a familiar rush of tingles overcame me, making me dizzy.

Ethon was near.

As I glanced up, Ethon appeared floating gracefully down from the hole in the ceiling. After pausing briefly, he flew toward the stairway.

"Emma," he called. "I know you're here. I've come for you."

Kade held tight to my hand. "Don't," he said. "Why would he want you to come to him in the midst of danger?"

"Emma, we have to seal the bond before it's too late," he announced. "Come to me, let me keep you safe and take you away from this danger."

Ethon stood in the stairwell, between the second and third level. He left his wings visible but folded them behind his back. He had on a black shirt with black jeans. Through one hand, he raked his raven black hair away from his crimson eyes, and in the other he held his long, sharp sword.

"Emma," he called again.

The bond acted as a magnet, pulling me away from Kade. As much as I wanted to stay with him, the bond seemed like it was getting stronger. It weakened me and caused my heart to yearn after Ethon. I had to go. The bond was forcing me to.

"I'm sorry. I have to go," I said.

Kade didn't say a word, but loosened his grip on my hand. He knew time was running out, and if Lucifer lived, he would use my oath against me.

As soon as I was free from him, I found myself running toward Ethon. My body was on autopilot. I didn't have as much control over myself as before, and I could feel my inner-self fading to the will of the bond.

I willed visibility and as soon as I did, Ethon sheathed his sword and held out his arms to me, a wide smile filled his face. "There you are, my love."

From the side, I saw a large figure shooting toward him. In a flash, Lucian had escaped from Lucifer. His face was hard-set, and his blackened eyes were narrowed and set on his new target.

"Ethon!" I screamed, a few yards away. He turned and ducked under Lucian's sword. Behind him, Lucifer caught up to him, grabbing his leg.

What happened next played out in slow motion, and I had a front row seat; an unwilling witness to every horrific and terrorizing detail.

As Lucian was being thrown backward by Lucifer, he resisted. His face hardened as he twisted, thrusting his right wing outward at the exact moment Ethon stood to unsheathe his sword.

I cried out helplessly, watching the tip of Lucian's wing impale Ethon's chest, exiting out his back.

A reverberating, earth shattering roar exploded from Lucifer, rattling the entire house as he watched the assault on his son. His rage quickly overpowered Lucian. As he slammed him backward into the ground, sending a shockwave of rubble, Lucian's wing ripped from Ethon's chest.

Enraged with a fire in his eyes I'd not yet witnessed, Lucifer pounced on him, hammering down on his face and body with such force it was sickening. Lucian was broken, barely moving, and hardly recognizable. But Lucifer continued, showing no mercy. He finally stood above him, his eyes filled with wicked intent, kicking him over to his stomach. He then took his wings, and with his sword, severed each one and tossed them to the side like they were trash.

Lucian wailed in agony as Lucifer kicked him back over to face him.

"Now... you die," Lucifer hissed.

He lifted his sword and then slammed it down right through Lucian's chest. Lucian wailed and clawed at the metal, struggling to remove it. The sounds of his last cries were nauseating.

With one final twist of his blade, Lucifer ended Lucian's life. But his revenge had not ended. He grabbed Lucian's hair, pulling his body upward, and then severed his head. He stood and raised it above his head, showing Lucian's Fallen what became of their leader.

During Lucian's extermination, Ethon dropped to the ground, grasping the wound in his chest.

"*Ethon!*" I screamed, running to his side. I fell down next to him, bringing his head to rest on my lap. Blood was pouring from the wound, pooling around and under him. His crimson eyes were becoming dim and dark; his breaths were raspy and shallow.

"Ethon. You can heal, right? You just need to rest. You're an immortal."

He looked at me, his eyes glossed over. "I'm sorry, Emma. Fate got the best of me," he said softly.

"No," I wailed. "Can't you heal yourself?"

My heart felt like barbed wire was being tightly wound around it. Throbbing in agony, I could barely breathe.

"Emma," Malachi yelled from below. I was glad to hear his voice.

As I turned to him, I noticed his eyes were filled with concern. "Look," he said, holding up Lucian's severed wing, showing us the tip which pierced through Ethon. "He attached immortal blades to them."

"What does that mean?"

"It means... there's nothing we can do for him," he said sadly.

"You can't die," I said, turning back to Ethon, bringing my face to his. My heart was torched with an intense and shooting pain.

"It's alright," he whispered, then smiled weakly. "Death is my final destiny. But you will live, my beautiful Emma."

"Ethon, no," I sobbed. The bond was literally bashing my heart, splintering it into the tiniest fragments.

He raised his hand and rested it on the side of my cheek. I held it tight.

"Don't cry for me, Emma," he said softly. "I've been in existence longer than I've wanted. This life was never meant for me, the bastard son of Darkness. I'm sick and tired of it all, and am ready to find peace and rest."

"I'm sorry, Ethon. I'm so sorry. I wish things could have been different between us," I cried. My heart was tormented as everything he had ever done for me replayed in my mind. I leaned over, and kissed his cheek, then whispered in his ear. "Thank you."

"For what?" He breathed out and gasped for air.

"For coming into my life. For protecting me. For loving me, even if it was for a moment. You showed me there is good in things that are seemingly dark."

"Be happy, Emma. That's all I ever wanted for you. I know you will find it." Ethon's eyes directed to Kade. "She's always loved you... that's never changed. I was always second choice," he said, his eyes weakening. "Make her happy."

"I promise," Kade said.

I watched the crimson in Ethon's eyes slowly changing... fading into a dull white.

"Emma?" he exhaled roughly, looking around but not seeing anything.

I placed both hands on his face and leaned over him. "I'm here, Ethon."

"Did you ever love me?"

Tears streamed down my face. "Yes, Ethon. I loved you. I still do, and I always will."

A smile lifted on his lips. "Remember me," he said, then took his last breath.

"Always," I whispered. Tears poured from my eyes and I placed my lips on his forehead.

Ethon's lifeless hand dropped to his side, and I found myself screaming uncontrollably. My heart felt like it was being ripped right out of my chest. The pain was indescribable. Fear, loss, and agony tore through every cell. I felt like I was dying.

Kade tried to pick me up but Dom held him back.

"Let her be. The pain she's experiencing is from the bond, and there is nothing anyone can do. It's a process she has to go through," he said with tears in his eyes. My pain must have been a reminder of what he'd lost.

It took a while before the agony subsided, but it didn't leave. It just became a bit more bearable.

SIXTEEN

EVERYONE'S ATTENTION WAS ON US and not the leader of the Underworld. Lucifer stood in the background, quietly mourning his son, but not for long. An ear-piercing wail echoed through the house, causing an earthquake.

His eyes were burning bright, erupting with flames of pain which licked the sides of his face. He strode forward, eyes locked onto the lifeless body of his son grasped in my arms. Hate and anger were embedded in his eyes and on his face.

I didn't know if I should say anything to him.

"If Ethon cannot have you, neither will the other," Lucifer roared, his flaming eyes narrowed on Kade.

Before anyone could decipher what was happening, he flew at Kade, wrapping his arm around his neck, pushing him backward against a wall.

Everyone charged forward, but froze in place when Lucifer pressed a long, sharp sword to Kade's side, right in line with his heart.

"Test me and see if I will not kill him," Lucifer shouted.

"*No!*" I screamed. I released Ethon's body and ran toward Kade.

"Emma, stop!" he yelled, holding his hand up. I was grabbed from behind, so I twisted and held the dagger up, pressing it against Dom's throat.

Dom's eyes landed on mine. "Emma, we're on the same team, remember?"

When I realized it was him, I fell into his arms and sobbed. Pushing away from him, I fell to my knees crawling toward Lucifer.

"I beg you. Please let him go," I pleaded. "Take me. I'm the one you wanted anyway." Blinding hot tears flooded my eyes and poured down my cheeks.

This could not be happening.

"Don't worry, Emma," Samuel spoke softly, appearing out of nowhere to lay a hand on my shoulder. "I told you I'd take care of this."

"Samuel, wait!" I cried, grabbing hold of his arm as he walked past me.

"It'll be alright, sweetheart," he said softly, disengaging his arm from my grasp.

"*Samuel,*" Alaine bellowed from the lower level.

"Stay there, Alaine," he commanded.

"Don't do this. I need you. *Please,*" she begged in anguish.

Samuel glanced down at her with a smile on his face. "I've always loved you."

Alaine cried out, trying to rush for him, but three of the Fallen immediately surrounded her. One of them slapped her backward and James charged forward, shoving his blade through the Fallen's chest.

Malachi joined to help him, but they were seriously outnumbered.

From behind, a Fallen grabbed James and threw him clear across the room where he was immediately surrounded. James stood, then crouched with his weapon in hand. A Fallen charged him from the front, and as soon as he swung to defend himself, another came from behind and sliced across his neck with a sword, instantly decapitating him.

"*James!*" Alaine's cries were piercing. She tried to run to him, but fell weakly to her knees. Thomas ran after her and folding his arms around her. She fell helplessly into his arms.

Malachi fought bravely, slaughtering three Fallen before he was struck in the back. His eyes went wide as he fell to his knees. He stumbled to get up, but was kicked down again.

"Malachi!" Dom roared as he turned to run to him, but he was blocked by four massive Fallen on the stairwell, their swords drawn and ready to spill blood.

Thomas held Alaine's head away from the scene; her screams were heart wrenching.

I cried, turning my head away as a Fallen held Malachi down, and the other raised his sword. My loud sobs didn't mute the sound of the blade as it took of his head, and Dom's howl of anger and pain.

I looked to Samuel trying to find some kind of sanity within the madness. Rage was carved heavily on his face, his body was tense, his chest was rising and falling with long deep breaths. This showed me how much restraint he had.

It must have been killing him to watch Alaine, and not do anything about it.

He took in one final deep breath, and turned to me. His eyes instantly softened.

"I love you, my daughter, and am so proud of you. Please take care of your mother."

"We just got you back. You can't leave," I cried.

Dom knelt behind me and wrapped me in his arms.

"What is happening? I can't handle this," I bawled.

"I know," Dom exhaled, his voice shaking.

"Dad," I yelled. "You can't do this."

Samuel turned to me, and a smile I'd not seen before lit his entire face. He was glowing and I knew it was because I finally called him by his true name. He *was* my dad, and he was the bravest, most selfless person I'd ever met.

He gave a slight nod to Dom, and his arms tightened around me.

"Let me go, Dom," I begged.

"I can't," he said. "I'm sorry."

I could hear Alaine's heartbreaking cries below, pleading with Samuel, her voice raspy from overuse. If he gave himself up, she would be mourning the three men who were closest her.

This couldn't be happening. It was the worst nightmare imaginable, with no way of waking out of it.

"Leave him be, Lucifer. Take me instead," Samuel said calmly. His shoulders were relaxed; his arms were extended out to his sides in surrender.

Lucifer's crimson eyes raged with flames, and narrowed on Samuel with burning disgust. "What is it with you immortals, willing to give up your life for worthless human insects who will die within a few years?"

"He was once an immortal - Emma's Guardian - who asked for mortality to lead her into the Underworld to seek you out. You and I will outlive him a million times. Let him go, and take me instead," Samuel courageously requested.

Ever since I met my father, he'd been my hero. He had defied death and come back to life to watch over me and Alaine, making sure of our safety. And here he was, still protecting us.

I flashed back to when I met him out beyond Alaine's gate. That was the first time he saved me, and from that moment on, he came to my aid whenever I needed him most. He was always there for me, and now I was witnessing him offering his life for me... for Kade.

I didn't know how much more pain my heart could take.

Lucifer paused, and his eyes narrowed on Samuel.

"No," his voice rumbled. "My only legacy, my son is dead because of her. My Ethon is gone." Pain and hatred burned in his eyes as he glanced over to Ethon's lifeless body, then back at me. "Now she will pay for the rest of her life. Her heart was torn because of this worthless mortal. And as per our agreement, his soul will become the final payment."

"*No!*" I hollered. "Let me go!" I struggled to break free from Dom's hold.

"Lucifer, don't," Samuel urged, stepping toward him.

Before he or anyone else could make another move, Lucifer slowly pushed his sharp blade into the side of Kade's chest.

My entire world collapsed right in front of my eyes.

Kade gasped, his eyes widened, his body drooped forward.

Lucifer drew out his blade, and let go of Kade. He fell to his knees, then grabbed at the side of his chest. Blood poured from the wound as he toppled backward, his legs bent awkwardly beneath him.

"Now, we are even," Lucifer hissed, with a wicked scowl.

"You bastard!" I bellowed in anger and hate. Dom's arms, which had been tightly wrapped around me, unfolded, setting me free.

Rage torched my insides, turning the world around me red; hatred grasped my entire being and exuded from my pores, squeezing the air from my lungs, trying to render me weak. Every negative emotion wrapped itself tightly around me, suffocating, gripping my heart and compressing it to the point of depleting every ounce of good left in me.

I wanted nothing more than having the pleasure of killing him and watching him suffer.

I charged toward Lucifer, crying out with every ounce of anger and pain I had inside me. I raised my trusted dagger above my head, hoping it would aid me in finding its mark, and sink itself deep into Lucifer's vile, amoral, merciless heart.

Samuel had also charged forward, but Lucifer had anticipated his move and thrust him to the side. He hit the bannister, cracking a few of the rails.

I pressed forward and dove for Lucifer, my blade aimed directly at his heart. As soon as the tip touched his flesh, he burst into a million black flies. They swarmed around us, biting at our exposed flesh, then disappeared up and out through the hole he'd entered.

I scrambled to Kade and saw his eyes roll back into his head. He couldn't be dead. I dropped down next to his body and felt for a pulse. It was faint, but there was one. He was still alive, but barely.

Blood pumped out from the wound in the side of his chest.

"You can't die. Please, you can't die," I grieved, the pain in my heart aching to the point of bursting. I pressed my hands against his injury to help slow the bleeding.

"Alaine," I screamed, as blood soaked my hands. Samuel and Dominic knelt next to me. Dom laid his hand on his shoulder.

"Fight brother. Don't give up," he said as tears welled in his eyes.

In a few seconds Alaine bounded up the stairs and knelt down beside me. After examining his would, her eyes pressed shut.

"Where is the potion? We need to get his potion," I yelled.

"His potion isn't going to help a fatal wound inflicted by an immortal blade," Alaine said with tears spilling down her face. "I'm so sorry, Emma."

"What are you saying? You can't heal him?"

Her lips quivered uncontrollably as she shook her head, and brought a hand up to brush his hair back.

"I'm sorry," she sobbed.

Samuel came up behind her. Alaine jumped up and wrapped her arms around him.

"I thought I'd lost you," she wailed.

He didn't respond, but held her tightly.

"Help me!" I bellowed, pleading with anyone. "There has to be a way. He can't die. We can't give up! Is there some magic I can use to give my life for his? Something? *Anything*?"

The true love of my life, my first bonded, my protector, my Guardian, was dying right before my eyes and there was nothing I could do about it. I was helpless, watching him quickly fade away. The horrifying dreams were becoming reality.

Then I remembered the last dream I had... the one where my kiss saved him.

I leaned over and kissed him. "Don't die. Please don't die," I spoke against his lips, hoping my words would travel down to his heart and magically heal him.

But they didn't.

In absolute horror I helplessly watched him take his last, weak breath and was gone. Just like that. I didn't get a chance to say goodbye. I didn't even have a chance to tell him how much I loved him.

My heart burst in agony, hot tormenting tears burned my swollen eyes.

He left me.

I had a chance to say goodbye to Ethon, why not my Kade?

"Kade," I wailed, clawing at his shirt. Trembling, I lay over his lifeless body. No one should ever be allowed to feel this kind of pain.

His body started to glow brightly, and I watched as he dissolved right from under me, disappearing in a fine mist.

He was gone from my grasp, and I lay alone in a pool of his blood.

"Where is he? What happened?" I frantically pleaded.

"His family must have called his body home," Dom replied. "I'm so sorry, Emma."

There wasn't much more I could take. My body, my mind, my soul was in utter anguish and disbelief. I was exhausted to the point of collapsing.

Strong arms lifted and cradled me.

"You'll be alright. I promise." Samuel pressed his lips to my forehead. I rolled my head onto his chest, and closed my eyes, too weak to move.

"You just need to *sleep*, my Emma."

With his words, I faded into darkness, hoping never to awake.

SEVENTEEN

MY EYES WERE BLURRY WHEN I woke in my bed. Someone had cleaned my bedroom, and fixed the door. The room was dimly lit from a lamp next to my bedside.

As I started to come fully awake, all the heinous events which had happened earlier came flooding back to me. I knew it couldn't have been a dream, because the pain and aching proved the reality.

Kade was gone. Ethon was gone. Malachi and James... gone.

My thoughts rushed to Kade. I would never again be able to feel his loving touch, his soft kiss, or his warm arms around me again. His gentle words, the buzz of excitement whenever he walked into a room, and the undeniable connection we experienced whenever our eyes met, were all gone.

They were gone, and I was left with nothing but memories.

I closed my eyes and tried to picture his face, but my emotions began to brim, and tears rushed back into my swollen, aching eyes.

Samuel was sitting on the floor and Alaine was sleeping with her head gently resting on his lap. He nudged her and when her eyes landed on me, she sat up.

"How are you, sweetheart?" she asked. Her eyes were also red and swollen.

In one day there had been so much heartache, so much pain. How could we ever get through this? I couldn't answer her. Tears automatically flooded my eyes, and began to spill down my tear stained cheeks.

"Emma," Samuel spoke quietly. "We will be here for you. I know your world looks lightless and gloomy right now, but it will only be for a season, and this season will pass. One day you will wake up, and the sun will be shining again. It is then when you will start to find your happiness."

I nodded, looking into both of their anguished eyes, knowing full well they wanted what was best for me, hoping everything would work out in the end.

"I'll be alright. I just need some time," I said, although my voice was weak and doubtful.

I knew those were the words they wanted and needed to hear. They needed to be consoled just as much as I did. But to even give them an answer I had to scrape from whatever remnants were left of me. I had been emptied, drained, and was now a shell of who I used to be. The butterfly in the cocoon had died along with Kade and Ethon.

"I'm sorry about James," I said sadly.

She began nodding her head, tears filled her swollen eyes. "He was a good friend, one of my best. He and Malachi will be sorely missed. We are still praying and hoping for Alex to hold on as well. We're still uncertain."

I nodded, fighting the urge to crumble apart again.

"Your transformation is tonight. Would you like us to stay with you?" Alaine asked.

I shook my head. "No, thank you. I need to be alone."

"Alright, sweetheart. We understand," she replied. She walked over to me, then leaned over and lightly kissed my cheek. "If you change your mind, just call. Either of us will be close at all times, just to be sure."

I nodded. "Thank you so much. Both of you. For everything."

"You're our daughter," Samuel said. "We would do anything for you."

"And we will always be here for you, should you need us," Alaine added. She took Samuel's hand and exited the room, closing the door behind them.

Now alone, sadness overtook me. I didn't see how there could be a glorious transformation. I was only existing, not living. Breathing, but just barely.

I didn't want it. I never wanted it... any of it. This life was shoved at me, then filled with nothing more than overwhelming heartache and pain. It was suffocating and killing me slowly. The meaning of life had been sucked right out of me, along with the will to live. I had nothing to look forward to.

Ethon and Kade were gone. Death had me in its clutches, and was pulling me deeper and deeper down into its fiery pit, with no one left to pull me out.

I closed my eyes and envisioned the two sets of eyes which had consumed my life over the past few months. Two men chosen to be my soul mates, both stolen away, leaving me shattered. My heart would never mend, and my bond would never be fulfilled.

I was cursed from the beginning. Everyone I had ever loved, aside from Samuel and Alaine, had died. As much as I loved them, they would never be able to fill the empty void that was left.

James and Malachi were gone, and I still hadn't even begun to mourn them yet.

I lay in bed terrified of what the transformation might bring. Merely thinking about it made my heart thrum a million miles an hour, and a cold sweat blanket over my skin. Maybe, I didn't want to be alone and endure whatever was coming.

Continued thoughts of Kade and Ethon swirled in my mind, but the one who I wished would be here to hold me, and see me through, was Kade. If the decision had been up to me, I would have chosen him. There was no doubt about it. It was always him. From the very beginning.

Ethon was an amazing guy, and had everything a girl could want, but he still wasn't Kade.

I could feel the sadness eroding away my insides, but I could also feel myself erupting, like a volcano ready to explode.

I pulled my pillow to my face and screamed.

"Why God? Why did you even allow me to be born into this misery? Why would you give me love, only to steal it away? Do you hate me that much?"

Fate was just as evil and hard as Lucifer.

Agony and torment kept poking their ugly heads in my face, taunting me.

But then Kade's face, his smile, his hazel eyes which were once filled with so much love and so much life, flashed before me. I wished I could replay it over and over.

"Kade," I anguished. Every part of my body ached. Intense pain ripped through my chest, puncturing my heart over and over again. My world had never felt so dark or so empty, and could never offer a cure, or a magic potion, for this kind of suffering.

I curled up into a fetal position and let my emotions bleed. Tears soaked my cheeks and my pillow, but the pain only intensified. "Help me," I cried out in desperation. "Someone help me."

"Emma," a voice spoke ever so softly, as if directly into my ear. I could barely hear it over my cries, so I paused. In between my convulsive gasps for breath, I heard it again.

"Emma."

I glanced up to witness a bright light emitting from my closet, illuminating the whole frame. It was as if I was experiencing déjà vu.

Was this real, or was I dreaming?

Then, even through my very stuffy nose, I could smell a familiar sweet scent which wrapped the room in a warm tranquility.

My eyelids were swollen, but remained frozen on the knob which appeared to be turning. My breath hitched. I couldn't scream, but I didn't feel like I needed to.

When the door opened, a light shined so bright I had to shield my eyes. Someone stepped forward and walked toward me. I slowly lowered my arm and froze. An impassive peace covered the area.

Before me stood the most beautiful angel I had ever seen. A golden aura radiated around him, and the most beautiful golden hair fell like silk around his broad shoulders. His features were strong and chiseled, and when I gazed into his dark brown eyes, a halo of gold encircled them. They seemed so familiar, but I knew I'd never seen him before.

"Emma." His voice was melodic and melted my anxiety.

The closer he approached, the more I felt as if we were connected.

"Are you God?" I exhaled. I figured I'd start at the top because he appeared nothing less than God-like.

"No," he chuckled, taking another step forward, leaving about four feet between us. "My name is Michael."

I gasped, clasping both hands over my mouth.

"As in Michael the Archangel?" My heart hammered against my chest, my pulse was racing.

He nodded and offered me his hand. As I placed mine in his, every ounce of sadness I'd felt inside instantly melted away.

"You've been through so much pain and suffering, Emma, but you've shown so much strength. You should be proud of the young woman you've become."

A tear trickled down my cheek, not knowing how to respond. I hadn't been strong. I'd been weak and feeble, barely holding myself together.

"It seems you've been in possession of my dagger?" he questioned, with a grin and a tilt to his head.

I nodded and found my voice.

"Yes. Yes, I have it. Dominic gave it to me, and it saved me, many times." I turned back to the dagger lying on my nightstand, now glowing just as brightly as Michael. I reached back and picked it up. It was warm and sent a buzz through my arm. I held it out and offered it to him. "Thank you so much for letting me have it for a while, Michael – Archangel... sir." I felt like a complete idiot, not sure how I should address him.

His face lit up and he laughed loudly, then reached out and took the dagger in his right hand. He held it out, and it magically hovered above his palm. I watched it slowly twist, then it floated back in front of me.

Michael's brow rose. "Peculiar. It seems my dagger would like to remain in your possession for the time being. Would you care to watch over it a while longer?"

I was in shock, looking at the dagger magically floating in front of me.

"Is that a yes?" he asked.

"Yes. Yes, of course," I sputtered, reaching forward and grasping it by its shaft. It tingled in my hand, and then the light went out. I carefully placed it back on the dresser. I was glad the dagger wouldn't be leaving me for now. "This dagger has watched over me more than I have of it," I smiled.

"Yes, it has grown quite fond of you," he acknowledged.

I glanced up to him. "It has? How can you tell?"

"Because we are connected, the dagger and I. It was a gift from the Creator. We were bonded by blood, which makes our connection even stronger. Magical."

"Blood? How?" I questioned. "Once the new blade touched my skin, it tasted my blood and took on my symbol, only revealing it to those it chooses."

I looked at the markings on its shaft, and traced it with my finger. "Wow," I said under my breath.

"Emma, this is why the dagger came to your aid. It is also connected to you."

Our eyes locked, and then he stepped forward and gently laid his hand on my shoulder.

"I've been watching over you from the second you took your first breath, seeing to it that you have had everything you needed to survive." He paused briefly and his smile widened. "I am the one who commissioned Kade to guard over you, and gave Dominic the dagger. And if you haven't figured it out yet, the note in your closet was from me as well."

My eyes stung with tears, already feeling a realization of truth, anticipating it to be spoken.

"Why?" I breathed, wanting to hear it from him.

He stepped closer, eliminating the space between us.

"Because I wanted my *granddaughter* to be safe."

I burst into tears, never expecting this day to come. I never thought I would get the chance to meet the one who created me and Alaine. It was like a dream, and he was standing in front of me.

"Grandfather?"

I broke down, then stood and stepped into his arms. Hot tears stung and spilled uncontrollably from my eyes.

"My sweet, Emma. You were never alone. And you will never be."

I was overwhelmed and felt so secure, so safe within his arms.

"There are a few more who would really like to meet you, but I need your permission before they can come."

"Who?" I asked.

"Friends who have also been watching over you," he added.

"Yes, of course," I nodded, wiping the tears from my eyes. "I'd like to meet them."

"Brother, come," Michael spoke.

Another bright light illuminated the closet, and this time, two figures stepped forward.

I gasped, recognizing them as soon as they came into focus.

"These are—" Michael said with his hand outstretched toward them.

"Kade's parents," I breathed.

He looked at me and smiled.

"They're exactly how he described," I said, breathless.

Both were beautiful beyond words, with strong resemblances of Kade which made my heart ache. His mother radiated beauty.

241

Her deep amber eyes had flecks of gold within them, and when she smiled at me, it reminded me so much of my mother.

"Emma, I am Arella," his mother spoke. I instinctively ran into her arms.

"I'm sorry. I'm so sorry he's gone. It should have been me. He didn't deserve to die. Not for me."

"Shhh—" She gently stroked my hair. "It's okay. It's okay, darling."

I didn't understand how they could bear to look at me, let alone touch or speak to me so kindly. Their son was dead because of me. But they didn't show an ounce of anger.

"Kade knew what he was doing." Arella's voice was soft and sweet. "He freely chose his path, and was willing to give everything he had for the one he loved. We are proud of our son. The choices he made were his alone, and no one can question why. He did it because he believed in you. Because he loved you."

"I never deserved him."

"Yes, you did. And right now, mourning his death is the last thing he would want. He would want you to celebrate his life," she answered.

"I'm so sorry we had to meet under these circumstances. I loved your son, and you're right. He wouldn't want me to mourn him. But whenever I close my eyes, I see his face, and it kills me a little more each time."

Kade's father, Raphael, sighed. "Come, child." He stepped forward and offered me his hand, then led me over to the bed. "Please sit." He nodded and smiled.

I did as he said, wondering why.

Arella moved behind him, and stood next to Michael. Their calm demeanors made me relax just a bit.

"Are you going to put me to sleep?"

They all began to laugh.

It was a rational question. I really didn't want to be put under, not when I still had so many questions. Not to mention the fact I had just met them.

"No." Raphael grinned, placing his hand on my forehead.

As soon as he touched me, a rush of dizziness and tingles jolted through my body. It felt similar to the effects of the potion, only much more potent. I felt woozy and grabbed his arm to steady myself.

"It's okay. Just close your eyes, relax, and breathe."

"What's happening?" I questioned.

"He's healing you," Michael answered.

Arella nodded kindly, her beautiful smile never left her lips. "Kade's vial was filled with Raphael's healing magic, which we shared with Alaine. The reason why Kade was in possession of the vial was because he knew from whom it came, and how it worked."

It was like a light flicked on in my mind as I remembered all the times I needed help, and Kade was there, offering me the magical potion.

After another a minute, Raphael stepped back. "You should be good as new. Now tonight, during your transformation, you shouldn't feel as much pain. And, you are now free from any infirmity."

"I had infirmities?"

"A few bruised ribs and a broken heart. The heart might take a while to mend, but eventually it will. I promise you."

I didn't see how. I knew as soon as they left and I was alone again, I would start to drown in my sorrow.

Arella walked forward and stood next to Raphael. They looked into each other's eyes, and for that brief moment, I saw nothing but pure unconditional love. It was a look Kade and I had shared.

His mom then turned, leaned over and hugged me. "Thank you, Emma, for loving our son. He never loved anyone as much as he loved you."

"He was everything I could have ever wished for." I fought a never-ending battle with tears that would not relent.

"Remember... it wasn't your fault. We all know what happened, and Lucifer will pay a pretty price for what he's done," Raphael added. "You don't have to worry about him. You have drawn the attention of the Creator, and he has made sure Lucifer is kept under tight reigns. He has been bound to the Underworld, with no portal to escape. And now that Lucian is gone, there will be no more senseless killings of Nephilim. You have fulfilled the prophecy."

"But the cost was great," I sobbed.

"There has always been death and mourning, and it will continue until the end of time. Those who have passed are no longer in pain. It's the ones who remain who suffer the most. But we must remember to celebrate their life, and not mourn their death."

"It's so hard."

"But don't you see, Emma? You haven't even transformed yet and you've already fulfilled the prophecy. Lucifer is gone, the war has ended, and all Nephilim will be free," Arella added.

"It's been a rough road, but we know you will make it. Look how far you've come. And we will all be watching over you," Raphael added.

"Thank you," I said, appreciatively.

"I have to leave on a mission, but my dear Emma, it was an honor to finally meet you. I hope it won't be the last time we see you," Raphael said, taking my hands in his. "And, don't fret my child. Have faith."

I nodded not seeing how faith would help.

Arella wrapped her arms around me one last time and kissed my forehead.

"Goodbye, Emma. If you ever come to Grandia, please come and visit us."

"I will," I smiled. "Thank you again. It was such an honor to meet you."

"The honor was ours," Raphael said with a nod, then grasped hold of his wife's hand.

They both turned and acknowledged Michael before they walked back into my closet. With a flash of bright light, they were gone.

Michael stepped forward, holding his arms out to me again.

"I'm so proud of you," he said as I walked into his embrace.

"Michael, grandfather, which should I call you?"

"Whatever you are comfortable with. I realize I've just appeared into your life and I won't be offended."

I smiled. "Could I ask you a question?"

"Of course," he said, with a glint in his eye.

"I thought all angels who mated with mortals were executed?"

A wide smile grew on his face. "Yes. It was a rule, but only if caught in the act."

"But then, why was Lucifer's brother killed if he wasn't caught?"

"Because some of the rules in the Underworld were altered after the Fall. Though they kept most of the rules, the ones which would be punishable by the Creator, the others were mildly amended. Lucian made his own rules. He wanted to overthrow Lucifer, and accusing him was his way of attempting that feat. Lucifer blamed his brother because it was the only way to turn Lucian's wrath away from him."

"So, you're not going to be executed?"

Michael roared with laughter. "No, dear child. I most definitely will not be executed."

"That's good," I exhaled. "You haven't met Alaine yet, have you?"

"No," he said. "And right now is not the time. I came because of you needed me most. But one day soon our paths will cross, and I will finally meet my daughter."

"Should I tell her I met you?"

"Let's keep it secret for now."

"She will just *die*. You're even more amazing than I ever could have imagined," I said. "Michael the Archangel is *my* grandfather."

Michael laughed. "The feeling is mutual. Such greatness in such a small package."

"It's in the blood," I acknowledged.

"Yes, I guess it is," he smiled. "If you like, I could send someone to help you through your transformation."

"No. I think I'll be alright."

He nodded with a proud smile. "If you change your mind, just speak the words. I have someone who is highly skilled to aid in the transition and will help you cope afterward."

"Okay. I'll consider it," I said. Maybe having someone with me who knew what to expect would be good for me.

"Good," he said, hugging me again. "I must leave, but you have a lot of people surrounding you who love you unconditionally. So don't fail to ask if you ever need help."

"I won't," I said. "Thank you for coming. You've helped me more than you know."

"I knew it was time. I'm glad you called out," he said, leaning over and kissing the top of my forehead. "Goodbye, Emma."

"Goodbye, Grandfather."

He turned and winked at me before stepping through the doorway and disappearing into a burst of light.

I fell backward onto my bed.

"Oh my God," I said out loud. I couldn't believe everything that had just happened. It was all like a dream. I never, in my wildest dreams, thought I would meet Kade's parents. They were the most amazing, caring beings I had ever met. They understood his motives and accepted his actions. I guess that's how they could cope with his passing so easily.

Being touched by all of them eased some of the pain.

I took in another deep breath, taking in their sweet scents before they faded away.

In a few hours, I would be transforming into who knows what. I would become immortal, but didn't know what gifts I would be given. Would I have invisibility, or something else?

The ache in my heart was a reminder that as an immortal, I would be spending the rest of eternity alone.

I still had the choice to become mortal. All I needed to do was go and see Ephraim. I guess I would have to see how it worked out. Even with the sleeper, I was still exhausted, and Raphael's healing touch made my body relax.

My eyelids were heavy, so I closed them and tried to rest.

EIGHTEEN

TWO HOURS BEFORE
TRANSFORMATION

THERE WAS A KNOCK AT the door, and Alaine entered with a tray of food and handed it to me.

"You need to eat," she said. "You'll need your strength."

My stomach growled as soon as the aroma hit my nose.

"Thank you," I said, lifting the cover. It was a bowl of steaming beef stew, and a hot buttered roll. I immediately took it to the bed and started eating. The meat was tender, like biting into soft butter.

"Will it be alright if Thomas and Dom come to see you?" she asked. "They've been very worried."

I nodded. "Sure. How's Alex doing?"

"He's stable. We will have to wait another day or two to be sure he's out of danger, but he's holding on. Luckily, Lucian missed his heart, but the immortal blade did a lot of damage."

I nodded sadly.

"I'll let the others know they can come up in a bit. You finish your dinner." She gave me a small smile and closed the door on her way out.

I was happy I would get to see them, but knew my heart would be battered again, not seeing James or Malachi.

I fought the tears. "No. Not now." I quickly focused back on my meal, trying to block everything else out, but it took a lot out of me.

When I finally finished and set the tray aside, there was another knock.

"Come in," I said, standing, waiting for them to enter.

I tried to paint on a smile, but as soon as Dom walked through the door, and I saw the look of pain in his eyes, I lost it.

"Emma," he said, holding his arms open to me. I ran to him and hugged him tightly.

"I'm sorry, Dom. I know how much you loved them," I sobbed.

"Yeah, I miss that big ol' grumpy brute," he said, trying to make light of it, but the look in his eyes said how much he truly hurt. "And Kade," he continued, placing his hands on my shoulders, tears filling his eyes. "Kade was my best friend. He taught me that there is so much more to life than simply existing. That if we take time to look at all of the beautiful things around us, it is easy to see how much we really have to live for.

"I know what it's like to lose someone whose heart has been connected to yours. It feels like your heart has been ripped out, bashed, and stabbed repeatedly, with no hope of the pain ever stopping. It kills your will to live. But you can and *will* live, just by waking up each morning, breathing, and making it through the day. Every single day will be hard, like taking your first steps, but as you keep at it, it will start to get a little easier. Then one day, you will realize you are running on your own." He looked into my eyes with sincerity. "You will live again, Emma."

"How could I not with all of you surrounding me?"

"I know we'll be heading back to Midway soon, but if you ever need me, I will drop whatever it is I'm doing and come. You just say the words. Kade made me promise to watch over you if anything ever happened to him, and I *will* keep my word. No assignment will ever be too important. Understand?"

"I do. Thank you," I said, wrapping my arms around him and kissing him on the cheek. "Thank you so much."

Thomas stood to the side, his hands folded in front of him. "The same goes for me. Kade was my friend and brother, and I will always be here for you should you need me."

"Thank you, Thomas," I said, hugging him.

He awkwardly hugged me back, like he didn't want to break me. Then he added, "But I doubt you'll need us. After you transform you'll probably be more kickass than both of us put together."

"Yeah, so I might be calling you instead," Dom added. "But we'll keep that between us. We wouldn't want rumors to leak about me needing help from a chick. I have a reputation to uphold."

"Deal," I said, giggling.

I glanced behind them and saw a faint smile on Alaine's face. I nodded to her and she nodded back.

"Well, I don't think any of us will be getting any sleep tonight knowing it's your transformation. I think we will all be like proud parents, waiting and anticipating the birth, or in your case... rebirth," Dom said.

"Well, hopefully I'll still be alive to show and tell you all about it in the morning."

"Someone better put the sleeper on me tonight. I'm not kidding. I still have a lot of healing to do," Dom said, rolling his eyes.

"I'll tuck you in," Thomas said.

"Fine, but don't you dare try to fondle me."

"Dude, you're disgusting."

"So I've been told," he said raising his brow. "And Emma, when you get up, come and wake me up. I'll be in the room next to yours. Thomas will be across the hall."

"I will. I promise."

"Good luck, princess," Dom said.

"Thanks." I smiled.

"Bye, Emma. See you in the morning," Thomas added.

I hugged them both once more, and they left.

Alaine stayed a bit longer and gathered my tray.

Before she left she turned back to me. "Remember, if you need us—"

"I promise to call."

She smiled. "I love you, sweetheart."

"I love you too," I answered. Her smile grew, then she turned and walked out.

ONE HOUR BEFORE TRANSFORMATION

I'd just come out of a shower, where I stood under the stream of water for almost a half hour. The uncertainty and unanswered questions of the transformation consumed me. My heart rate elevated, and my stomach was twisting.

My mind began to spin, rewinding to all of the horrific images of death which had been hardwired into my mind, and I couldn't stop it. It was making me relive the deaths of Ethon and Kade, over and over again, and it was making me sick.

I then realized being alone wasn't working out like I'd planned. At least, not while I was still so weak. I needed help. I was scared and didn't really want to be alone. If there was someone to help me through it, maybe my mind wouldn't constantly be focused on the negative.

I remembered Arella and Raphael's words to me... to celebrate life instead of mourning death.

All of my good and positive memories were stored in my photo album, and the only reason they were here was because Kade went all the way back to L.A. to collect them. He knew having them would help me through the hard times.

I reached under the foot of the bed and pulled it out. The last person to touch it was Kade. I held it to my heart, not sure if I was strong enough to open it.

Laying the album down in front of me, I slowly flipped the cover.

There on the first page were my parent's smiling faces beaming back at me. God I missed them so much. I closed my eyes and tried to revisit them in our old house. But as soon as I did, the negative would jump right in, and take me to the accident and the hospital. I hated I had to fight against my own mind.

The next few pages were of me, Lia, and Jeremy. Random shots of our school years together. I smiled at their wide smiles, wild poses, and goofy faces.

As I flipped to the next page, I couldn't breathe.

It was filled with pictures of me and Kade. Lia had taken them while she was here. How did she develop them? And when did she find the time to put them into my book without me knowing? I didn't remember Lia taking half of these pictures... my own little paparazzi.

It was as if he were still alive, his beautiful face radiated so much joy as he held me in his arms.

My eyes landed on one particular photo. It was the night of the masquerade ball, and we were the only two on the dance floor. He looked so unbelievably handsome; his hazel eyes were fixed on mine. We looked so happy, so perfect, so in love. That picture defined who we were.

I traced the outline of his face, and my insides ached with a mixture of happiness and extreme sadness. Tears dropped down onto the pages, so I closed it and pushed it back under the bed.

I was a mess, and could feel myself slowly start to crumble. There were forty more minutes until my transformation, and I wrestled with the decision of having someone with me.

Thirty minutes remained, and I finally agreed I was going to do this alone. I clicked on my lamp, turned off the overhead light, and crawled into bed. Closing my eyes, I tried to slow my breathing. But as time grew closer I began to get more apprehensive, and found myself jittery and uneasy. Maybe I should have asked for help.

As I lay quiet and still, I was filled with a sudden charge of warmth and tingles flowing through me, causing a wave of dizziness, making my breath quicken. I sat up, addled and shaken.

An invisible force slammed me again, forcing me backward into my bed. I frantically struggled to sit back up, my arms weak, I felt like I'd just been struck with a lightning bolt. I was disoriented, gasping for air. I felt as if I had been shot up with adrenaline; my pulse quickened, my insides were tingling, and I became dizzy. I closed my eyes and took in long deep breaths.

What the hell?

When I opened my eyes, a brilliant white light illuminated from the closet.

Michael must have sent someone to help.

As the door swung open, my eyes were blinded by the brilliance of the purest light. I could feel the frantic beating of my heart coursing through my veins. The room filled with warmth, and electricity buzzed heavily in the air. I struggled to focus, but had to shield my eyes.

As I lowered my hand and narrowed my eyes, the figure stepped forward.

My eyes began to water, my heart palpitated, and a cold sweat overcame me. My fingers gripped the edge of the bed, my body trembling uncontrollably.

A familiar sweet scent filled the room, enveloping me. I suddenly felt like I was being ripped from the depths of darkness and the pieces of my heart slowly began to mend as the most mesmerizing eyes fastened upon mine.

As the light diminished, the figure came into focus.

My breath seized, my heart stopped, and I was frozen.

It was as if I were looking at a ghost.

He smiled and slowly raised his arms, opening them up to me.

"Kade?" My voice was quivering and unsure.

He nodded and stepped forward. My insides reacted like they were entrapped and being lured toward him. His smile was enchanting, captivating every part of me.

"How? I watched you die?"

"The Creator brought me back to life. He told me my time wasn't over; that I needed to come back to you."

I couldn't speak. Tears erupted from my eyes, and emotions overwhelmed me.

"Come to me, Emma," he spoke softly.

I didn't hesitate. I leapt from the bed, directly into his arms. As soon as he caught me, I was zapped. A million tingles surged through my body.

"It is you," I cried. "It's really you. You're alive. You've come back to me," I sobbed and clutched tightly to his frame.

I felt his warm breath on my neck as he hugged me. "I'm here now, and will always be."

He pulled back a little, causing me to look at him. With no hesitation, he leaned over and kissed me. Words could not describe the sensation as soon as our lips touched. It was magical, and took me to a place we had never been before. It felt like love was being wrapped around us, intertwining us, and binding our hearts together.

He pulled back and grinned.

"What's happening?" I gasped, breathless.

"Don't you know by now?"

I shook my head, unsure. "The bond?"

He smiled and nodded.

"But I thought—"

"When the creator resurrected me, he told me he had been watching. He said he knew about my decision to change from immortal to mortal. Because I was willing to risk everything, including my immortality, along with the fact my father and your grandfather are his Archangels — he made me immortal."

"Oh, Kade," I wailed, throwing my arms around him.

"I promised you, if it was within my power, I would be here for your transformation," he whispered.

"I didn't want to share it with anyone but you," I wept. "It was you. It was *always* you."

His lips turned up and his face beamed. He then turned to the clock. "You still have a few more minutes. I'd like to show you something before your transformation begins."

"Alright," I said, shaking with excitement.

"Step back a bit."

I took a few steps back and paused.

He grinned at me.

"What?" I smiled.

He held his arms out to his sides, and then in the still silence, two of the most beautiful wings magically appeared behind him. Layer upon layer of flawless white feathers looked as soft as silk, and shimmered in the dim light of my lamp. I was completely spellbound by him in all of his glory.

An ethereal golden glow encircled him. This is who he truly was. Who I'd always envisioned him to be. He had been reborn and was now complete.

"Emma?" he spoke softly.

Uncontrollable tears filled my eyes, and there were only two words I could manage to push out.

"You're beautiful."

Kade's eyes were filled with so much love, compassion, and tenderness.

"It's time," he said.

His wings folded around me, encasing me in a cocoon of white. His protective arms held me tight.

As soon as he did, I felt like I was bashed in the chest. My body went limp, but Kade held me tight. Intense pain began to rain down on me, igniting the top of my head. Inch by inch the pain blazed, slowly torching everything on its way down. As much as I tried to relax, I couldn't; my body was rigid, tensed and trying to cope with the pain.

"Kade," I moaned. "It burns."

"I'm here. We'll get through this together."

An unexpected gentle breeze brushed against my face, cooling me and taking some of the pain away. It was Kade, blowing his magic on me.

When the fire hit my chest it settled, and then a force slammed me again, jolting my body backward. It felt like something was punching a hole straight through my heart. I moaned, and Kade's arms tightened around me.

"I'm here, Emma," he whispered, trying to comfort me.

The fire raged on, consuming me, incinerating what was left of my mortality. As it passed below my chest, I began to bear the pain a bit, but it depleted nearly all my energy. I kept my breathing steady as it continued down my legs, thighs, calves, and exited out my toes.

When the pain finally subsided, I slowly opened my eyes.

I was face to face, inches away, from the most beautiful angel I'd ever seen.

He was perfect, and he was alive. This wasn't a dream.

I thought I'd lost him forever, but here he was, holding me, covering me, and protecting me, like he had from the very beginning. I could feel his unconditional love. He was my soul mate. My one true love. My bonded.

His hazel eyes, swirling with gold, were narrowed with concern and distress.

"Is it over?"

"No. It's just beginning," I whispered.

His brow furrowed.

"My life... with you," I explained, giving him a weak smile.

His eyes softened, and then he leaned forward and kissed me. As soon as his lips touched mine, something inside of me awakened. At first it was a small tingling sensation, but as his kiss deepened, the feeling intensified. It was as if refreshing cold water was pouring over me, washing away my internal blaze.

His kiss was healing me, from the inside out.

When I could breathe easy, I slowly pulled back.

Kade's eyes carefully studied mine. "Are you okay?"

"I am now," I answered, breathless.

"Can I ask you something?" he said, kissing my forehead.

"Of course."

He placed his hands on my shoulders and stepped backward. He then folded his beautiful wings behind his back and knelt down on one knee.

"Kade?" I was trembling, my knees weak.

He took hold of both of my hands and looked into my eyes with sincerity. His touch immediately strengthened me.

"We've both been reborn, transformed from one life and one being, into something much greater. I once made a decision which nearly took you away from me. It will never happen again.

"Emma, I want to spend the rest of eternity with you. I want to wake up every day and see your beautiful smile, feel your touch, and wrap you in my arms whenever you need strength. I want to be your protector for the rest of *our* immortal lives."

His face was blurred from the flood of tears in my eyes. My stomach twisted with a million butterflies, and my knees became weak.

He kissed my hands. "Emma Wise, will you marry me?"

It felt as if the floor disappeared from beneath me. I collapsed and fell into his arms.

"Oh, Kade," I wept, throwing my arms around him, kissing him.

"Was that a yes?" he chuckled against my lips.

"Yes. Yes. A million times, yes!" I exclaimed. Then, for the first time, I saw his mark. It was simple; a spiral with six triangles around it. It reminded me of a sun. A perfect symbol for Kade and who he was to me – my light in the darkness. Since the day we met, his presence brightened and filled me with such warmth and hope.

I kissed his mark and then wrapped my arms around him. As my fingers grazed up his back I gasped.

"Kade?" I exhaled.

"They're gone," he answered. "I guess a new body came with the transformation. No more scars."

I leaned back, laughing and crying at the same time. "I still can't believe all of this is happening. I – I can't believe you're here, and we're going to be married."

"I still have to ask Samuel. I know it's a mortal tradition, but Alaine is half-mortal, so I don't want to offend."

"They don't even know you're alive." I said, wondering what they would think when they saw him, raised from the dead.

"No, they don't," he grinned. "And I can't wait to see the looks on all their faces, especially Malachi and Dom."

My face suddenly dropped, and my heart began to ache.

"Emma? What is it? Are you unwell?"

I shook my head, fighting my emotions.

"You don't remember?"

"Remember what?" he asked, his brow furrowed.

"I'm so sorry, Kade. Malachi and James are gone, and Alex is barely holding on to life as we speak."

"What?" His face turned sorrowful, filled with grief.

I nodded, hating to dampen his spirit, but he needed to know.

He closed his eyes for a long time, and when he opened them again, his face brightened.

"They will be missed, but their memories will live on forever."

"They will never be forgotten. Not in our lifetime," I said.

"Yes," he breathed. "Now, you need to rest. Your gifts will be revealed once you've healed from the transformation. You'll be much stronger when you wake in the morning."

"I'm afraid to close my eyes."

"Why?" he questioned

"Because if this is a dream, I don't want it to end."

His fingers softly grazed the side of my cheek. "This is not a dream. I promise to be here when you wake."

"Will you stay with me?"

"Forever," he smiled as he swept me off my feet. Up into his strong arms he carried me to bed. Once I was situated under the covers, he crawled in next to me. We held onto each other tight, and it felt so natural and so unbelievably magical to be in his arms again.

I yawned, starting to feel the effects of the transformation weighing heavy on me.

"Want me to put the sleeper on you?" he asked.

"You can do that?"

"Of course I can. Whatever I did before, I can do now... only much better." He winked, and my heart melted.

"Assure me you're real," I whispered.

"I'm real alright. And once you heal, I'll show you exactly how real I am."

My insides twisted. "I can't wait to be married to you, Mr. Anders. Wait, is Anders your real last name?"

"No," he chuckled. "Angels don't have last names. We are just given titles. Like Archangel or Cherubim or—"

"Aren't Cherubim those cute little angels?" I asked.

His brow raised. "There is no such thing as a cute, little Cherubim. They are actually very offended how the mortal world has painted them to be as such. Cherubim are large, strong, and powerful beings. They are skilled warriors who surround the Creator, and are highly trained to defend him from any contaminations of sin."

"Wow," I exhaled. "I guess I still have a lot of learning to do."

"You have a lifetime, and I will gladly be your instructor. If you're good, I may even give you some hands-on training," he said, wiggling his brow.

"I can't wait to start, professor." I giggled, then automatically yawned. I could feel my body quickly draining of energy.

"You need to rest," he said.

I nodded, knowing as much as I wanted to stay awake and talk to him all night, the healing wouldn't allow it. My eyes were already getting heavy and my body was weakening.

"Don't leave me, okay?"

"Never again," he whispered.

"Thank you," I breathed, closing my eyes.

"Goodnight, my Emma. *Sleep* sweet."

"Goodnight," I whispered, fading into a deep, restful sleep.

NINETEEN

I OPENED MY EYES, AND noticed the bed next to me was
empty... fear flooded me, my limbs tensing.

"Kade?" I whispered to myself.

The door to the bathroom opened, and he stepped out.

"Don't worry, I'm still here," he said with a grin. He'd taken
a shower, and I had no idea why he thought he needed one.
Steam escaped around him, and the only thing he was wearing
was a towel wrapped around his waist. Lucky towel.

My face burned with embarrassment as he caught me
gawking at his perfect body. I couldn't help it. He was magnificent,
as if God had chiseled him himself. A flawless masterpiece... and
he was mine.

His hair was towel dried and disheveled; his body was
glistening and damp.

"I thought—"

"I promised I'd never leave you."

"I know, but I still can't believe it. I almost had a mini heart attack wondering if it was all just a dream."

"I'm sorry," he said, coming closer. As he did, I could feel my insides twisting.

"How are you feeling?" he asked.

I stretched. "Much better."

"Rested?"

"Mostly. I still feel a little tired."

"Give it another day, and you'll be showing off your new self."

I smiled. "I wonder what new gift I'll have? How will I know?"

"You'll figure it out, and whatever it is, it will be amazing. I'm sure of it."

"How can you be so sure?" I asked, raising my brow.

"Even without any gift, you're already amazing. The gift is just a bonus."

I shook my head. "You are the one who is amazing."

He smiled and held out his hand to me. "You should get ready. The others will be waking soon, and coming by to check up on you."

"You're right," I said. "They were really worried about me last night."

As soon as I grabbed his hand, an electrical current shot through me, sending me falling forward into his strong arms.

"I don't know if I'll ever get used to that," I said nearly breathless.

"You will once you've healed," he said with a sexy crooked grin.

I looked up into his mesmerizing eyes and became lost.

"Emma?" he said softly.

I shook my head. "How did I get so lucky?" Emotions began to bubble. "God *must* love me... enough to have given me my heart's desire."

"Yes, he does." He leaned over and kissed me.

"One day I will thank him," I said, hugging him. "And thank you for helping me through it all last night."

"It was my pleasure."

I inhaled deeply as a thought crossed my mind.

"Do your parents know about you? Do they know you're alive?"

His smile widened. "Yes, they do... and they told me they met you."

"And?" I questioned, wondering what they thought of me.

"They absolutely loved you," he answered.

"Are you sure?"

"Positive. I also told them I was going to ask you to marry me."

"What did they say?"

"That they were proud you were going to be part of our family, and they can't wait for us to visit them in Grandia."

"I'd love that." I smiled and took his hand. "Did they tell you I met my grandfather?"

His eyes softened. "Yes, they did. *And?*" he asked, his lips rising into a half smile.

"He was even greater than I expected, but I bet you already knew that," I answered.

"Your grandfather and my father have been very close friends and allies for centuries. They've worked very closely together."

"Which is the reason why I met you," I said.

"Yes. But I didn't know he was the one who had given the order to appoint me as your Guardian. Ephraim is the one who gave me the orders while I was at Midway. I swear... I didn't even know Michael was your grandfather until recently."

A door slammed shut outside, reminding me about the others.

"I better get ready," I said, grabbing my clothes and running for the bathroom. "Hey, where are your clothes?" I noticed the bathroom was clean.

He grasped the edge of the towel, and ripped it away.

I gasped and then realized he was wearing shorts, so I quickly snapped my mouth shut.

"Tease."

He laughed. "You should have seen the look on your face."

"Well, I was expecting a different outcome," I said, as heat rushed to my face.

"Maybe next time," he winked.

"Maybe," I giggled, and shut the bathroom door. I pressed my back against it and took in a deep breath, still trying to wrap my head around the fact that Kade was back. He was back and so was the bond... stronger than ever.

I quickly showered and brushed my teeth, then dressed in jeans, and a long-sleeved, plain white T-shirt. I wiped the steam from the mirror and looked at myself. I didn't see anything different. I looked like the same girl.

As soon as I exited, Kade was sitting on the bed, staring at me.

"What?" I asked; a smile was glued to my face.

"You're stunning."

"Thanks," I breathed, as a soft knock interrupted us.

"It's probably Alaine," I whispered. "Maybe you should hide in the bathroom until I can explain."

"How are you going to explain?"

"I have no idea," I said, my heart was thumping wildly.

He chuckled and made his way to hide.

"Wait," I said, making him pause. "Don't disappear into any portal, okay?"

"I promise," he said, holding his hands up.

There was another knock.

"I'm coming," I called, walking calmly for the door. When I opened it, Alaine was standing there, with a worried look on her face.

"How are you feeling?" she asked.

"I'm actually doing great; better than great," I said, smiling widely.

Her brow furrowed with confusion.

"No, really. There's something I want to show you, but I'd like you to get the others and bring them here first."

She leaned forward and hugged me, looking completely baffled. "Alright, I'll be right back."

When she left, I shut the door, and Kade peeked his head out.

"Oh my God, they are going to *freak* when they find out. Alaine's face was twisted when she saw me smiling. Imagine what will happen when they see you *alive*."

There was another knock on the door.

"That was fast," I mouthed to him. He quickly ducked back in the bathroom and closed the door.

I opened the door, and was elated to see Samuel, Dominic, and Thomas with Alaine.

"Come in," I said, stepping to the side.

"You look good, and happy," Dom noted, hugging me. His face just as baffled as Alaine's.

"Well, today I just... woke up happy," I said, feeling a bit awkward.

"Well, that's wonderful, sweetheart," Samuel said, wrapping me in a hug and kissing the top of my head.

They all came in and stood around, bewildered, waiting for me to give an answer as to why I called them in.

"How's Alex?" I asked Alaine.

"He's alive, but still very weak. It will take him about another week to recover. We've kept him in the sleeper so he can rest and heal without pain."

"That's good to know. When he gets better, I'd like to go visit him."

"Of course," she said.

I stood nervously in front of them. "Well, why don't you all have a seat? There is something I'd like to show you, and I don't know if you should be standing."

"Don't tell me you can shoot fireballs from yer eyes, or bolts of lightnin' from yer ass," Dom blurted in an awful Scottish accent.

I rolled my eyes. "Have you been watching *Braveheart*?"

"I fell asleep to it last night," he shrugged.

"Well, no. I can't do that... I think. But what I have to show you is something even *greater* than that." My smile widened even more. My heart began to race, anticipating their reactions.

"Are you going to show us, or are you going to make us beat it out of you?" Dom exhaled, rolling his eyes.

"If you lay a hand on her, I'll have to break your arm," Kade said, stepping into the room.

All four heads snapped in the direction of his voice, faces frozen, trying to analyze what the hell they were seeing.

"What the—" Dom exclaimed, his face completely tweaked.

"Kade?" Alaine exhaled. She grasped Samuel's arm like she was about to collapse. Her eyes were wide with either terror or shock, probably both.

"Hey guys," Kade said smiling and waving gingerly.

"What the? How the?" Dom stuttered. "Holy shit."

"Are you real?" Thomas questioned.

"Dude, look at me. Of course I'm real," Kade answered.

"But... how?" Alaine asked.

I walked over to Kade and held his hand. "The Creator did have his eye on us. He saw Kade's selfless act of giving up his mortality, and then his mortal life for me. So, he decided to resurrect him," I answered proudly. "He came to me last night, right before my transformation. He helped me through it."

"Oh my," Alaine breathed, running over to him and hugging him. She stepped back and looked at him again in disbelief. "I can't believe it."

"It's good to be back," he said.

Samuel walked up to him and held out his hand. Kade shook it, then Samuel pulled him into a hug. "It's great to have you back."

Thomas and Dom were next to hug him.

"Sooo...," Dom drawled. "Are you still mortal or what?"

Kade and I looked at each other and grinned.

"Show them," I urged.

He shook his head.

"Why not?" I really wanted them to see him in all of his glory.

"Dude!" Thomas interjected. "Just spill."

A smirk crossed Kade's face. "Alright, you asked for it."

I stepped away, while he took his shirt off.

"Yeah, there he goes, showing off his six pack," Dom teased.

He smiled then spread his arms out, and glorious white wings extended out to his sides.

"Holy shit," Dom cursed. "You freaking got your wings?"

"How?" Thomas asked.

"Does it matter?" I said. "He totally deserves them. He *earned* his wings."

"Yeah, I guess after all the crap he was put through... he does deserve them," Dom agreed.

"Kade, they are beautiful," Alaine said. Her hands were clasped over her mouth.

"You got wings, so that means you're immortal, right?" Thomas asked.

"Yep," Kade said proudly, tucking his wings back behind him.

"Congratulations, Kade," Samuel said. "They're stunning."

"Thank you, Samuel," he nodded.

"No wonder Emma had the biggest, goofiest smile on her face," Dom laughed.

"Hey!" I huffed.

"We all thought we were going to walk in and see the walking dead. We didn't expect you to be so... chipper. But I don't blame you. I'm just sayin', now I understand why," he explained.

"Yeah," I said looking at Kade. "I thought I was looking at a ghost. It took me a while to believe he was real."

"Sooo, was there any bond sealing?" Dom asked, eyebrows raised.

"Dom!" I snapped.

"It's a reasonable question."

"No, we didn't," Kade replied. "But I'd like to speak to Samuel and Alaine for a moment before they leave, if that's alright," Kade asked.

"Sure," Samuel answered, and Alaine agreed.

"Man, it's so unbelievably freaking amazing to see you," Dom said, throwing his arms around Kade. "You don't know how happy your handsome face makes me. I almost cried, dude. Like seriously. I was on the verge. Thomas had to put the freaking sleeper on me 'cause I was so freaking distraught."

"I love you too, man," Kade laughed, hugging him back.

Dom stepped to me next, and hugged me. "We can't ever have a thing now."

"*We* were never going to happen," I laughed.

"I know. But now that Kade's back, we never will. I'm sorry, Emma. Do you need a moment to mourn?"

"Man, get the hell out of here," Kade laughed, pushing him away.

"I can't compete with wings, man," Dom grinned. "Those things are sexy as hell."

"Dom," Alaine sighed. "Why don't you and Thomas go whip up some breakfast."

"Sure. I'll be the manservant until Miss Lily returns. I'm fine with that," Dom said as he made his way out. Before he completely disappeared he stuck his head back in. "By the way... breakfast will be ready in an hour." He spoke with an English accent.

"He is something else," Alaine said.

"He helps make life bearable," I noted.

"He makes life complicated," Thomas added. "Which is why I should get down there before he makes a mess."

Thomas hugged Kade. "Good to have you back."

"Thanks, Thomas," Kade said.

He hugged me next and then walked out.

I walked over and shut the door while Kade stood in front of Samuel and Alaine.

"Last night, when I came back, I realized how much I needed Emma. I know the bond is a huge part of it, but, I just... I don't know how else to explain it. It's—"

Samuel chuckled. "Son, you don't have to explain a thing. I know how the bond works, and I know exactly what you're feeling." He turned to Alaine and they shared that special look. She stepped to him and he put his arm over her. "We know firsthand what you two are experiencing."

Kade exhaled and his face washed with relief. "Thank you. But what I really wanted to ask is..." he looked at me and I could tell he was nervous. I smiled and nodded at him.

He exhaled then turned back to them. "Samuel, Alaine... could I have permission to marry your daughter?"

Samuel paused, then with a wide smile, stepped forward to Kade. "Of course you both have my blessing. As a father, I can honestly say she will be in the best hands. You've proven yourself to all of us, and showed you will love and protect her. She is truly blessed. You both are."

"Thank you," Kade said, hugging him.

Alaine's eyes instantly filled with tears. "I always dreamed of this day, but I guess I was never prepared, especially since I've only had my daughter back for a year, actually less than a year, but you know what I'm trying to say. As far as I am concerned, the answer is yes. I knew from the moment you brought her here, you were meant to be together. I saw it on your faces. She needs you, and you need her. You complete each other."

She moved to stand in front of him. "I'm so proud of you, and what you've done to protect our daughter. She couldn't find a better person. And I know you didn't have to ask, but thank you for considering us."

"I wouldn't have it any other way. Thank you, Alaine," Kade said, hugging her.

"Oh, Emma," she said, hugging me next. "I'm so excited for you. Samuel and I will be here for you both, and will help in any way we can. I never had a wedding, so this will be the greatest party I will ever plan.

"You never had a wedding?" I asked.

"No, we never really talked about it, and before we even had a chance to, Samuel was taken from me."

"Why don't we have a joint wedding?" I exclaimed. "It will be fun, and we can plan it together."

"No, no, no. This will be your day. Samuel and I will have a small, simple wedding. Just the way we like it."

"Are you sure?"

"I am very sure. My greatest joy will be to help plan your day. It will be spectacular, and I can't wait to start planning."

"Oh, now you've got her started," Samuel laughed.

"Well, it's not every day our only daughter will be getting married," she replied. "Besides, I am looking forward to watching Samuel walk you down the aisle."

I hugged her tightly. "Thank you so much."

"So, how long do I have to plan? Have you both set a date?" she asked.

"I was thinking in about a month," Kade said.

"A month?" I gasped, and Kade smiled.

"A month?" Alaine said under her breath. "That's not much time."

"Alaine, they are dealing with the bond. They don't need to have a wedding. They are only doing it as an outward celebration."

"Alright, a month it is. We can work with a month and it will be fabulous."

"You've awakened the inner wedding planner," Samuel chuckled.

"Good!" I smiled. "Okay, I'm starving. I need sustenance."

"Then let's go," Alaine said. "Have you had any indication of what your gift might be?"

"Not yet. I think I'm still too weak."

"Just give it another day or two," she said, and I nodded.

"Alright, let's go check on breakfast." Alaine took hold of Samuel's hand. "See you soon," she said, as they walked out of the room.

I turned to Kade. "A month? That's not much time."

"If it were up to me, we'd be married tomorrow," he said, pulling me into his arms. "I can barely be away from you right now. One month will practically kill me."

"Well," I said rubbing my hand across his chest. "It will be worth the wait."

"It will be," he said, kissing me quickly.

"Now let's go eat."

I took his arm and he led me down to breakfast.

TWENTY

A FTER BREAKFAST, I WENT BACK to my room and took a nap. I was still healing and my limbs were still very weak.

When I finally woke in my room, the sun had already gone to sleep. I checked the clock on my nightstand, and it said 9:09 pm. I'd totally slept the day away, but I did feel rested.

Kade told me earlier he was going to Dominic's room to play some cards, and as I listened, I could hear them laughing. I smiled inside, so glad he was still in my life.

Pulling the blanket off, I stood from the bed and stretched my body.

Wow. I actually felt great, like there was no more pain and my tired achy muscles were now strong.

I grabbed some clothes, jeans and a T-shirt, and headed to the bathroom. When I clicked on the light, I paused, staring at my reflection. *What the heck?* There were no dark bags, and my skin was luminous... like I'd put on some kind of shimmery make-up.

I stepped closer to the mirror and examined my eyes. Within the chocolate brown were swirls of gold. I pulled my lids open to make sure. Dropping my hands, I almost freaked out. "Holy crap," I breathed out loud. My healing must have been complete, which also meant my transformation must have been too.

My insides started to somersault with anticipation, wondering what my new gift would be. I had a feeling it might be invisibility, so I thought I would start with that. You know, process of elimination.

I stood in front of the mirror, sucking in a very deep breath. This time I would keep my eyes open so I could bear witness, and see for myself if invisibility was or wasn't one of my gifts. With apprehension, I willed invisibility, just like I had when wearing the suit.

A tingling started at the top of my head and I gasped, immediately watching my reflection flicker in the mirror, then completely vanish.

I knew it! I knew I would have invisibility!

Then as I did before, I willed visibility and watched my reflection reappear. I squealed quietly, and had a little dance party all to myself.

I wondered if I should go invisible, sneak up on the guys, then reappear right in the middle of them.

No, I better not. An instant flash of Dom, Thomas, or even Kade, smacking me with their instinctual Guardian reflexes would not make it fun. The last thing I needed was a superhuman karate chop to the face. It was a cool thought though, and would have been hilarious if they weren't warriors.

I was thrilled to have the same gift as Alaine, but was aware I didn't feel drained or tired at all. I actually felt strong and... powerful.

I raised my arms and flexed them in the mirror. Sadly there was no change; just the same thin un-muscular arms. I guess that's what was expected for someone who never worked out. I sighed and thought of Kade, and how he was given his wings. How unbelievable would it have been if I had wings?

Just for fun, I held my arms out to the sides and wished for wings, dreaming about what it would have been like to be able to fly whenever or wherever I wanted.

Pain tore through my chest and felt like it ripped straight through my back. I gasped, doubling over, grabbing hold of the sink to hold me up. *What the hell was that?*

As the pain subsided, I took in a deep breath and straightened up.

I screamed as I saw my reflection, then quickly covered my mouth. My breath seized, my heart stopped, and I froze.

Oh. My. God.

I was completely floored, trying to wrap my head around what I was witnessing.

Was it real?

It couldn't be. I couldn't have been given more than one gift, right?

But as much as I blinked, what I saw didn't go away.

Folded behind me, were two of the most glorious white wings I had ever seen. They were perfectly shaped and the purest white... completely flawless. Excitement bubbled inside of me, and began to spill over into a squeal. I took in a deep breath and tried to calm myself.

Still a little doubtful, I reached backward and brushed my fingers across the side. They were as soft as silk and ruffled under my touch, sending a tingle down my spine.

I couldn't believe it. How? How was I worthy of such magic?

I had wings.

I—had the most amazing, magnificent wings.

Hidden wings.

Overwhelmed with adoration, my eyes began to water. Then, I whispered quietly, hoping the Creator would hear my words. "Thank you."

I wiped the pooled tears from my eyes and leaned closer to examine them. They were shimmering: gilded with strands of gold which were intertwined within the delicate pure white feathers.

I stood up and exhaled. "Oh my God. No one is going to believe this."

I needed more room.

Overcome with excitement and disbelief I slowly backed out of the bathroom into my bedroom, so could still see myself in the mirror.

"Now, how do you work?" I whispered to my wings.

My wings softly fluttered behind me, shooting a rush of electricity through my veins.

None of the others had to speak to get their wings to work, so maybe it was just a thought process, like how it worked with invisibility.

Well, I was about to give it a try.

In my mind I willed my wings to spread out. As soon as the thought was released, I was almost thrown off balance as they unfolded spreading out to my sides.

"Holy smokes," I squealed quietly. I tried to settle myself, but this was too freaking exciting. I mean... who the heck gets wings for their eighteenth birthday?

And these things didn't come with an instruction manual. It was learn-as-you-go.

They were extended out so long, beyond the door frame, so I couldn't see them in their full glory. As I looked to the sides, I was dumbfounded and dazed at how perfectly symmetrical they were. Fully extended, they were approximately seven feet long on each side.

Laughter from the guys next door snapped me back into reality. I wondered what they would think when they saw *my* wings?

Then I had an amazing idea. I would keep my wings a secret and reveal them on the day of the wedding. That would be the shocker of the century, and I was totally in. But I also hated surprises and had the hardest time trying to keep them.

In the meantime, I would show them my invisibility, hoping my wings wouldn't magically pop out in the process. That would be shocking, but not the full reaction I wanted.

I wondered what it felt like to fly.

As soon as the word *fly* entered my mind, my wings gave a strong flap.

It happened so fast, I couldn't control it. The force of that single wing flap thrust me forward, slamming into the bathroom wall. I screamed as my body came to a crashing halt, then fell backward onto the floor.

I heard a door slam and I knew they must have heard.

"Disappear. Disappear. Disappear," I frantically repeated, willing my wings to vanish.

The door to my room suddenly opened and I heard Kade's distressed voice as he crossed the floor to the bathroom. "Emma? Emma, are you okay?"

He stood in the doorway, his brow furrowed with concern.

I glanced to my sides, and noticed my wings were gone, but one single feather lay right next to my hand. I quickly covered it, then burst into laughter. I couldn't help it, and I couldn't stop it. I laughed so hard my belly and face began to hurt.

Kade stood there, with a look of confusion on his face. Then Dom and Thomas peeked around him with similar looks.

"Did the transformation make her mad?" Dom asked.

"Is she alright?" Thomas whispered.

"I'm fine," I giggled. "There was a bit of water on the floor and I slipped. Being surefooted certainly wasn't my gift."

"Are you sure you're alright?" Kade asked, reaching his hand out to help me up. "I heard you scream, and thought something bad happened."

"Yes. I'm totally fine, and I'm sorry for scaring you."

I took his hand and immediately felt the familiar electrical current.

Kade grinned and pulled me up into a hug.

"I'm glad you're okay," he breathed.

"Hey, Emma. Did you discover your gift?" Dom asked.

I nodded, and while in Kade's arms, willed invisibility.

We instantly vanished.

"Damn. That is so freaking cool, but it's also kind of unnerving. I would never know if you were invisible... watching me... maybe even stalking," Dom said with a straight face.

I willed visibility and we reappeared.

"Don't worry, Dom. I'm not a creeper."

"Well, if you ever wanted to be... I guess I wouldn't mind. As long as I'm not in the bathroom."

"You're so gross," I laughed.

As I exited from Kade's embrace, Dom threw a playful punch at me. Without really knowing what was going on, my hand automatically grabbed hold of his arm, and launched him in the air over my head. He slammed into the ground with a thud.

I gasped and let go, stepping back, holding my hands up.

Kade and Thomas were frozen, staring at me with the widest eyes.

"Shiiiit," Thomas breathed.

"What the freaking hell?" Dom yelled, holding his side.

"Dom, I'm so sorry. I don't know what happened. I couldn't control myself. I'm so sorry," I stepped forward, begging for his forgiveness.

"Don't touch me," he warned, leaning away from me.

"Emma. It's alright," Kade said softly, walking over to me slowly and gently backing me away.

"It's not alright," Dom moaned. "Your chick just picked me up like a child and body slammed me. I'm surprised she didn't jump from her bed and finish me off with the People's Elbow!"

He looked up at me, his eyes were narrowed and I felt horrible. Then suddenly, his demeanor whiplashed.

"Holy crap, Emma. You freaking kicked my ass," he howled with laughter. "Oh my God. She's a beast!"

I didn't know what to say. I still felt horrible, but his outburst of laughter made me feel a little better – and a bit embarrassed.

"We seriously have to warn everyone not to make any sudden moves around her." Dom got up from the floor; groaning like an old man.

"She'll be fine. She just needs to learn how to control her new gifts," Kade said. Then he and Thomas began laughing beside me.

Dom stretched his back. "Damn... that's gonna leave a mark."

"I'm really, really sorry," I repeated.

"I'm fine. It'll heal in a day," Dom said, shaking his head. "You really are something."

"Yeah, she really is," Kade said, looking at me with appreciation. "Two gifts? Invisibility *and* super strength? Makes me wonder what else is in there," he said, throwing his arm around me.

"You know what's not in me? Food. I'm starving," I said, trying to change the subject.

"Sounds good to me. Let's go get the Warrior Princess some grub," Dom added, walking out the door.

"Ha-ha-ha," I said, not amused.

As we made our way downstairs, I saw the complete destruction of the home for the first time since the attack. My heart began to ache replaying the horrifying events which took place only a few days ago. So much death and destruction had happened in such a short time.

But over those past few days, Alaine had flown in a few highly skilled workers who she paid well to work round-the-clock. The windows had been reinstalled, the door was back in place, and they were hanging new sheets of drywall to cover the damages.

In the middle of the foyer was a huge heap of rubble, and I noticed pieces from the crystal chandelier and stained glass. As I glanced up at the large, clear plastic sheet spread across the hole in the ceiling, I wondered how in the world Alaine tried to explain the damages. Maybe she paid them not to ask questions. I certainly would.

There were about five men working on different sections of the room. None of them stopped to look at us. They tediously continued what they needed to.

As we made our way down toward the bottom of the stairs Kade wrapped his arm around my waist. "Be careful where you step," he warned.

I nodded, laying my head against his shoulder to keep my eyes from wandering to the places I'd last seen James and Malachi.

As we made our way through the rubble and into the kitchen, I was glad to see it hadn't received too much damage. The lights were already on, and I could hear voices in the dining area.

"Do you guys care what you eat?" Thomas asked.

"Nah," I answered. "I'm just really hungry."

"Alright, you two go ahead. Dom and I will fix something quick and bring it in."

"Are you sure?" I asked.

"Yes, he's sure. This is your time to share your gifts with your parents," Dom winked.

"Thanks, guys," Kade said.

"Yes, thank you," I repeated.

"Oh, and Emma," Dom called out.

"Yeah?"

"Please don't kick their asses. That would be a complete tragedy."

I rolled my eyes. "Don't worry, I won't. I'll even sit across the table from them."

"Good thinking," he said, giving me a thumbs up.

As Kade and I made our way into the dining area, Samuel and Alaine's faces lit up.

"Emma," Alaine said, standing to her feet. She stood and came towards us, but Kade stepped in between and held out his hand.

"It's okay," I said. "I won't hurt her."

Alaine stopped and looked at us puzzled.

"Kade was just protecting you," I said.

"From what?" she asked.

"From me," I breathed.

"I don't understand," she said, shaking her head.

"One of Emma's gifts is strength. Dom threw a fake punch at her, and she reacted without control. She grabbed his arm and tossed him over her head like he was a pillow."

"What?" Samuel asked. His face lit up.

"Yeah, and that's not the only gift she has," Kade explained.

I was relieved he was doing all the talking. It made it so much easier for me because I had no idea what I was going to say, or how I was going to explain it.

"What's your other gift?" Alaine asked.

Kade stepped to the side so she could see me fully. I smiled and disappeared.

"I knew it," she gasped. Tears flowed from her eyes, then she slowly walked up to me. I became visible again, and threw my arms around her.

"A chip off the old block," Samuel chimed. Little did he know, I was a chip off of his block as well.

When he came to me, I could see a look of pride glowing on his face. "Look at you, all grown up. You're radiant," he said.

"Thanks," I said, hugging him tightly.

"And don't worry about not being able to control your gift. There are some gifts which take longer to tame than others. In time you'll get it, and I can help you if you want," he offered.

"I'd like that," I said, and his smile widened.

During our late night meal, we discussed everything from the renovations on the house, the return of Courtney and Caleb, and details of the wedding. It was going to be a small affair, on a big budget.

Although Samuel had already performed his magical Angelic cremation ceremony on James and Malachi, he did collect their ashes knowing I would want them.

I requested for each of them, including Danyel, to have a small headstone placed outside in the graveyard; an area where we could go to remember them; where all our loved ones would be remembered, for as long as we were alive.

Alaine agreed.

The wedding would be held in the back yard, and the reception in the ballroom. Alaine said she would have gardeners come and trim the labyrinth all the way down to waist length, and then cut away the center to make it large enough to hold the ceremony. She promised it would be transformed into something unforgettable, and I didn't doubt her.

I was about to begin a brand new journey.

TWENTY ONE

THE NEXT MONTH WAS EXTREMELY BUSY.

Alex lived and began his healing process, and after a few weeks, he was up and walking. Courtney and Caleb returned home and were overjoyed to see me and Kade alive, but were also heartbroken over the loss of James and Malachi. They had become close to James the last few weeks before they left.

The workers continued day and night, taking shifts to finish the renovations on the house, and after only a few short weeks, it was looking even more charming than before.

The wedding planning was in full force. Alaine had made arrangements to fly Jeremy and Lia up for the wedding, and was also busy finding the perfect flowers, centerpieces, cake, and formal attire for the whole party. I wanted the ceremony to be simple, just Kade and I, because if we had a wedding party there would be no one sitting in the seats.

Alaine suggested at least one person should stand with us, like a best-man and maid-of-honor. So, I chose Lia. When I called her, she screamed and then started bawling over the phone. Half the time I didn't understand what she was saying, but I knew she was ecstatic. In a few short weeks I'd see their faces again.

I told Alaine she could make most of the decisions without me. I didn't really care about all the details, or how frilly it was, and since she was such a stickler for detail, I let her have the reins. The only thing I wanted to be a part of was choosing my wedding dress. For that, I chose a simple but elegant design, and then she took all my measurements and called them into the designer who would hand sew it.

As far as invitations went, there weren't too many people on the list, but I did have a secret list of my own. Michael told me to call on him if I ever needed, so I sent up a dozen verbal requests for him and Kade's parents to attend the wedding. I wasn't sure if they would come, or even if they wanted to, but I extended the invitation to them anyway. I knew this outward celebration was only a mortal tradition, but thought it would be a nice surprise for Alaine.

Every moment I was alone, I called my wings. Each time I practiced, it became easier and easier until it came to the point there was no more pain. I would extend them and fold them back behind my back, exercises to try and to get control over them, and they seemed to respond perfectly to my thoughts. The only thing I hadn't done was fly, and I was looking forward to that moment.

Samuel also helped me with my gift of strength. He taught me how to train my gift not to react without my consent. It took some time, but I finally got it under control.

Kade stayed down in his room because the pull of the bond was becoming much too hard for us to resist, especially when we were alone. My heart ached the moment he left, but I knew in a short time, he would forever be mine. That fact made resisting just a little easier.

The day before the wedding, Lia and Jeremy flew into Fairbanks airport, so I went with Dom and Kade to pick them up. On the way back, Dom drove, Kade rode shotgun, and me, Lia, and Jeremy sat in the back.

Lia grabbed my hand. "I am so excited for you. Oh my God. I can't believe you're getting married," she squealed.

"I know. This has all been like a dream," I breathed.

"We both knew you were going to get married first. It's not like me and Jeremy have people fighting to be with us," she laughed, and Jeremy rolled his eyes. "By the way, how is Caleb?"

"He's good," I replied. "And, he can't wait to see you."

"Really?" Her face lit up and she actually clapped.

"Yep, and Courtney is excited to see you too, Jeremy."

His eyes widened and he began nodding. "Yeah, she's really cool. It will be nice to see her again."

"Oh, don't even act like your insides aren't throwing a party right now, Jeremy," Lia giggled.

"I'm excited, alright. I just don't go around like a toddler, clapping my hands and squealing."

"Whatever," she exhaled. Lia leaned over to me and whispered. "I knew you and Kade were meant for each other. You read my email didn't you? I *told* you. Best friends intuition." She nodded, tapping the side of her head.

"Yeah, you did," I acknowledged. Kade's head slightly turned to the side and I could see a smile on his face.

"So what ever happened to Ethon?" she asked. Kade and Dom quickly glanced at each other. I didn't tell her Ethon died because Lia would never understand. It was best to keep her out of the affairs of the paranormal, and give her the simplest answer.

"He's gone and won't be coming back," I answered.

"Well, it's probably for the best. He was a cool guy and all, but you ended up with your soul mate," she said matter-of-factly.

"Yeah, I agree with that," Jeremy said.

"Thanks guys," I said, wrapping their necks with my arms and pulling them in for a group hug. Their heads collided.

"Ouch," Jeremy and Lia yelled.

"Sorry!" I replied, releasing them. Being around them made me briefly forget I had super strength.

They both sat back, rubbing their foreheads.

"Have you been working out?" Jeremy asked, straightening his glasses.

I shrugged. "Maybe just a little," I answered.

"I knew something was different about you!" Lia snapped. "I couldn't put my finger on it. But you also look really happy, like you're glowing. Are you wearing makeup?" she asked, studying my face.

"A little," I answered.

"You have to give me the name of your brand. Your face looks flawless."

"It's called Transformation," Dom blurted.

"Transformation? I'll have to remember that," Lia said.

I could see Dom's eyes in the rear view mirror, so I narrowed mine on him. He began laughing.

"Was he joking?" she asked.

"Yes, he was joking. I'll show you what I have when I get home," I said, and she sighed.

The rest of the ride was filled with tales and horrors of the school year and graduation. It was great to have my human friends back here with me. They brought laughter and reality back into my life.

When we arrived back at the house, Alaine immediately collected Jeremy and Lia, bringing them up-to-date on the wedding ceremony and reception. She then took Lia to try on her dress, which was supposed to be another surprise.

As night fell, Courtney, Caleb, Jeremy, and Lia hung out in my room. We laid around talking and laughing all night long, while Kade and the guys hung out in the cottage, playing games and filling up on junk food.

I couldn't help but think about him, and Lia caught me several times staring blankly into nothingness.

"You're thinking about him aren't you?" she giggled.

I nodded. "My insides twist when I think about him."

"I am so jealous of you two. You are so perfect for each other it's disgusting... in the best possible way, of course," she added.

"Yeah, I guess we are," I giggled. She rolled her eyes, and then we continued on with our pointless conversations until our eyes got heavy and we all fell asleep.

When I opened my eyes the next morning, the boys and Courtney, had already left the room. Lia was still on the floor, and if I didn't hear her snores, I would have thought she was dead. Her hair was a knotted mess, her mouth was hanging wide open, and I swear there was drool on the pillow.

"Lia," I said, poking her with my finger, knowing anything short of an alarm wouldn't wake her up.

A few moments later, Jeremy knocked and slowly opened the door.

"Alaine wanted me to wake you guys up. Breakfast will be ready in thirty minutes, and the hair and face people will be coming after."

"Alright. I'm up, but," I thumbed to Lia and shook my head. "I have sleeping beauty over here."

"More like sleeping beast," he said with a twisted face.

"Jeremy," I scolded.

"I've come to awaken the Kraken," he said, his face narrowed on her.

"Oh no," I exhaled.

"Oooh yes," he said excitedly. "And I brought back up."

From behind his back he revealed an air horn.

"You can't do that," I gasped. "She almost killed you last time."

"I can and I will," he said, with a grin the size of the Cheshire cat.

"Where in the world did you get an air horn?"

"Caleb," he answered flatly.

"Well, I am going to proceed to the bathroom and lock myself in. Don't do anything until I'm safe," I said, quickly running and grabbing clothes, as Jeremy stalked toward Lia. "And you'd better leave that door wide open for your quick escape, because she will pounce on you and eat you for breakfast," I laughed, quickly shutting the door behind me.

I jumped as the air horn blasted. It wasn't just a simple honk... Jeremy held it for a good three seconds. It was the loudest, most horrifying sound which carried straight through the door and vibrated my chest.

Lia screamed directly after, making me cringe.

Then I heard her yell at the top of her lungs.

"I hate you, Jeremy!"

Jeremy's laughter quickly diminished as his footsteps carried him away. Shortly after, Lia's thudding, angry footsteps followed.

Oh, he woke the beast and he was definitely going to get it.

It was great to have them back.

Excitement buzzed in the air as we made our way down to breakfast. When we entered the dining room, all the curtains were drawn to keep the back yard a secret.

Kade was already at the table with everyone else, and when he saw me, his bright eyes lit up. He looked unbelievably sexy this morning. His face was glowing, and I could see the definition of muscles under his simple white T-shirt.

He stood and walked over to me, wrapping me up in his embrace. I closed my eyes and inhaled, letting his scent fill me.

"Hey, beautiful," he whispered gently, kissing my cheek.

"Get a room," Dom teased.

"Don't worry. We will," Kade answered, then turned to me with a wink.

My heart thrummed and my stomach twisted. Today was the day I was going to marry him. Immortals never had a wedding or celebration. But Kade was doing this for me, and for Alaine. He knew I wanted a wedding, and he wanted Alaine and Samuel to be a part of it. That made me love him even more... if that were even possible.

"There are children here," Dom sang.

"I'm not a child," Courtney huffed.

"I didn't say you were."

"You were implying it."

"Oh, she's using big words now. I'm sorry...there are *teens* in our midst," he corrected.

"Yeah, get it right," Courtney playfully snapped back.

"Feisty this morning," Dom chuckled.

"Oh, she's tame compared to that one," Jeremy said, thumbing to Lia.

After breakfast, I knew it was the last time I'd see Kade before the ceremony, so I hugged him extra tight.

"I'll see you in a few hours?" he said softly.

"I can't wait to begin my life with you," I breathed.

"I'll be waiting at the altar," he grinned, then brushed his hand across my cheek. He leaned in and kissed me quick. "See you soon."

"See ya," I said, breathless.

Lia took me by the arm and dragged me out. "Come on Cinderella. Time to get you ready for the ball."

A few hours before the ceremony, the make-up artist and hairstylist were working on me at the same time. I refused to look in the mirror until I was fully put together. When they were done, they all stood around me, gawking and gasping. I assumed they had nailed their jobs.

Alaine, Lia, and Courtney were in the room. All of our make-up had been applied, but Lia was still in a tank top and jeans. Her hair was all down and straightened, with just the ends curled. They put false eyelashes on her and liner around her eyes to give them depth. Her cheeks were rosy and her lips were a dark shade of red. She looked like a porcelain China doll.

Courtney was wearing a delightful light-pink gown with sparkles all over it. Her hair was half-up, with ringlets flowing down her shoulders. Her make-up was natural with a slash of pink gloss over her lips. She looked like a princess.

Butterflies began to stir in my stomach as Alaine headed toward me carrying my gown in her arms. She carefully zipped the garment bag open, and I found myself shaking, taking in deep breaths and exhaling slowly.

"Oh my goodness, Emma. It's gorgeous," Lia gasped, holding her hands to her mouth.

"Wow! It's so lovely," Courtney added.

Alaine helped me slip into it, and as soon as she zipped it up, I could feel the weight of the fabric. It was strapless, and the back dipped down a little lower than usual, for one very specific reason... *just in case.*

The bodice was fitted down my waist, and was adorned with the most exquisite beading. The bottom was silk, flowing around me in layers. Alaine insisted on a train, but I didn't want anything too long, so we agreed on one which extended about seven feet behind the dress. I was glad she talked me into it because it really was beautiful. Along the border of the train was a very lightweight lace with intricate embroidery, intertwined with delicate designs of feathers, combined with some beading.

The top part of my hair was pulled back into some kind of fancy updo, so the hairdresser could attached a jewel-studded crown and a veil which hung behind me. The rest of my hair hung down in big silky curls.

Alaine stood in front of me after she spread out my train. Courtney and Lia came and stood next to her with unreadable expressions on their faces.

"What?" I asked.

Alaine's eyes began to water. "You are beyond gorgeous," she breathed.

"I agree," Courtney said. "You look like you should be on the cover of a magazine."

"They're right, Emma. You look like royalty," Lia exhaled, her eyes starting to tear.

"Don't do it," I said, fighting back tears while laughing. "If you guys start crying, I'll start crying, and then all this painted stuff on our faces will start running. It will ruin all of our pictures."

"Okay. Okay," Alaine said, fanning her eyes. "We all have a little something for you."

They each held a small box in their hands.

"Here's mine," Alaine said, handing me her box. I opened it and inside was a necklace. It was a very elegant, dainty golden heart filled with diamonds, hanging on a delicate gold chain.

"Go ahead, open it," she whispered.

"Oh my," I breathed.

Inside of the locket were the markings of Samuel and Alaine engraved in each side. Alaine's, the same as Michael's. "I don't know what to say. This is the best gift I've ever been given. Thank you so much," I said, hugging her tightly.

She took it and fastened it around my neck.

"The chain is from your grandmother, so it's very old, but the locket is new."

"Mine is next," Lia said, handing me her box.

When I opened it, it was an elegant golden bracelet.

"Oh wow," I exhaled. "It's beautiful."

"It's actually Alaine's. It's something borrowed, so you'll have to discuss giving it back to her later," she added.

I giggled putting on my wrist. "Okay, I will. Thanks, Lia," I said, hugging her.

Courtney was next and handed me her box. When I opened it there was a tiny blue pin, in the shape of angel's wings. "Thank you so much, Courtney," I said. "I love this."

"I actually found it in a little store in Washington. It reminded me of you, so I bought it. I guess it was for this moment."

"It couldn't be more perfect," I said, pulling back the top of my gown and pinning it inside. "There," I said patting it. "Hidden wings." I winked and Courtney smiled.

"Now you're set," Lia said. "Something old, new, borrowed, and blue."

"Thanks to all of you. I cannot tell you how lucky I am to have you here. This day would not have been the same without you. I love you guys," I said.

They all leaned in carefully for the most awkward group hug, all not wanting to mess up the masterpieces just done by the hairdresser.

Alaine peeked out the window. "Alright ladies, it's just about time. Lia, you should go get ready, and Courtney, you can go down and take your seat."

"I'm already gone," Lia said, slipping out of the door.

"Me too," Courtney said. "I'll see you soon, Emma."

"See you," I said, my voice trembling with excitement.

"Okay, Emma," Alaine said standing in front of me, doing another quick look-over to make sure everything was in perfect shape. When she was done tucking and fussing, she placed her hands on my shoulders and gazed lovingly into my eyes. "All you have to do is wait here for Samuel. He'll come escort you down. I'm going to go down now and make sure the guys are ready. Alright?"

"Okay," I replied. "Thank you so much."

When she left, I took in a deep breath and walked over to my closet. On the inside of the door was a floor length mirror. Glancing down, I opened the door, and then backed away. Slowly looking up, I saw myself for the first time.

"Oh my God."

I couldn't believe the transformation. I hardly recognized myself. I felt like I was in a fairytale, and I *was* Cinderella getting ready to marry Prince Charming. I slowly turned to each side trying to soak in all the intricate details of the dress. It was perfectly fit for a princess.

TWENTY TWO

THERE WAS A SOFT TAPPING at the door.

"Come in," I called.

When the door swung open and his eyes landed on me, Samuel paused. His face softened and his eyes began to tear.

"Emma," he exhaled, shaking his head. "You're enchanting."

He was wearing an all-black tuxedo, with a matching black bow-tie and cummerbund. His hair was slicked back and he was clean shaven. He looked so handsome, and definitely not old enough to be my dad.

I smiled. "And, you look very dashing... dad."

His face beamed with happiness.

"I can't believe how fast this is all happening. It seemed like only a moment ago I was holding you in my arms. We thought we'd lost you, but look at you now. You've grown up into a beautiful young woman," he said softly, stepping in.

"I just got both of you back into my life, and I will make sure our relationship continues to grow. You can't get rid of me that easily."

His smile grew even brighter. "That really means a lot. You were the missing part of our lives for so long."

"And little did I know, so were both of you."

"I would hug you, but I don't want to ruin any of *that*," he said gesturing to my wedding ensemble.

"Dads get hugs no matter what," I said, wrapping my arms around him. He carefully hugged me back and then held out his arm to me.

"Are you ready?" he exhaled loudly.

"I am," I said, linking my arm around his.

He carefully led me down the stairs, and as he did, a few of the male helpers stopped and stared.

"Isn't my daughter exquisite?" Samuel proclaimed.

"Very beautiful," they replied, and then headed back toward the ballroom, carrying large boxes in their arms.

"For a second, I thought they were gawking at me," he laughed.

"Who knows? You do look very handsome in all black. Imagine if you flashed your magical, matching wings. Instant bromance," I giggled.

"Bromance?" he asked, his eyes narrowed.

"It's a bro – romance. You know... guy – guy," I explained.

"Oh no," he said. "No bromance for this immortal. I'm bonded," he said. "And here she comes now."

Alaine came around the corner in an elegant white and golden gown. Her chocolate hair fell in ringlets around her shoulders, and her face had an ethereal glow to it. She looked like an angel.

In her hand she held the perfect bouquet of white roses, wrapped with a silk ribbon.

"Here you go, Emma," she said, handing it to me.

"Oh my goodness," I said placing them up to my nose and smelling their sweet floral scent. "They are gorgeous. Better than I could have ever imagined."

"You look stunning, Alaine," Samuel said, leaning forward to kiss her.

"And you look as handsome as the first day I laid eyes on you," she said, adjusting his bow-tie.

"Still keeping me straight and tidy, I see," he smiled warmly. Alaine blushed.

"I am going to go out first, and you guys will follow. Lia and Dominic are already in place, and ready to walk once the music starts. Samuel, you and Emma will start walking as soon as you hear the violin play, okay?"

"We've got this," Samuel said, holding her hand.

She quickly glanced at me. "Kade looks... well you'll see. He's anxiously waiting."

Those words immediately brought a thrill of excitement. All I could think about was seeing him.

"How many people are here?"

"Everyone I invited is already here. There are about twenty total," she replied.

I felt a little sad Michael and Kade's parents didn't make it, but they were Archangels, and must have had missions. I was still surrounded by everyone I loved.

Alaine walked out of the front door, and continued until she disappeared around the corner. As soon as Samuel took his first step my nerves kicked in, making me feel lightheaded, and dizzy.

"Are you alright?" he asked.

"I'm fine," I said, pulling myself together and smiling, because in front of us stood a photographer, snapping away with her large camera.

"We'll take it one step at a time. Together," he said quietly.

"Together." I repeated.

In the air I could hear the music start to play, and it soothed me. As we rounded the corner of the house, I froze. I was literally walking into a fairy tale.

The labyrinth did not look the same. It was trimmed down, and at the entrance, adorning each side, stood two glorious trees, filled with white blossoms in full bloom. It was illuminated by thousands of tiny white lights strung intricately around its limbs.

As we stepped closer to the entrance, the sweetest floral smell wafted in the air. I took in a deep breath and smiled. Then, as I was about to take another step forward, Samuel held me back.

"Not yet," he whispered.

I nodded and exhaled. "I'm so glad you're here with me."

"So am I," he said, kissing me on the forehead. "I can see how mortal fathers cherish this moment."

The music stopped and a glorious melody of strings swelled in the air. The sound of the violin filled me with such emotion I could hardly contain it. As the musician's bow glided across the strings, it created the most beautiful ballad of love.

My heart began to patter as we took our first steps down the pathway leading to Kade. The ground was covered in a blanket of white rose petals, and above us hung tall arches, filled with every kind of white flower imaginable.

As we drew near, I could feel him; the bond pulling us together. When we exited the pathway, the dimming sky became our canopy. Beautiful pastel colors painted across it created a picturesque backdrop.

The pathway of petals continued all the way to the altar, ending where Kade stood.

His presence stole all breath from my lips. He looked unbelievably handsome in his all-white tuxedo. His face was ethereal, and his hair was perfectly disheveled.

I wanted to run to him, to hold him and never let go.

As Samuel continued to walk me down the aisle, everyone stood, and I began to recognize most of their faces.

Thomas, Courtney, Caleb, Jeremy, Miss Lily, Henry, and then Alaine. But in between, there were more than a few I hadn't met yet. Next to Alaine I saw a familiar face, and when she smiled, I had a flashback. She was the woman who visited me in the hospital. Miss Reed. Abigail Reed. I remembered her name because she was the one who worked with Alaine to send me here. She must have been an angel.

I had a feeling all those faces glowing and smiling at me, had some part to play in our lives. Or they were somehow connected.

As we neared the front I couldn't help but notice Lia's bright shining face, and it made me smile. She was wearing a golden gown, and clasped tightly in her hands was a white bouquet of roses, similar to mine.

Dominic was standing on the other side of Kade. He looked handsome with his light brown hair and gleaming green eyes. His smile was wide, revealing his perfect white teeth. He was wearing a white tuxedo with a gold bow-tie and gold cummerbund, to match Lia.

But as beautiful as they were, there was only one who took my breath away. As our eyes focused onto each other, I couldn't help but get emotional.

When we reached the front, Samuel held out his hand and turned to me. Leaning over, he kissed me gently on my cheek, and then placed my hand in Kade's. The bond, as strong as ever, surged through us, filling me with a great want and desire. As if this moment wasn't already magical enough.

Kade didn't speak, but the affection in his eyes spoke louder than any word.

When the minister began the ceremony, I looked up and recognized him. He was the same person who led my parent's funeral.

I held tight to Kade's hands, knowing if I let go, I wouldn't have been able to stand. He was my strength, as he had always been from the very beginning. If I could have, I would have rather been wrapped tightly in his arms.

When it was time for our vows and the exchange of rings, our voices wavered with emotion, the words simple, but true

For Kade's ring, I'd chosen a simple white gold band, engraved on the inside with my markings. He was thankful, and his eyes pooled as I placed the ring on his finger.

The ring he gave me was also of white gold, but had three rows of diamonds which merged into a very large heart shaped diamond in the center, and on the inside, his symbol was engraved. I sobbed as he placed it on my finger.

For the remainder of the ceremony, I kept my eyes on him.

Then, the minister finally announced…"I now pronounce you man and wife. Kade," he said with a grin, "you may kiss your bride."

Gently holding the back of my neck he pressed his lips to mine and the guests cheered. Rose petals were thrown in the air as we finished our kiss and turned to them.

As we proceeded down the aisle we were stopped when someone stepped in our path, and I gasped as soon as I realized who it was.

"Michael!" I said, throwing my arms around him. "You came."

"Of course I came," he said, hugging me back. "I can't stay for long, but since you invited me at least a dozen times, I couldn't say no." He gently caressed my face in his hands. "You're a vision."

"Thank you," I blushed.

"Kade," Michael said, extending his hand to him.

"Michael," Kade nodded, shaking his hand in appreciation.

"Your parents couldn't make it. Your father was called on a mission. I'm sorry."

"I understand. But I am glad you came," he answered.

Alaine came and stood next to me, her eyes fixed on a man she had never met before.

"Hi, Alaine," his beautiful voice sang.

"Do I know you?" she asked, then glanced at me, and back at him.

"I've been with you your entire life, but have never had the pleasure of meeting you."

Alaine shook her head, completely baffled, and then she turned back toward me.

"Mom, I'd like you to meet your father, my grandfather," I slowly introduced.

She turned back toward Michael, her eyes perplexed. "My father?"

"Yes, Alaine." His smile radiated like a beam of sunshine.

"My father?" she repeated, her eyes welled with tears.

"Yes. Michael the Archangel is your father," I said softly.

Samuel placed his hand on her shoulder, and when she looked back at him, he nodded.

Michael held his arms open to her. "Come, Alaine," he spoke, and she fell into his arms weeping like a child.

After a while she straightened up, wiped her tears, and faced him.

"I'm sorry. I just never thought this day would ever come," she sniffled, looking at him in complete wonderment.

"It's been long overdue," he agreed.

"How did you meet Emma?"

"She called out for help before her transformation and I could not deny her."

"He did," I affirmed. "I had to keep it secret because I didn't think you would believe me, or understand."

"You're right. I wouldn't have," she admitted. She then turned back to Michael with a pained look in her eyes. "Why didn't you ever come to me? I called out many times."

"I know you did, my dear child, and it made my heart ache. But I could not answer because there is an order to things that even I cannot break," he confessed.

Alaine sadly nodded. "Did you send Emma the dagger?"

"I did."

"And you sent me the amulet and suit?" she questioned.

He nodded.

"Thank you," she said appreciatively. "Those gifts saved her life. She probably wouldn't be here today if it weren't for them."

"I only did what any father, or grandfather, would do to protect those he loves. I wish I could have done more, but like I said, my hands were tied."

"I understand," Alaine said.

Michael's eyes softened as he looked at her. "I'm so proud of you. You rose above all of the darkness in your life, and still became a beacon of light for all those around you – touching so many souls."

"I only try to do what is right," she said.

"You've been doing what is in your heart, a heart which is pure and unselfish," he acknowledged with pride. He then turned to Samuel and extended his hand. "Samuel, it is a pleasure to meet you. I realize things happened a long time ago, but I want to personally thank you for taking care of Alaine and Emma."

"I love them with my life," Samuel replied, with a simple bow of his head.

"I know. And you are highly regarded."

"Thank you, Michael," Samuel said.

"I have a mission to take care of, so I must bid you farewell. But be assured this will not be our last meeting," he said to Alaine.

"I will be looking forward to our future encounters," she said, hugging him again.

"Good bye, Emma. Congratulations to you both. I will be seeing you around," he said, winking at me.

"See you, grandfather," I giggled.

He laughed, and in a flash, dissolved into a million sparking gold flecks.

Alaine threw her hands up, holding the sides of her head as if they were going to explode.

"Oh my God," she whispered. "Oh my God."

"He's unbelievable isn't he?" I said.

"This whole moment has been unbelievable," she said, turning and squeezing me in a hug.

She then linked her arm into Samuel's, ushering him to head out toward the reception. The guests began to follow, but when I turned around Lia's eyes were fixed on mine.

"Oh no," I exhaled.

"Emma," she respired, her face filled with disappointment. "There are some *major* things you've been keeping from us."

"I know, and I'm sorry. But there are things about my new life I didn't think you would understand," I tried to explain.

"I'm your best friend, and best friends share secrets. They stick by each other through thick and thin... no matter what."

"*We* are your best friends," Jeremy said, stepping next to her.

"You both *are* the best friends anyone could ever have, and when this is all over, I promise I will explain it *all* to you."

"Promise?" she asked.

"Cross my heart."

"Alright. 'Cause I'm trying to make sense of it all. First, there was that big, handsome guy who popped up before vanishing into thin air, and then you were over there calling him grandfather, and Alaine *mom*... I'm going to need some affirmations soon or my head will explode."

"Yeah, we both will," Jeremy added.

"And you will. As soon as this whole celebration is over," I promised.

"Okay," she said, hugging me. She grabbed Jeremy's arm and pointed. "To the ballroom, where the food is! Take me now."

Jeremy rolled his eyes, and then led her down the pathway of rose petals.

TWENTY THREE

JUST AS KADE AND I made our way toward the pathway, I gasped, feeling a rush of heat twist in my stomach. It felt like a warning.

"What's the matter?" Kade asked.

"I don't know. But I feel like something bad is about to happen."

A faint smell of a sweet smokiness caught my nose.

"Fallen," Kade whispered, and as soon as he spoke, his beautiful hazel eyes went black.

"Emma, stay behind me," Kade said, stepping in front of me.

"Oh, how sweet," Azzah's words dripped with disgust. He and Bane appeared in the corner of the open space.

"What do you want?" Kade asked, in a not so friendly tone.

"Bane?" I questioned, trying to read his expression. He looked torn but he didn't answer.

"We came for the girl," Azzah spoke in a deep, growl.

"You aren't touching her," Kade crouched. "What happened with Lucifer is over."

"It's not over," Azzah roared with laughter, slowly stepping closer. "Lucifer is imprisoned in hell, unceasingly tortured by the death of his son, and his heart is unwilling to rest until one thing has been accomplished."

"And what is that?" I asked.

"Your death." His black wicked eyes fastened on mine.

I would normally freeze with fear, but instead, a deep seeded fury overcame me, burning like an inferno. I was glad everyone else was gone from the area, still making their way out of the labyrinth.

"He can't touch her," Kade said, "Lucifer has been bound to Hell."

"Yes. But his legion has not. They will come, and they will *keep* coming until there is no breath left in her."

"Let them try," Kade threatened.

"We will," Azzah implored.

My fury erupted from within, and I could not contain it. I felt myself being involuntarily thrust toward Azzah.

It all happened so fast, like a flash of lightening.

Before anyone could react, Azzah pulled a huge, sharp sword from behind him and charged toward me. I could hear Kade yelling my name, but everything inside of me was muted and focused.

I went invisible, momentarily throwing him off, and then reappeared right at his side. Grabbing hold of his arm, I thrust him to the ground. He twisted his body and kicked me backward with such great force I flew upward into the air about twenty feet.

And then it happened.

My wings suddenly appeared, fully extended, stopping my backward momentum with one brisk flap. Below me, collective gasps and screams filled the air and a look of utter astonishment filled everyone's faces as they watched.

Alaine and Samuel had just exited the labyrinth and were standing next to one of the trees. Alaine's hands were clasped over her mouth, and her eyes were wide with terror. Samuel's face was filled with concern as I watched him immediately call his wings.

But Azzah had also called his wings, and was heading toward me. Kade tried to intercept him, but when Bane moved in his peripheral, he changed directions and flew forward to take him down.

The fury within me continued to burn.

With a flap of my wings, I shot forward like a rocket to meet Azzah head on. I was on autopilot now, my body a slave to my gifts.

In a microsecond, we collided. The raw strength in my arms crashed against his chest, ramming him backward. His body impacted the ground with such violent force, it sent a shockwave of energy outward, sending the chairs flying back, crashing against each other.

I landed on top of him, and for a moment, his black eyes were filled with shock and awe.

With a quick twist of my chest, my right wing swung around and beheaded him.

I stood as Samuel landed in front of me, and looked upon the scene with pride and adoration.

Everyone rushed back toward us, but Thomas and Dom kept them back. Samuel quickly spoke his angelic words, and Azzah's body burned into ash.

Kade brought Bane forward, holding one of his wings under his neck.

"I don't want to hurt you," Bane said, his arms extended out to his side.

I knew he was telling the truth.

"Lucifer sent us. We *had* to. We are slaves to his will."

"I know," I said, stepping forward. "I know."

Samuel stood next to me, his striking black wings still spread, anticipating any danger.

I folded my wings behind my back, and touched Kade's hand. "It's alright. He won't hurt me."

"Emma," Kade said, his eyes landing on my wings.

"I was going to tell you," I breathed. "I just didn't think it would be like this. I'm sorry."

His expression softened. "It's alright," he smiled and nodded. "We'll talk later."

I nodded in agreement.

My gaze went back to Bane. "You tell Lucifer where he can shove it."

"I'm not returning to the Underworld. I don't care if others are sent to seek out and kill me. I want to live. I want to be free."

"As you should be," I said, gently lowering Kade's wing from his neck.

"Thank you," Bane said with a nod. "You will never see me again."

"And hopefully it will be because you have stayed hidden," I grinned.

He smiled then bowed his head. "Live well, Emma."

"Live well, Bane."

Bane called his wings and with a single flap he was gone.

Everyone rushed back into the area, and Alaine was the last to enter. She didn't say a word as she ran to me, but tears were flowing from her eyes.

"Are you alright?" she cried, her face was filled with fear and concern.

"Not a scratch. See?" I showed her my arms. "But my hair is sort of a mess, and my dress is a bit damaged."

She gathered me in her arms. "Emma," she sobbed. "I was terrified. But you have proven to everyone that you *have* fulfilled the prophecy. You've become utterly transcendent."

Thomas stepped forward with Lia in his arms. She was lying limp, her mouth wide open.

"Did you put the sleeper on her?" I gasped.

"No, she did this herself. She fainted as soon as she saw your wings."

"And the photographer?" I asked, pointing to her still body, flailed out on the ground.

"Dom put her out right before the action started. We didn't want photos of us flying floating around the internet," he laughed.

"Emma?" Jeremy asked, stepping around Thomas.

"Hey Jeremy," I grinned apologetically.

"How?" He shook his head in disbelief, his eyes locked onto my wings. "What—?"

My face twisted a bit, knowing I had to give him an answer.

"I know," I exhaled. "Well, for starters... I'm not entirely human."

He pushed his glassed up on his nose. "I can clearly see that."

I turned to Samuel, Alaine, and then Kade. "We're angels. Immortals."

"And you were like this the whole time?"

"No. I transformed on my eighteenth birthday."

His brow furrowed. "But, your birthday isn't for a few more months."

I shook my head. "My true birthday was a month ago."

He exhaled loudly. "Well, I guess that makes a lot more sense. I thought it might be a little fast; you know... getting married at seventeen and all."

"Are you mad?" I asked.

His eyes looked at me, and then the hugest smile filled his face. "Are you kidding? Our best friend is immortal. That's the most freaking amazing thing ever!"

"Good," I said, walking to him. I hid my wings, and then hugged him.

Behind Jeremy, Dominic stood shaking his head.

"What?" I asked.

"I've got nothing. You have rendered me speechless." He grinned and shrugged.

"Now *that* is a miracle," Kade laughed, and everyone else joined him.

"I know we all have some major questions and things we need to discuss, but there are guests and a celebration that needs to be attended to first." Alaine said, wiping the black mascara from under her eyes. "So, let's all head to the ballroom!" She then paused and turned. "Dom, will you please take the photographer to the kitchen and revive her first. Give her some of your charm, and hopefully she'll stick around."

"You got it," he said, tossing the limp photographer over one shoulder, and holding her camera in the other.

Everyone started out of the Labyrinth and when I turned to Kade, his eyes were fastened on mine. A look of passion and desire swirled within them.

"Come here," he said, stepping closer.

His arms wrapped tightly around my waist, pulling me firmly against him.

"Wings?" he asked, his eyes smiling with adoration.

I nodded.

"When did you know?"

"The day I showed you my other gifts. They were the reason I was on the floor."

He laughed. "I had a feeling something was up. You're very sneaky."

"I wanted it to be a surprise," I said.

"Well, you totally pulled off the surprise factor. Even the Fallen were shocked. They weren't ready for you."

"Are you ready for me?" I asked.

"Are you kidding? I've been ready since the day we first touched."

"Well, I'm not sure if I'm ready for you," I grinned.

"Oh, you won't be," he affirmed. I narrowed my eyes and shook my head. "Are you ready to go to the reception?"

"No. How about we ditch the party and find a place to be alone?"

"Alaine will kill us," he answered slowly.

"I know," I sighed. "But it sounds like a great plan."

"Don't worry," he whispered softly in my ear. "Tonight, I will give you an after party you will *never* forget."

His words left me blushing and breathless.

"Let's go," he said, swooping me up into his arms, and carrying me out of the labyrinth.

As he carried me down the hall toward the ballroom, I could hear soft classical music playing in the background.

When we entered the room, Kade paused at the entrance.

"Wow," he gasped.

I was dazed and incapable of words.

The ballroom had been transformed into an enchanted dreamland, filled with the most exotic trees and flower arrangements, all done in white. Thousands upon thousands of golden twinkle lights filled the room. The light from the chandelier was dimmed, while up-lights, lowlights, and spotlights accentuated every floral masterpiece with a soft golden glow.

In the center of the room were five circular tables, with golden table cloths and white china table settings. The center of each table held tall crystal vases, filled with bouquets of white roses.

It looked like a golden wonderland, a place of magic.

As soon as everyone saw us, they began clapping.

Kade set me down, and I wrapped my arm around his. As we made our way in, the song we had our first dance to, the night of the masquerade ball, started playing.

Kade turned to me with a smile, then unhooked his arm. He bowed in front of me, then held out his hand.

"May I have this dance?" he asked.

I placed my hand in his and he led me over to the dance floor.

The music played, but the world around us began to fade away. Wrapped in his strong arms, I laid my head on his chest and curled my arms around his neck, never wanting the music to stop. His sweet scent swirled around me, and with every inhale, filled me with desire. I wanted to disappear, and finally be alone with him.

As the night continued, there was so much laughter and happiness, it was the celebration of our lives. But before we knew it, it was over.

TWENTY FOUR

AFTER ALL THE GUESTS LEFT and everyone else went to bed, Kade held my hand and walked me outside. The night air was cool and crisp, enlivening me as it brushed against my bare skin.

"Where do you want to go?" he asked.

"What do you mean?"

"For our honeymoon," he replied, as a crooked grin adorned his perfect lips. "Where would you like to go?"

"What are my options?"

His magnificent white wings appeared behind his back.

"Anywhere your heart desires."

"Right now?" I squeaked.

"Yes, right now." He winked making my pulse race. "I don't want to wait another minute."

"What about packing?"

"You don't need to pack," he answered.

"How long will we be gone?"

"As long as we like. Alaine and Samuel already know."

"Well," I said, knowing there was no way of making a decision. "Why don't you surprise me?"

His lips turned up on both sides. "I was hoping you'd say that." He grabbed me by the waist and secured me firmly against the length of his hard body. I wrapped my arms around his neck, and he shot up into the air. I screamed and laughed as we entered the darkened sky. The stars sparkled extra bright tonight, as if they were celebrating with us.

He secured me in his arms, against his solid chest; his silky white wings glistened lightly under the stars and moonlight. The cool night air whispered in my ear, sending a chill down my spine, so I hugged him closer. Each flap of his wings sent a charge through me, filling me with want and desire. I felt his arms tighten even more, pressing our bodies even closer.

His eyes were secured on mine and I was spellbound, mesmerized by the swirling liquid gold within them. His lips brushed against my cheek, and slowly found my lips, kissing me ever so gently.

"Where are you taking me?" I breathed.

"To our place," he answered.

"We have a place?"

"We do," he grinned.

"And where exactly is this place?"

"You'll see in just a minute." He kissed the tip of my nose, and flapped his wings, flying faster and higher.

"You aren't taking me to the moon, are you?"

"I could, if that's where you want to go," he grinned.

But then I saw it, a tiny shimmer in the atmosphere, a ripple which was invisible to the human eye.

"Is that a portal?"

"It is. I'm taking you home."

With another flap of his wings, we entered the portal and went from darkness to a brilliant light.

"This has to be heaven," I said breathless.

He placed his warm cheek against mine and whispered in my ear.

"Welcome to Grandia, Emma."

Excitement and anticipation filled me and then he asked, "Would you like to fly?"

My answer was quick. "No," I breathed, "I don't want to leave your arms."

He kissed me and carefully twisted me around so I could take it all in.

Each one of my senses were on overload. The air was filled with the most unbelievable and indescribable sweetness. As I breathed in, I felt an overwhelming serenity come over me. There was a constant but gentle charge in the air, a transcendental promise of peace.

The scenery below was beyond breathtaking, stimulating my sight. The variations of the glorious greens in the trees and grass, along with the kaleidoscope of colored flowers were the brightest and most picturesque I had ever seen. The sky was the bluest blue, the clouds the whitest white, and the water was crystal clear, in soft hues of turquoise.

Grandia was a world untainted and unpolluted by mortal hands. Here existed the perfect utopian world, a fantasy designed for immortal beings to dwell. It was pure and without blemish, a place filled with warmth and light, where darkness was nonexistent. A place free of corruption and sin.

Kade dove down and flew across a field of green, making the velvety grass wave as we passed over. In the distance, I saw a small cottage settled close to the edge of a river. The landscape was what I imagined being around a palace. It looked so inviting, like it was created just for us.

I gasped. "Is that—?"

"Ours," he whispered.

As he landed, I turned toward him. The bond was powerful, unyielding, and vigorous. Although Grandia was beautiful, beyond what I could have ever imagined, at this very moment there was nothing I wanted more than him.

"And now, my wife," he spoke with a tender voice. "We seal the bond."

He led me to the front door, and twisted the knob to open it. Before I could take another breath, he swooped me up into in his strong arms, kicked the door open, and carried me inside.

He placed me down, and we stood in the quiet, facing each other. The dim light of candles flickered against his porcelain skin. The soft sound of his measured breaths slowly started to calm the thunderous beating of my heart.

He took his shirt off, throwing it to the side. His finely sculpted muscles were tight, and gleamed in the light. I lifted my hand and slid my fingers down his defined chest; his body tensing under my touch.

A breathless whisper escaped his lips. "Emma."

When I looked up, his eyes were glazed over with desire. I stood there motionless, as intense emotion filled me. Every fiber in my being longed to touch him, and to be touched by him.

His hands suddenly brushed over my head, settling at the back of my neck. And then, he kissed me. His tongue, warm and wet, swept across my lips; his hand pressed on the small of my back making me arch into him. Waves of ecstasy and longing raged out of control.

He picked me up and carried me into another room, and laid me on a bed as soft as a cloud. As his body pressed on top of mine, I clung to his shoulders.

Abandoning all restraint, we became slaves to our carnal desires.

Caressed in his arms, we lay uncovered. Our bodies intertwined, gliding and trembling with unfathomable pleasure and fulfillment, finally melting together in sacred union. Our hearts and bodies bound, sealed with an invisible and unbreakable bond.

TWENTY
FIVE

WE STAYED IN GRANDIA FOR a few days, before
returning to the mortal world. As much as I wanted
to stay, I knew we needed to go back.

Jeremy and Lia returned to L.A. and we kept in close contact.
I spent some time explaining everything in detail; from the crash
to the wedding. Being my best friends, they completely
understood, and continued to love me for who I was. Lia assured
me we were, and would always remain 'best friends forever'.

I believed her.

Alaine had headstones made and placed in the family
cemetery, and we had a small ceremony in remembrance of our
fallen heroes – Danyel, Malachi, and James. I asked for a special
area to plant a tree, in memory of Ethon, and I chose an oak. It
reminded me of the portal into his secret escape. Kade helped

me plant it, knowing the significance and how he affected both our lives.

Dominic and Thomas returned to Midway to await their next assignments, and as soon as they left, I missed them. They were a part of our family, but promised to visit us from time to time. They also assured us that if any trouble should arise, they would be there for us. We knew we could always count on them.

Alaine gave us the cottage at the back of her house, and we agreed to stay there for a while so we could continue to build our relationship. But we did travel back and forth to Grandia to visit his parents, and to have some quality alone time.

It was night in the cottage behind Alaine's house, and we were snuggled under the covers. I shared the dream I'd once had of us lying on the grass, watching our children play near the water.

"It will happen one day," he whispered, kissing my forehead.

"Yeah," I agreed. "Maybe down the road... a long, long way down the road. I won't bring children into this world, knowing at any given moment we could be attacked. Do you think we will ever be free from Lucifer or his Fallen?" I questioned.

He smiled, wrapping me tight in a warm embrace.

"No one here is ever completely free from darkness. When the darkness comes, we will meet it head on. And we will defeat it *together*."

I nodded and snuggled closer to him.

"I love you, Emma," he whispered, brushing his fingers down my back.

"And, I love you," I replied automatically. The words came without effort, flowing straight from my soul and out through my mouth. They were the surest and truest words I had ever spoken to anyone.

We lay in each other's arms, our bodies consummated, and our hearts sealed by the powerful magic of the angelic bond. It was all we ever needed. The strength of our bond, the certainty of our love, and the rest of eternity to live it...

IN OUR LITTLE PIECE OF HEAVEN, HAPPILY EVER AFTER.

ABOUT CAMEO:

 Cameo Renae was born in San Francisco, raised in Maui, Hawaii, and recently moved with her husband and children to Alaska.

She's a daydreamer, a caffeine and peppermint addict, loves to laugh, loves to read, and loves to escape reality. One of her greatest joys is creating fantasy worlds filled with adventure and romance, and sharing it with others.

One day she hopes to find her own magic wardrobe, and ride away on her magical unicorn. Until then...she'll keep writing!

CPSIA information can be obtained at www.ICGtesting.com
Printed in the USA
LVOW12s1301080415

433719LV00025B/106/P